PRAISE FOR

A Rush of Wings

Transportive and beautiful. Each page turned
in *A Rush of Wings* is the smell of salt and the spray of seawater.
With lyrical prose and a steadfast protagonist fighting against
her world and then some, this is a story forged with strength."
—CHLOE GONG, *New York Times* bestselling author
of *These Violent Delights*

"*A Rush of Wings* is a lyrical, moving retelling of one of
my favorite fairy tales. Rowenna's determination to save
her family and journey to claiming her own strength will
sweep you away."
—REBECCA KIM WELLS, author of *Shatter the Sky*

"Fierce, lush, and lyrical, *A Rush of Wings* feels simultaneously
like a story passed down through ages and something entirely
new. A must-read from historical fantasy's best."
—HANNAH WHITTEN, *New York Times* bestselling author
of *For the Wolf*

"*Outlander* meets an old classic in Laura E. Weymouth's
retelling of the wild swans. Chock-full of cold, coastal
atmosphere and ancient magic, *Rush* also features Weymouth's
signature, a fully drawn cast of characters who are by turns
prickly, stern, deceptive, cruel, and vulnerable. Another
success from a brilliant author."
—ANNA BRIGHT, author of *The Beholder* and *The Boundless*

"Atmospheric and lyrical, Weymouth spins magic and whimsy like she was born of it. A Rush of Wings bewitched me body and soul, and I love . . . I love . . . I love it!"
—LAUREN BLACKWOOD, author of *Within These Wicked Walls*

"A gorgeously rendered retelling—lovely, raw, and fierce."
—JOANNA RUTH MEYER, author of *Echo North* and *Into the Heartless Wood*

"*A Rush of Wings* is a fierce, dark-hearted fairy tale that yearns toward the light. Readers will love the book's passionate, loyal characters, beguiling monsters, and subtle, sea-scented magic. With her usual immersive and beautiful writing and a resilient, powerful heroine, Weymouth has crafted another book that feels like a classic but speaks perfectly to this moment in time."
—ERICA WATERS, author of *Ghost Wood Song* and *The River Has Teeth*

"Once again, Laura Weymouth's storytelling is unmatched. Calling to mind childhood fairy tales and teeming with original interpretation, *A Rush of Wings* is a refreshing blend of nostalgia and unpredictability. Her prose will lift you up on white wings before plunging you from sharp cliffs, and her characters will dazzle against a world framed by history and colored by magic. There are stories to read and stories to live in—and this is a world readers will never want to leave."
—ALEKSANDRA ROSS, author of *Don't Call the Wolf*

A
Rush
of
Wings

A Rush of Wings

of

Wings

LAURA E. WEYMOUTH

MARGARET K. McELDERRY BOOKS
New York   London   Toronto   Sydney   New Delhi

MARGARET K. McELDERRY BOOKS
An imprint of Simon & Schuster Children's Publishing Division
1230 Avenue of the Americas, New York, New York 10020
For information about special discounts for bulk purchases, please contact Simon & Schuster Special Sales at 1-866-506-1949 or business@simonandschuster.com.
The Simon & Schuster Speakers Bureau can bring authors to your live event. For more information or to book an event, contact the Simon & Schuster Speakers Bureau at 1-866-248-3049 or visit our website at www.simonspeakers.com.
Interior design by Debra Sfetsios-Conover
The text for this book was set in Athelas.
Manufactured in the United States of America
First Edition
10 9 8 7 6 5 4 3 2 1
Library of Congress Cataloging-in-Publication Data
Names: Weymouth, Laura E., author.
Title: A rush of wings / Laura E. Weymouth.
Description: First edition. | New York : Margaret K. McElderry Books, [2021] | Audience: Ages 14 up. | Audience: Grades 10–12. | Summary: In the eighteenth-century Scotland Highlands, untutored cailleach Rowenna must master her craft to free her cursed brothers, thwart a charismatic tyrant, and save her village. Identifiers: LCCN 2021010326 (print) | LCCN 2021010327 (ebook) | ISBN 9781534493087 (hardcover) | ISBN 9781534493100 (ebook) Subjects: CYAC: Witches—Fiction. | Blessing and cursing—Fiction. | Brothers and sisters—Fiction. | Water spirits—Fiction. | Scotland—History—18th century—Fiction. Classification: LCC PZ7.1.W43757 Ru 2021 (print) | LCC PZ7.1.W43757 (ebook) | DDC [Fic]—dc23 LC record available at https://lccn.loc.gov/2021010326
LC ebook record available at https://lccn.loc.gov/2021010327

For Lauren,

who wouldn't let me give up on the girl

with the swans.

The seas of publishing are rough at times,

and I couldn't have anyone better

to navigate them with than you.

Prologue

"When will you show me how to do that?" Rowenna Winthrop asked her mother. She was newly turned nine, and Mairead had been promising for years to teach her the secret of working craft. They were out on the headland beyond the village of Neadeala, where the cliffs grew steep, dropping from a breakneck height to narrow spits of shingle where waves shattered and foamed. Mairead had a shovel with her and was digging up stones, which she laid in waist-high cairns and infused with protective power.

"Not yet, love. Not for a while," Mairead said absently, but a frown drew her golden brows together. Rowenna flushed with shame—she knew what her mother was thinking of. Only that morning Rowenna had let her brother Duncan, the closest to her in age, tease her into a towering passion. She'd thrown herself at him, pummeling her brother with her small fists while he only laughed.

"If I could, I'd string you up by your toes," Rowenna had hissed at Duncan. "I'd skin you alive and pull your guts out and feed them to the cliff wyverns. That'd teach you a lesson."

Mairead, fair haired and forever composed, had overheard it all from across the single long room of the Winthrops' cottage. She'd been standing before the tall, warp-weighted loom at which she wove fine woolen broadcloth to sell. Her hand holding the shuttle had stilled at Rowenna's sharp words, but she'd said nothing—just taken it all in and carried on with her work.

Rowenna knew, though, that this was why Mairead would not teach her craft—the making of stone cairns into wards and the fashioning of green and growing things into charms or possets. You must have control of yourself in order to work with power, Mairead reminded Rowenna often.

And Rowenna knew Mairead saw no signs of that control in her yet.

"Maybe next year?" Rowenna asked hopefully, and Mairead smiled, her cornflower-blue gaze soft with affection.

"Aye, love. Maybe next year."

"Do you think I'm ready now?" Rowenna asked, trying vainly to keep impatience from creeping into her words. It was midsummer of her thirteenth year, and two summers back she'd begun to hear the voice of the wind. It made little sense to her, but Mairead had told Rowenna it was a good sign, that she'd work powerful craft when her time came, for a piece of nature itself had chosen to be her ally.

Yet her time never seemed to come.

Once again, they were on the cliffs, but today they kept near home. The Winthrops' stone cottage stood a hundred yards away, smoke spiraling from the chimney. A shaggy cow cropped grass at the end of a picket, and Rowenna's youngest brother, Finn, who was only two, lay napping on a blanket in the sun.

Mairead, who'd been burying iron nails at intervals in the rich peat soil, straightened and glanced at Rowenna.

"What did George Groom say to you on Sunday after church?" she asked. "I know he can be a difficult lad—Duncan's fought with him a dozen times if he's done it once."

Rowenna looked down at her feet.

"Enna," Mairead coaxed. "What did the boy say?"

"He said you're a witch," Rowenna answered reluctantly. "And that I must be a witch too. Not just that, either—he said . . ."

She faltered. But Mairead was waiting, her beautiful face mild and expectant.

"He said I must be the spawn of a union between you and the devil himself, because I look nothing like you or my brothers or like *Athair*," Rowenna finished, using the Gàidhlig word for "father," as was her practice.

"I'm sorry," Mairead said. Pity underpinned the words, but with a sickening drop of her stomach, Rowenna guessed what would come next. Her mother was too shrewd and too clever by far.

"What did you say in reply?" Mairead asked. There was no accusation in the question. It was just an inquiry after fact, but Rowenna felt pinned down, like a gutted herring staked out to dry.

"I said he was right and that I'd lay a curse on him," Rowenna replied. "I told George I'd ask the devil, my father, to drag him down to hell for fighting with Duncan and speaking ill of you."

Even now she couldn't keep a note of anger from ringing out with her words. How *dare* George say such things, when everyone knew how hard the Winthrops worked, and that the Grooms were shiftless and lazy, the whole lot of them?

"Hm." Mairead took an iron nail from her apron pocket and

set it into the earth. "Go check on Finn, won't you, love? I think he's waking."

And Rowenna knew she should not ask about craft again for some time.

⌘

"I'm fifteen today," Rowenna said desperately to Mairead as they stood side by side, washing the breakfast dishes. "*Athair* reminded me this morning before he left."

There were English soldiers billeted at a few of the homes in Neadeala, and Rowenna's father, Cam, was in a rage about it, though no troops had come to the Winthrop cot on its lonely cliff top. Cam had kissed Rowenna upon waking and told her happy birthday and gone straightaway to Laird Sutherland to see what could be done about the redcoats in the village.

Likely nothing, Rowenna knew. Ever since the English king had sent his youngest half brother to Inverness to be rid of him, small battles and uprisings had sparked intermittently across the Highlands, like so many torches guttering to life only to be snuffed out. The boy in Inverness was ambitious, folk said, and determined to set up a court to rival that of his kin in the south. He'd come with troops of his own, and Rowenna had overheard Cam say time and again that the Highlands were a scapegoat England had used to avoid yet another bloody civil war.

But they were not used to servitude in this wild and free place. Fealty to a laird was one thing. The tyranny of a distant king's inconvenient relation and the yoke of bondage that came with him was quite another. In the Highlands, that could not be borne.

"Fifteen today!" Mairead gasped, her face lighting at the reminder. "So you are. I'm sorry it slipped my mind with all that's going on. Poor Enna, scrubbing the porridge pot on her birthday. Dry your hands and come sit a moment with me—the dishes will keep."

Obediently Rowenna wiped her hands and let herself be drawn over to the hearth, where Mairead settled into a rocking chair and Rowenna sat on the floor, resting her head against her mother's knees. Mairead ran one hand over Rowenna's black hair, and the girl shut her eyes, knowing what would come next. It was tradition between them, that every year Mairead would recount the story of Rowenna's birth.

"The night you were born, the sea raged at our shores," Mairead began, and Rowenna smiled. She knew this story by heart but loved to hear it told. "I'd never seen weather to match it—the waves beat so hard at the cliffs that their spray hit against our windows, along with the rain. It was as if the ocean and I had chosen to make war with each other, both of us laboring away as the night dragged on. Finally, near dawn, you slipped into the world. But as you did, the breakers below the cliffs surged so high and the wind gusted so fiercely, one of the storm shutters tore from its hinges. When the midwife held you up to the lantern to look at you, salt spray caught you full in the face. You squalled at the sea and the sea squalled back, and that was your first baptism, by the wind and the ocean, before ever a priest laid hands on you."

Mairead's touch was gentle as she combed through Rowenna's hair. Opening her eyes, Rowenna stared at the peat embers burning on the hearth and gathered her courage.

"All I want this year is for you to teach me our craft," she said, and regretted the words the moment they'd left her. Once she'd spoken her heart's wish, it could not be unsaid.

Mairead's hands stilled, and Rowenna knew at once that the answer would be no again.

"I saw you," Mairead told her, and a hint of reproach crept into her mother's gentle voice. "I saw you in the village, Rowenna, when that redcoat passed you by."

Ice lodged itself in the pit of Rowenna's stomach. Only the day before she'd gone into Neadeala with Mairead, to buy sugar and lamp oil. One of the billeted redcoats had brushed against Rowenna and said something foul as he did.

The wind had been rustling about her, restless and longing, murmuring over and over to itself in its senseless way.

Rowenna Rowenna Rowenna, our love, our own, our light.

And Rowenna, who had not yet received a moment's instruction in craft, yielded to temptation and tried to curse the redcoat. With one piece of her, she reached out to the wind, and with the other, she focused all her hurt and spite and shame on the retreating soldier. What she wanted to bring about with her unschooled craft, she didn't know. But she longed to sting, as she had been stung. She'd found herself spineless and powerless, though, and that had cut her deeper than even the redcoat's words.

"I can't teach you yet," Mairead said decidedly. "But you must keep asking, my saltwater girl."

Her hands began to move again, once more running through

Rowenna's hair. "Even rock wears away before salt water in the end. One day, you'll be ready."

Rowenna was relieved to have her mother at her back, so that Mairead could not see the hot tears yet another dismissal brought to her eyes. For the first time, despair washed over the girl. She would never be free of anger. If that was the requirement for learning craft, then she'd have to live all her life in ignorance and cut off this part of herself entirely.

"Yes, *Màthair*," she said dully. "I can wait."

But in her heart of hearts, Rowenna knew she would not be able to bring herself to ask for her mother's help again.

Chapter One

THREE YEARS LATER

Rowenna found her mother on the cliff tops to the northeast of the Winthrop cottage. It was a storm-tossed March night—the sky was a boil of approaching thunderheads, and Mairead Winthrop crouched on her hands and knees, scrabbling for stones in the scant, unyielding earth of the cliffs.

It hadn't been hard for Rowenna to find her mother. A nameless something, a pull at her bones, had alerted her to the fact that Mairead was missing and drawn her here. The untapped craft within Rowenna led her places of its own accord with increasing frequency now, but she said nothing of it to anyone and ignored the call when she could. Mairead had made it clear enough that Rowenna was ill-suited for this sort of work and too undisciplined for power. And Rowenna had resolved not to grasp for power if that was so. If she had to wait a lifetime to be taught her craft, then wait she would, even if the wordless pulls and yearnings within her tore her apart.

"*Màthair*, come inside," Rowenna begged. "This is no weather to be out in."

Anxious things clawed at the insides of her rib cage at the sight of Mairead. The oncoming storm hadn't yet swallowed up the last gray light of dusk, and she could see that her mother was filthy. Dark soil stained Mairead's clothes and clung to her skin, and her nails were broken and bloodied from wrestling with rocks she'd dug up and built into a lopsided cairn. Far below them, the angry sea worried away at the cliffs, its constant muttering having built up to a discontented roar.

Whatever Mairead was doing, Rowenna did not understand it. All her life she'd sat by, observing her mother's craft, trying to still the shards of it that lurked beneath her own skin until such a time as she was deemed ready. An all too familiar sense of frustration and confusion washed over Rowenna, bitter enough for her to choke on.

"Go home, Enna," Mairead pleaded. "There's nothing you can do to help."

Rowenna stayed as she was, wracked with indecision.

You're not ready yet, Mairead had told her so many times, with or without words. *Perhaps you never will be.*

But there was hunger in Rowenna Winthrop, no matter how she strove to keep it in check. A hunger to know her inexplicable pieces better. A starveling desire to be whole and understood, even if only by herself.

"Enna!" Mairead insisted.

Rather than do as she was bid, Rowenna sank to her knees at her mother's side. A cold, fitful rain was starting up, and she knew if her father, Cam, had been there, he'd have dealt with this very differently. If he'd been home, he'd have coaxed Mairead in out of this weather, taking her back to the Winthrop cot and warming her by the fire. He'd have soothed her with quiet words and his steadfast presence, the way he'd done for all of the Winthrops at one time or another.

But Cam was gone and had been for months. The English tyrant in Inverness still kept his upstart and unwanted court, and the disparate sparks of rebellion had been fanned to full flame by his cruelty. Cam had left to join the Highlands uprising, and in his absence there was only Rowenna to manage Mairead's fey moods, for her brothers found them entirely unnerving. Well, so did Rowenna, but she did not have the luxury of casting off her mother's care onto someone else.

Setting her lantern down, Rowenna pushed up the sleeves of her oilskin and slowly began to dig at Mairead's side. It seemed simple enough—to pull rocks from the earth. There was no craft in that on its own. No witchwork. Her mother was sobbing with fear, the whites of her eyes gleaming in the lantern's feeble glow. It was catching, that fear, and however benign the work, soon Rowenna's belly roiled with nerves. She'd seen Mairead compelled to do things before—to build her cairns on the cliff tops at the solstices and equinoxes, to spin yarn and knit new pullovers for every one of the Winthrop boys well before their old clothes had worn out.

But none of it had ever been like this.

This wasn't just a compulsion. This was raw panic.

The wind died down for a moment, and Rowenna realized with a chill that the strange, rhythmic sound she'd heard beneath the gale was not the omnipresent sea, breaking against the shore, but Mairead herself. Her lips moved constantly as she muttered the words of the Our Father, over and over again as she worked.

Our Father, who art in heaven

hallowed be thy name;

thy kingdom come,

thy will be done. . . .

Deliver us from evil

Deliver us from evil

Deliver us from evil

"*Màthair?*" Rowenna finally managed to get the word out. She pried a rock free from the iron-hard earth and handed it to Mairead, who took it with a shamefaced look. "What is it you're afraid of? What are you doing? And how can I help?"

It was the first time in three years that Rowenna had put a question to her mother about the nature of her work.

Mairead glanced toward the sea, her eyes owl-like in the gloom.

"I'm making a ward," she said. "A hedge against the devil and his creatures. A work of protection, built of hard stone and unshakeable intent."

Rowenna's throat tightened, and she let the mud-slick rock she held fall from her hands. "I can't help you then. I don't know how to make a ward. You know that."

"Just go," Mairead ordered, her voice ragged with despair. "Please, Enna. There's nothing you can do here."

Slowly Rowenna got to her feet and looked down at Mairead. And despite her own ignorance, despite the mistrust that had driven a wedge between them, Rowenna loved her. Loved Mairead with a fierceness and wildness made sharper by the tension of knowing her mother saw her as too quick tempered to help in this work.

"Come with me," Rowenna pleaded. "Whatever you're doing can wait. No one's asked you to take on the burden of protecting this land—it's too much, and you'll get no thanks for it in the end. Leave it, and come home."

When Mairead looked up, there were tears shining in her eyes, but she shook her head. "I can't, Enna. I just can't. Someday you'll understand."

That cut Rowenna to the quick, because were it not for Mairead's resistance, she'd understand already. All around them, the wind keened across the moorland, repeating stormy words in a hollow, rain-sodden lament.

She comes, she comes, she comes.

Scrambling to her feet, Mairead disappeared into the deepening twilight. Wind howled over the cliffs and set the rain to stinging like bees by the time she returned. Rowenna glanced up, and a strangled gasp escaped her, for under one arm her mother bore an incongruous burden—a great white swan, which remained oddly quiescent with Mairead's hand covering its eyes. Rain beaded off its soft plumage, and its neck arched gracefully.

"What are you—" Rowenna began, but Mairead shook her head. She set the swan down atop the completed cairn, and the bird stood up, ruffling its feathers.

"*Eala,*" Mairead said, calling the bird by its name in Gàidhlig. "For years I've helped your kind on their long journeys across the sea. Now I stand here in need of an offering from something wild and pure to make fast my ward, and protect this land. Will you do as I ask? Will you help me?"

Rowenna shivered as the swan bowed low. Since she was a child, she'd fed the swans with her mother when they stopped in their wandering from north to south. A handful of times, when birds arrived exhausted or injured, she and Mairead had taken them in, tending to them at the Winthrop hearth until they were well enough to carry on.

Mairead bowed back. "Thank you, beloved."

But when Mairead reached into the pocket of her overskirt and pulled out a sheathed gutting knife, Rowenna could watch no longer. It was one thing to be up on the cliffs laying out wards in a gathering storm. To do harm to a living creature with this strange work, though—that was more than even Rowenna with her hunger had ever wanted. That felt like darkness.

Her eldest brother, Liam, with his priest's leanings, would have a thing or two to say about all this. Ungodly, he'd call it. Unforgivable.

"No, *Màthair*," Rowenna said breathlessly, hurrying forward and taking hold of Mairead's arm. "Surely there's another way to finish your work."

"Enna, I asked you to go for a reason. But it's only a little blood," Mairead assured her, quieter and calmer now that her work seemed to be near finished. "Just a drop or two. The swan will be fine, love. We've done it before, the swans and me."

"You've done *this* before?" The knowing that her mother had repeated this ritual in secret burned through Rowenna. It was as if an entire other life existed, beyond the one Rowenna knew, and Mairead had struggled to keep her out of it. Yet it should be hers by rights—didn't her bones cry out for power and craft, just as her mother's did?

Betrayal made Rowenna angry, and she chose her words with the intent of wounding.

"I didn't realize that all this time, you've been just what they say you are in the village." Rowenna spoke with defiance, and for the first time that she could remember, Mairead met her sharpness with answering anger.

"Say the word if you're bent on doing harm," Rowenna's mother snapped.

"You know what it is," Rowenna answered.

"I do. But I want you to speak it."

Rowenna drew herself up. "They call you a witch. And they call me a witch too, though I've none of the craft of one. I bear all the blame, and none of the power."

Her voice wavered a little at the last, and Mairead winced.

"Enna, I'm sorry," she said, her words hardly audible over the wind's cries. "I'm sorry I was cross with you, and I'm sorry for what they say. I didn't want any of this for you. Believe me when I tell you that all I've ever wanted is to keep you and our village safe."

"Then let me help in earnest," Rowenna pleaded. "Show me what needs to be done. Teach me. We'll finish this work together, and when it's complete we can go home together too. The boys are waiting. Finn's asleep, but Liam will read aloud, and you and I can help Duncan untangle his nets. Then in the morning, let me *keep* helping you, *Màthair*. Stop trying to cut me off from who we are and what we can do."

Mairead hesitated, glancing from the swan to Rowenna and back again.

"You're a good lass, Enna," she said. "Truly you are. I don't know what your father and I have done to deserve you, my salt-water girl."

Rowenna swallowed back tears and waited, hardly daring to breathe.

"All right," Mairead said at last. "I need you to show me your courage now, if you're to be a help."

Still standing on the cairn, the swan regarded them both with knowing dark eyes. But as Mairead and Rowenna turned to it, something startled the creature. It half ran, half flew past them, wings buffeting the air as it fled.

"*Eala!*" Mairead called, and started after the swan. "Don't leave me. Our work's not done!"

From somewhere in the gathering dark, the creature let out a riotous trumpeting that echoed off the stormy cliff sides. Rowenna ran after Mairead, who chased the swan, until abruptly, the clamorous sounds of the white bird were cut off. Mairead froze, and Rowenna fell still at her side.

"What is it, *Màthair*?" Rowenna asked, her voice little more than a whisper that the wind caught and carried away.

"I don't know." Mairead shook her head. "I don't know, but my work will have to stay unfinished. We'll be safest at home now. Come with me, and hurry."

She grasped Rowenna's hand and pulled her along, and Rowenna went willingly, heart beating so hard within her that it hurt.

They were just passing Iteag Burn, where a stream rushed over the cliff face and down a steep track to the sea, when Rowenna tripped and nearly stumbled. Pausing, she lowered her lantern, only to find one of Mairead's cairns in a scattered heap. Atop what remained of it lay a shapeless white-and-crimson object.

Rowenna's pulse quickened, and for a moment her breath refused to come.

"Is that your swan?" she finally managed to get out.

Without answering, Mairead stepped forward. When she set a hand on the white shape, the once-elegant head and neck of the swan lolled over her broken ward. The creature's breast feathers were sodden with gore, for it had been torn apart, its rib cage split and all the soft and vital pieces inside stolen, so that it was no more than an empty husk. No more than the twisted idea of a bird, rather than the thing itself.

"What did this, *Màthair*?"

She comes, she comes, she comes, the wind sang desperately to Rowenna, as unreasoning fear woke inside the girl.

"I won't speak the name of the thing that's done this. Not here, not tonight," Rowenna's mother said with a tense shake of her head. "But I mustn't leave the bird, not when it would have offered me blood to keep us safe. I must at least give it back to the sea."

Mairead glanced at Rowenna, and the girl's chest ached with fierce devotion, and with familiar hunger and longing.

"I think I've been wrong, to keep you in the dark," Mairead

said slowly. "And I think you're ready. You are who you are, and there's no changing that. We'll work together from now on, my saltwater girl. Just as soon as we get through this night."

When she pressed a kiss to Rowenna's forehead, it felt like a benediction. Like a new beginning. Like the moment Rowenna had waited for all her life.

Mairead bundled up the broken swan and carried it to the edge of the cliff. There she lingered, murmuring something to the lifeless bird, but her voice was stolen by the wind. Toeing blank space with the breakers pounding endlessly against the shore below, she let the dead swan slip from her arms. There was a flash of white, and the darkness and the distance swallowed the creature up.

At last Mairead turned back to her daughter, and to the blur of the Highlands, shrouded in stinging rain. She reached out, and for the briefest, tantalizing instant, her fingers brushed warm against Rowenna's own.

In spite of the storm, Rowenna smiled, overcome by a surge of pure relief. Things would be better now that they'd come to an understanding. Mairead smiled back, and Rowenna's fear quieted.

Then, with a strangled cry, Mairead was torn away as something reached out of the darkness and dragged her down the wet and treacherous track of the burn.

Chapter Two

Rowenna sat with her back to one of Mairead's cairns, half a mile north of home. The earth beneath her was damp and cold, and she pulled her knees closer to her chest with a shiver. It was not yet dawn, and the waves beyond the cliffs of Neadeala were brushed with scant silver light by a moon that scudded between clouds. All around her the wind danced about, murmuring endlessly.

Rowenna, Rowenna, Rowenna, our love, our light, our dark-hearted girl.

Scowling, Rowenna paid it no mind. They were at odds now, Rowenna and the wind and the land and the sea. It felt, some days, as if watching Mairead go had stolen all Rowenna's goodness and brightness and set her against the world. Today especially, she felt full of fear and anger and sharp edges, so she'd slipped out of the Winthrop cottage early to spare her family such company.

At least, she'd tried to spare them.

"Two months to the day since she went, isn't it?" Cam Winthrop said with a sigh as he approached from across the heath and lowered himself down heavily beside Rowenna.

Rowenna tore her eyes from the sea and glanced at her father. Cam was a towheaded bear of a man, who'd returned from the Highland rebellion's devastating last battle only weeks ago and found his wife dead and his household in disarray. Though he'd loved Mairead and made sure she and every one of the Winthrop children knew it, he'd weathered the news of her death the way a stone weathers a storm. With immovable stubbornness. With a refusal, for the sake of his children, to be ground down or toppled by grief.

"Aye, two months," Rowenna answered quietly, resting her chin on her arms. She wondered, not for the first time, what it would be like to be able to speak of that night. To be honest and not to constantly swallow the truth of what she'd seen. What she'd really witnessed lay like ice inside her—a weight and a worry, a bitter secret from which she was never free.

"Is Duncan home yet?" Rowenna asked Cam. Older than her by only a year, Duncan was the wildest of the Winthrops and often missing till sunrise. But he was Cam's right hand aboard the family's fishing boat and had done the work of two men while Cam was away. No matter how he wandered, Duncan always appeared when he was needed.

"Not yet," Cam said. "I'll go down to the harbor from here— he'll meet me there, no doubt, or you can send him along if he turns up at home first."

Rowenna gnawed at her lower lip. That was a worry too—she hated for any of her family to be unaccounted for. And today the wind was restless, which added to the constant backdrop of low fear she lived with.

Rowenna, the breeze sighed as it roamed across the cliff tops. *Beware, beware, dark-hearted girl.*

"I miss how it felt, walking into the cot when she was here," Cam said abruptly, and Rowenna held her breath as tears started behind her eyes. It was the first time her father had owned to missing Mairead. He'd never shared even a fraction of his grief with Rowenna or her brothers, choosing to keep his sorrow private, but Rowenna could sense it inside him—a counterpoint to her own heartsick longing. "You've done so well, Enna—so well, looking after things, but no place feels like home without her."

"I know," Rowenna said, swallowing around the tightening in her throat. "Nothing's right with *Màthair* gone."

It wasn't just the house, either. In the weeks after Mairead's death, Rowenna had *felt* something emanating from the wards her mother had frantically cobbled together along the cliff tops. A soft, comforting warmth. A sense of safety and watchfulness. It had faded over time, though, and in Mairead's absence, Rowenna was powerless to restore whatever virtue the wards had been imbued with. She'd tried adding stones to them, or rearranging the rocks they were already built of, or keeping their surfaces clear of moss and dirt. None of it served any purpose. Rowenna still stood on the threshold of a whole world of craft she could not understand, and without a guide, she was unable to enter it.

With one calloused hand, Cam reached out and ruffled her black hair, as he'd done when she was a small girl.

"We'll just have to keep muddling through," he said. "We're all right, though, aren't we? You and me, and the boys?"

It was the first hint of uncertainty he'd shown since coming home, and Rowenna's heart broke a little to hear it.

"Aye, *Athair*," she answered, with an uncharacteristic attempt at brightness. "We're all right. Things can only get better."

But the warding stones behind her were lifeless rock, and the wind sighed away across the heath.

Beware, beware, our love, our light. Beware, beware, dark-hearted girl.

As Cam got to his feet once more, Rowenna couldn't help it. Her hand shot out of its own accord and grasped his. She couldn't shake the last image she had of Mairead—that one terrible memory that had set fear inside her.

"*Athair*, don't take the boat out today," Rowenna begged. "Stay safe ashore. Just this once. Just until tomorrow. We'll keep Duncan and Liam and Finn home too, and all stay together. I know *Màthair*'s gone, but maybe I can—"

The words died on Rowenna's lips. She could what? Safeguard her family the way Mairead had once done? The craft her mother exercised was beyond her, and perhaps now it always would be. Rowenna had no way of protecting them from the fate that had befallen Mairead, only the fruitless wish that she might keep them all within her sight forever.

Cam gave her a look that served as a gentle reproach. It was an unspoken rule in the Winthrop household that no one should try to dissuade him or Duncan from their work. The sea was a fickle and dangerous place, but without Cam and Duncan's fishing, the Winthrops would not eat. Liam and Finn would not have a chance to better themselves, Liam being meant for life as a priest, Finn for work in trade. And Rowenna—well, Rowenna would not have a roof to live under or a reputation to speak of, which was all the world had ever seen fit to offer her.

"Fear won't keep us fed, Rowenna," Cam said, and as he did, she recalled that he'd told Mairead the same thing the day he left them to fight for the freedom of the Highlands. Mairead had been beside herself, but Cam was adamant about going. He felt it right, and he'd been offered compensation from Laird Sutherland that would bring in more money than half a year of him fishing and Mairead selling woolen-work.

Rowenna fell silent. For the briefest moment, she considered speaking the truth, rather than the lie she'd told after Mairead's death.

The cliffs were slick with rain. The night was dark. She slipped and fell.

It had been an easy story for the villagers to believe. But the truth wore away at Rowenna always, like salt water against stone. The prospect of confessing everything to Cam—the entire appalling truth of what had happened the night her mother died, and how Rowenna, kept untaught, had been powerless to save her—was a tempting one. But it was hard enough to bear Mairead's absence believing her death had been an accident. Rowenna feared it would finally break her stalwart father to know his wife's last moments had been filled with malevolence and terror. And it might break Rowenna to have Cam know she could have saved Mairead, if she'd only known more, and been more.

"We'll make a short day of it," Cam promised when she remained quiet. "Duncan and I'll be home before sundown, you'll see. You're a good girl, Enna, and there's no need to fret."

Rowenna stood and watched him go across the heath and toward the harbor. As he went, the wind whipped at her skirts, muttering and moaning, its words a warning.

The dark, the deep, the drowning sea. She comes, she comes, she comes.

Athair's expecting you at the harbor, Duncan," Rowenna said peevishly as she arrived home and caught sight of a golden-haired boy under the cottage's thatched overhang, a dainty girl in a cloak and hood standing on her toes to kiss him, long and slow and soft. "Where've you been all night, anyhow? You're a fool to go wandering in this wind—it cuts like a knife."

At the sound of Rowenna's voice, the girl startled and glanced up. Rowenna caught sight of her small, expressive face and stifled a sigh.

Alice Sutherland. The laird's own daughter. Just like Duncan to step out with someone so far above his station he might as well be making sheep's eyes at the stars.

Duncan shrugged amiably, a red-cheeked disaster of a boy. His nose was crooked from having been broken not once or twice, but three times—once in a fall, twice in fights—but his hazel eyes shone like sea glass, if sea glass had a wildness and a will of its own. Rowenna would have killed or cursed or died for him, whichever was needed, and Duncan took shameless advantage of that fact.

"I've never claimed to be anything but a fool," he told Rowenna with a grin. He casually draped an arm around Alice Sutherland's shoulders, and Alice, at least, had the good grace to bite her lower lip and look acutely embarrassed.

"Good morrow to you," she said politely to Rowenna, in a voice soft as lamb's wool. "You're up early, Enna."

"And you're up late," Rowenna shot back. It wasn't that she disliked Alice in particular. But the villagers in general were rarely kind to Rowenna, so she kept to herself when possible, and any run-in with the people of Neadeala generally served as a stark reminder of why she'd made that her habit.

Alice seemed determined to make herself amiable, though. She said nothing in her own defense, and Duncan shot Rowenna a warning look.

"You're right" was all Alice said. "I've kept Duncan out till dawn, and now he's got a day's work ahead of him. It was thoughtless of me, and I won't be so foolish again."

Her softness took the edge off Rowenna's ill humor.

"I doubt it was your fault," Rowenna offered, relenting a bit. "Duncan's never had much sense when it comes to managing time, and he's powerless against a pretty face."

Alice drew her cloak tighter about herself and squinted up at Duncan. "Is that so? I'll have to be wary of competition then. Duncan. Rowenna."

Nodding to the two of them, she set out across the moors, back toward Neadeala.

Rowenna turned on Duncan immediately.

"Was it only her last night?" she asked, sounding every inch a scold, but with Mairead gone, *someone* had to scold Duncan. And Rowenna had done everything she could to fill the gaping holes Mairead's absence had left in the fabric of their lives. "Or do you plan to break the heart of every young lass and lad in the Highlands? And if you manage that, will you be satisfied?"

"I'm not sure." Duncan put his head to one side. "There's a lot of land here, caught between the seas. But perhaps I'll get bored in time, and have to go wooing in the Americas as well."

Rowenna gave him a long-suffering look, and Duncan nudged her shoulder with his own as she came up beside him. "You'll be proud of me, little sister. As it happens, I'm nearly reformed these days."

"Really? So you're stepping out with two admirers at once, instead of three?"

Duncan let his ruffian's face grow mournful. "Just the one, I'm afraid. How the mighty have fallen."

He moved out of the shelter of the cot's overhanging roof, ready for a day's hard work regardless of how he'd spent the night, and Rowenna called after him. "It's her then, Duncan? You've finally set your cap at someone and *that's* who you chose?"

"Aye it is," he said, shoving his hands into the pockets of his oilskin coat with a regretful sigh. "God help me, there's only Alice now."

Rowenna made a noise of disapproval and disbelief. "You could have anyone from here to Inverness and you choose the *laird's* daughter? You've got seawater for brains, you know that?

Old Sutherland will have you horsewhipped if he finds out."

Duncan grinned irrepressibly. "I suppose that's half the fun of it."

He started out across the bare land that stretched between the Winthrop cot and the harbor. But after a few steps, Duncan stopped and glanced over one shoulder, as if he'd forgotten something.

"Enna," he said, his mocking voice uncharacteristically serious. "You'll be all right today, won't you? Only I know you've taken *Màthair*'s death especially hard."

Rowenna swallowed. She couldn't renew the request she'd made to Cam—Duncan would have even less luck trying to persuade their father to stay onshore than she had done.

Instead she nodded. "I'm all right. Get on with you—don't keep *Athair* waiting."

And then Duncan was gone too, vanishing into the mist that lay across the moorland. Shivering, Rowenna ducked indoors. Liam and Finn had already left for the day, and the cot stood empty and silent, the embers of a peat fire smoldering soundlessly on the hearth. There was a forlorn air about the place, despite the signs of habitation. It felt as if everyone who'd ever lived there had just stepped out, but that unbeknownst to them, they'd never return.

It's only a mood, Rowenna reassured herself as she cleared away and slowly washed the breakfast dishes, which had been left waiting on the table for her. *You're being a fool. What happened with* Màthair *was already impossible the once. It can't repeat itself.*

At midmorning, as if to rob her of any last shred of comfort, wind slammed against the cot with sudden force. It raged around the eaves and howled down the chimney, wordless and furious now, and bringing rain that tore at the thatch. Down in the village the church bell rang endlessly, calling for any of the fishing boats that had already left harbor to return home.

The day passed in a haze of work and worry. At last the storm faded, letting light through as the sun set behind banks of lingering cloud. The wind had calmed into sullenness rather than rage, but Rowenna's restlessness had reached a fever pitch.

Rowenna, the breeze whispered, all its passion spent. *Come out, come out, dark-hearted girl.*

By the time a commotion sounded outside the cottage's door, Rowenna could bear no more uncertainty. She flew to the door and wrenched it open, only to find her eldest brother, Liam, standing on the threshold with little Finn behind him.

Liam said nothing as he stepped inside. His thin, expressive face was unreadable, but Finn, the youngest of the family at only seven, hung up his oilskin coat and went to Rowenna at once. She put her arms around her smallest brother and fixed her eyes on Liam as Finn buried his face in her apron.

"What is it?" she asked. "What's gone wrong?"

A muscle worked in Liam's jaw. The leanest of the Winthrops, he reminded Rowenna of an altar painting, or of a reed that bent and never broke. She envied that strength sometimes—that serene and untouchable calm he'd learned to cultivate. It would serve him well if he took holy orders as Mairead had intended.

"They never came into harbor," Liam said. "The Grooms were out last and said they saw what looked like *Athair*'s boat, foundering in the storm. But they couldn't get close enough to help."

Rowenna stood rooted to the spot with her arms still around Finn. Then, slowly, she smiled down at her youngest brother.

"Nothing to worry about, Finny," Rowenna said. "*Athair* and Duncan are the best sailors we know. I'm sure they put down anchor in some cove to wait out the storm. Why not get yourself some bread and milk and take it to bed with you? You look worn out after a day with Liam and Father Osric—no doubt they've been making you study too hard."

Finn smiled back, tentatively, and Rowenna watched him do as she'd said. Only once he'd disappeared behind the curtain that sectioned off the alcove where her father and brothers slept did Rowenna let her gentle demeanor slip. She strode to the door and snatched an oilskin from the row of pegs there.

"Where are you going, Rowenna?" Liam asked, his voice a warning.

"Out," Rowenna snapped, her hand already on the latch.

"To do *what*?"

With a helpless sigh, Rowenna turned to face her brother. He was seated by the hearth, a book open on his lap, firelight gilding his ascetic face. A saint's face, made for suffering without complaint.

But Rowenna was no saint, and she refused to lose yet more of her family without a fight.

"I don't know," she answered. "I don't know if there's much I can do, but Liam, I have to try. Whatever craft I have, if it can help—if there's a way to see *Athair* and Duncan come home safe . . ."

Liam looked up, and it stole her breath how beautiful he was, this eldest brother with whom she seemed forever at odds. Yet it had been Liam and no one else to whom Rowenna had confessed the truth of Mairead's last night, and of her dying. More fool, she. He had not believed a word of it.

"There's no devil in this storm, Enna," Liam said gently. "There was no devil that night, either, no matter what you think you saw. Storms happen. Falls happen. There doesn't have to be ill intent behind them, and you can't fight what's just an act of God. *Màthair* did you no good, letting you think her oddness was anything more than idle superstition."

Liam spoke with infinite patience, and Rowenna winced. She stared miserably at the cottage door, through which Mairead would never walk again. Through which Duncan and Cam—but no. She would not number them among the dead, not yet. Not even in her mind. For once in her life, she refused to be powerless or to let ignorance get the better of her.

"I know what I saw that night," Rowenna gritted out as she slung the oilskin over her shoulders and reached for a satchel she kept ready by the door, packed with a wool blanket and a flask of fresh water. "But you can misbelieve me if you like, and I'll count it a mercy, Liam. Because if you'd seen what happened to *Màthair*— well, I don't think you could bear it."

"What is it you're planning to do?" Liam asked again, a wariness in the way he looked at Rowenna.

"I don't know," she answered. "But I do know this—I won't give up until *Athair* and Duncan come home. I'm not losing someone again, not if I've got a chance of stopping it."

Without another word, she stepped into the dying storm.

Chapter Three

Trudging through the fading rain with the wind muttering about her, Rowenna could not help but remember. The panic swimming in her veins and the fear weighting down her bones threw her right back to the night Mairead had died.

However Liam doubted, whatever uncertainty he liked to cast on Rowenna's memories, she always recalled that night the same way—with perfect and startling clarity.

The warmth of Mairead's hand in hers.

The shock of their fingers parting as her mother was torn away.

Ragged screams, descending down the cliff track.

The agonizing pull of something lost, something desperate, something in need of Rowenna's help, burning through her like unforgiving fire until the pain of it drove her to her knees.

A flash of lightning, illuminating the little strip of rocky beach at the bottom of the burn.

And the vision that stark light had seared across Rowenna's mind, never to be forgotten: her beloved mother, lying on her belly on the shifting stones and staring up at the cliff top with a look that said she knew death was a heartbeat away. For pinning her to the shingle was a creature the like of which Rowenna had never seen before and hoped never to see again.

It was a twisted, malevolent thing, its deepwater skin mottled and slippery with salt. The lightning limned it with white fire, gleaming from a row of needle-sharp teeth that jutted at odd angles from the creature's hungry maw. With limbs like a mockery of human arms and legs, it kept Mairead down, webbed and many-jointed fingers tangled in her golden hair.

Rowenna could *feel* the craft surging from her mother—a torrent of it, a lifetime's worth of magic. But it did no good. Mairead's craft was as golden and harmless as any other part of her.

Help me, she mouthed to Rowenna.

For a brief and devastating instant, Rowenna locked eyes with the creature that had laid hold of her mother. It stared up at her with unfeeling, incandescent orbs, made for plumbing the sea's lightless depths. And Rowenna tried. She tried with everything in her to dredge up her untouched craft and fashion it into a blade with which to kill this monstrous thing.

The creature only blinked. Then, with a wrench of its plunderer's arms, it snapped Mairead Winthrop's neck and dragged her into the sea.

Tonight would be different, Rowenna swore to herself. Tonight, she wouldn't let ignorance stand in her way. If she had to cut the heart out of her own chest to access some spark of her craft, she'd do it, and gladly.

On sure feet Rowenna walked away from Neadeala, to a hidden cove past the Winthrop cot where Cam had taught all his children to swim on the warmest summer days. She made her way down a worn path between cliffs, headed for the rocky beach around the cove, the wind slackening and the icy rain ceasing as she went. Overhead, the moon showed now and then through shreds of cloud.

At least there was no worry of meeting anyone out in the wake of such a storm. God knew what any of the villagers would think if they found her at the work she was about to attempt.

As Rowenna slipped and slid down the incline that led to the beach, the wind skipped and sang about her.

Come out, come out, beloved girl. The dark, the deep, the drowning sea.

Only twice before had Rowenna tried to work her craft: the night her mother died and the day she attempted to curse the redcoat and was chided by Mairead. Both times it had come to naught. But now more than ever before, she was desperate, needing her uncanny, bewildering abilities to fledge into full power.

"Please," Rowenna called to the wind, which so often called to her. "Tell me where *Athair* and Duncan are. Let them be not lost but found. Lead me to them."

She waited, breath catching in her throat, for anything. Any sign that she had been heard and understood. But it did not come. There was only the deep, abiding chill of the Highlands, and the rumble of waves against the rock-strewn shore.

What is it I always tell you? Mairead's voice said in the dark recesses of Rowenna's mind.

"That I'm like the sea," Rowenna answered aloud. "And that even rock wears away before salt water in the end."

If the wind could not help, perhaps the sea would.

Standing on the shingle, with the white teeth of the waves

eating away at the shoreline before her, Rowenna cast a glance over each shoulder. Then she shed her thick woolen clothes like a selkie peeling off its sealskin. In nothing but a thin shift, she walked to the water's edge and, without hesitation, carried on into the breakers.

Fear rose in her at the thought of grasping fingers and deep-water eyes, but Rowenna tamped it down ruthlessly. She'd make a deal with the devil if it meant bringing Cam and Duncan home.

As frigid water rose up Rowenna's legs and higher, the cold of it was like catching a fist in the soft skin of her belly. She gasped and went a little faster, feet flat and steady as waves buffeted her. At last, Rowenna took a great breath and went below the surface, into the quiet moonlit depths, where the crash of the waves was but an echo of a distant world. Standing on the rocky seabed, she looked out past the cove, toward the place where the wild waters of the North Sea foamed. Dark and dangerous they were, but Rowenna Winthrop, who had suffered heartbreak and seen monsters, looked into the heart of the sea without quailing. Her long black hair rose around her head, turning her into something half-wild—a siren or a Gorgon, perhaps, the sort of creature that brought men to ruin. She felt her doubts and hesitation and fears melt away as she stared into the watery depths, tasting both salt water and something gloriously like freedom.

Rowenna had spent all her life restraining the craft that lay within her. She'd waited for so long, avoiding and diminishing her gifts, never pushing at the strangeness that made her more or less than ordinary and stoked suspicion. But tonight she reached out to the fathomless expanse of the sea, and the sea came to her as she beckoned.

At first it looked like nothing more than a ripple in the black, but as it grew closer and closer, the North Sea's emissary resolved into the shape of an enormous moray eel, stone gray and sinuous, its wide eyes shining like small moons. The creature stopped before Rowenna, and the muscular length of it undulated in the current.

Up above, the wind cried out, its voice a muffled wail. *Take care, take care. Mind what you wish for, saltwater girl.*

But Rowenna ignored the keening wind. She summoned the image of her missing family and held it with all the fierceness of her troubled heart. She thought it at the sea and the wind and the sky. At the heather and the earth and God above.

Give them back, her blood sang.

Give them back, her heart cried.

Let the proud waters surrender what they've taken. Let the waves give up what they stole. I will have what is lost returned to me.

The eel darted forward, quick as a knife strike. Rowenna felt the sharp sting of razor-edged teeth cutting into her flesh, and when the cloud of blood that blossomed from her bitten hand cleared, all that could be seen of the moray was its serpentine shape retreating back into the midnight water.

With one swift kick of her feet, Rowenna surged upward and broke free of the sea's embrace, taking in sobbing breaths of air. She let the waves batter and push her in to shore, stumbling the last few yards to where she'd left her clothes and a wool blanket.

Though her teeth chattered and her limbs shook so hard it hurt, she dried herself off with the blanket at once, peeling out of her wet shift and leaving it abandoned on the beach. After pulling her clothes back on and wrapping the blanket around her shoulders, Rowenna hurried up and down the shore, halfway between a walk and a run, until the blood flowed fast through her veins and warmth flushed her from head to toe.

The moment she stopped, it slammed into her—the *pull* of work waiting to be done. She'd never felt it so strongly. But then again, she'd only ever been sought out by the wind and the sea before, and never sought them out herself. The efficacy of her craft startled Rowenna, leaving her filled with a heady sense of triumph. For once, she'd taken control of her power and managed to find a way to use it rightly. But she had no time to stop and wonder at the nature of her gift, not with that pull dragging her northward.

It was less than half a mile to her mother's old cliff top wards, and to where the swift, rain-swollen waters of the rushing burn cut their way down the cliffs to the sea. Rowenna ran all the way, in danger of turning an ankle on the uneven ground. Though no outside force worked on her, it felt as if she was dragged across the moor by the fearsome pull of her lost kin.

But at the top of the burn, Rowenna stopped short. Of all the places to be led, it had to be here, to the very spot where Mairead had met her end. Staring down at the cliff's edge, memories of her mother's last moments were like a grasping hand at Rowenna's throat.

Gathering her courage, she peered down into the windswept darkness below. The track the stream had carved through the cliffs was treacherous at the best of times, let alone on a storm-tossed spring night. Rainwater rushed over the loose stones, churning them up into a mess of mud and pebbles.

But Rowenna's pull dragged her onward, toward the one place she despised most.

Take heart, take heart, saltwater girl, the wind moaned as she hesitated on the brink.

Letting out a ragged breath, Rowenna began her descent.

She crept, inch by slow inch, down the track of the burn, beside the rushing rainwater, testing every bit of earth before placing her weight on it. By the time Rowenna reached the small patch of rocky shore at the base of the cliffs, she was slick with mud and shaking, from exhaustion rather than cold.

There it was, though—the ruined remains of a boat, mast and torn sailcloth and snapped timbers strewn about the beach, visible by moonlight now the sky had nearly cleared.

"Athair!" Rowenna gasped, and ran to peer under the largest piece of the vessel that had washed ashore. All she found was an irritable crab that snapped its claws at her and scuttled off.

"Athair," Rowenna called out, her voice carrying above the boom and hush of the sea. "Duncan!"

The only answer that came was the shrill cry of a trio of small cliff wyverns, who launched themselves from the nearby crags and circled overhead, rain glinting on their silvery dragon bodies and leathery wings.

At the sight of them, Rowenna's breath caught in her throat, and she spun on one heel, hurrying to the base of the cliffs, which lay in deep shadow. Cliff wyverns were carrion creatures who slept during the day and came out to scavenge at night. Their presence could only mean one thing—easy prey was nearby.

Even as she thought it, Rowenna's foot connected with something heavy and yielding. Something decidedly not stone or hard earth or snapped timber. For a moment, her courage nearly failed. She imagined a hundred terrible things, not least of them that the creature she'd watched kill her mother lay waiting at her feet.

"*Athair?*" Rowenna sobbed, steeling her nerves as she dropped to her knees and blindly ran her hands over oilskin and thick, tightly knit wool. The figure before her stirred and let out an anguished groan.

"Rowenna Winthrop?"

Everything in Rowenna revolted at the realization that it was a stranger's voice—not Cam or Duncan or anyone she could recognize from two spoken words. Her name came out of the stranger raw and hoarse, and suddenly a pair of hands grasped Rowenna's, holding on so tightly, it hurt.

"Are you Rowenna Winthrop? There's no one else who'd have known to look for me down here."

Not Cam.

Not Duncan.

Rowenna's heart broke inside her chest, and she could think of nothing beyond that fact. Her work had failed because, yet again, she'd been too ignorant to save her own flesh and blood.

As her silence stretched on, the stranger let out a shuddering sigh, laden with the sound of despair. "You're not her, then."

With a supreme effort, Rowenna collected herself. "I am. But you'd best tell me your name and quick—there's no one missing from these shores but my father and my brother."

"Not from here," the stranger rasped. Hard as Rowenna squinted, she couldn't make out his face in the shadows. Couldn't tell if he was in one piece or not. "I'm Gawen MacArthur. But I was on my way to Neadeala to find you, when I got caught in the storm this afternoon."

"Coming to find me?" Rowenna asked, dull surprise underscoring the words. "What could anyone from elsewhere possibly have to say to me, when I've never been more than five miles from home?"

The stranger took a moment, his breath coming short and fast. Then: "My father knew—knows—yours. And I heard from him that Camden Winthrop of Neadeala has a wife and a daughter possessed of strange craft. I'm looking for something that's gone badly astray, and I need your help. I don't think anyone else can find it."

A consuming grief shot through Rowenna at his words, coupled with a hollow sense of defeat as the pull she'd followed while sliding down to the beach vanished. Cam and Duncan were as lost as ever, gone without a trace. Whatever craft she had was wholly beyond her ken, and as such, no more than a useless burden.

"No," Rowenna said, her voice flat. "You've got the wrong girl, and the wrong village. My *màthair*'s dead, my *athair*'s gone missing, and I can't help you. I can't even help myself."

"But you found me," the stranger insisted.

"It's not you I was looking for," Rowenna told him bitterly. "You're just a mistake. Another thing gone wrong."

Whoever the stranger was, he let out a faint, pained sound. And he'd not moved from where he lay on the shingle since Rowenna reached the bottom of the burn. Softening a little, she amended her refusal. "I can't help you with my craft, at any rate. But I can fetch someone to haul you up this cliff, and get you warmed and tended."

She tried rising to her feet, but Gawen wouldn't let go of her hands.

"Don't leave," he begged. "I've been down here for hours. I thought I was going to die."

"I have to go," Rowenna said. "You're all right now, and I'll fetch help. I'll be back before you know it."

"No." Gawen tightened his grip on Rowenna's hands. "You can't leave me."

One of the cliff wyverns squalled overhead. Their small, scaly forms still hung on the air, gleaming by the light of the moon. Rowenna glanced up at them and sighed.

"How bad is it?" she asked Gawen.

"I think I might have broken a leg," he answered. "At least a few ribs. Don't know about my insides."

"I'm going. I can't leave you down here, and I doubt I'd be able to get you up that cliff alone," Rowenna said, wrenching free and hurrying toward the narrow path left by the thin stream. But at the base of the burn she stopped for a moment, wrapping her arms about her waist and stifling a sob as the reality of her failure hit her anew.

Oh, Màthair. *If only you'd known what keeping me in the dark would mean. Your own undoing, and* Athair's *and Duncan's, too.*

Gawen's voice came low from behind her. "If you go, I may not be here when you get back. I saw something out there, in the water."

Rowenna turned slowly to look at him again, her face lit by sudden moonlight that stole through a rent in the clouds. Gawen himself was near invisible, just a patch of darker shade in the looming shadows.

"I'm not mad, I swear it. And it's not fever, or thirst. There's something waiting out there. Something . . ." His voice trailed off, as if he could not speak of it.

"What?" Rowenna snarled, fear setting every nerve in her on fire. "What did you see?"

But he did not answer. Rowenna crossed the bit of rocky beach between them and dropped to her knees at his side once more. She reached out and took his face in both hands, turning it toward her, forcing him to look.

"What did you see?" she repeated.

The set of his jaw was iron hard beneath her palms, and he shook his head.

"Sit up," Rowenna ordered. "I'll drag you to the top of that cliff if I have to."

She could never really say afterward how they managed it. But somehow, Rowenna Winthrop managed to coax and shove and chivvy Gawen MacArthur along as he crawled up the slippery track of Iteag Burn on his hands and one knee and sometimes his belly. He swore and sobbed under his breath, and once was sick into the mud, but Rowenna snapped at him whenever he tried to stop, more sharply than she'd ever snapped before. At last, after what seemed like a lifetime of dirt and toil and anguish, she got them both over the cliff side and onto the cold, wet ground.

Gawen rolled onto his uninjured side and lay panting, his eyes glazed over and faraway.

Rowenna had seen that look once before—on her mother's face, the day she bore Finn. Rowenna knew what it meant. Knew that in that moment, Gawen was far beyond her, caught in a world entirely composed of pain. She let him be. For her own part, she stared out at the boundless sea and sank into a futile dream of family, in which every last member of hers was home and safe and well. Gradually, her heart slowed its frantic racing and her hands ceased to tremble. When she'd calmed a little, she stole a glance at the stranger.

He was younger than she'd guessed at first, not Liam's age, but nearer hers. The sea and the wind had worn his pale face raw and split his lips, and salt matted his thatch of black hair. And yet Rowenna couldn't deny he was comely in spite of that, though it was in a way entirely unlike her brothers. Gawen had all her own paleness and darkness, down to the stern set of his jaw and the subdued fire in his eyes. It was as if, in her request to be given her kin back, the sea had thought to better what Rowenna asked for and dredged up a matching soul.

Unnerved by the thought, she turned away again, fixing her eyes on the horizon.

"I'm going to leave you, but not for long," she said at last. The words came out quiet and flat, offering no sign of the fact that if Rowenna could trade this unfamiliar boy's life for Cam's and Duncan's, she'd have done so in a heartbeat, no matter their outward similarities. "I'll borrow my uncle Morris's cart. You'll hardly miss me, I promise."

Gawen nodded, and Rowenna fetched the wool blanket from where she'd left her bag, in the shadow of a nearby rock. She tucked it around Gawen and hurried off, refusing to allow herself a backward glance or to think of the cliff wyverns, still circling overhead. Refusing to think of her father and her brother, still at the mercy of the sea, and of all the things that lay offshore, lurking beneath the waves.

Chapter Four

The storm had blown over, and the eastern horizon was beginning to lighten by the time Rowenna arrived at home with Gawen in the bed of the cart she'd borrowed or stolen—she wasn't entirely sure which. She'd never been on good terms with her uncle Morris and hadn't bothered to wake him. The night of missed sleep had her head spinning, but she led the pony along with grim determination. Liam and Finn would be home, and they could sort things out between them. Even with Cam and Duncan gone, she wasn't entirely alone in the world yet.

Rowenna drew up in front of the cot, tied the pony to a gorse shrub, and slipped inside, only to find the cottage empty.

"Liam?" she called out. "Finn?"

No answer.

"Hello?"

She looked behind the curtain that separated the boys' pallets from the rest of the cot. No one. Rowenna stood in the empty cottage and pressed a hand to her forehead, swallowing back disappointed tears.

Rifling through the wooden hutch in one corner that served them for a pantry, Rowenna took out a flask of whiskey Cam kept on hand for the longest winter nights. She pulled back the curtain hiding the boys' sleeping quarters and tugged a pallet out to the middle of the room, then shoved it over to one side of the hearth. Rowenna set the whiskey down beside it and went back outside.

Along the way home, as the cart bumped over the uneven heath, Gawen had lost consciousness. Rowenna looked down at him—pale and drawn, with deep shadows under his eyes—and it felt like something had shattered within her, as well.

"Wake up," she said at last, prodding him in the arm. "We're home. All that's left to do is get you inside. Can you manage, if I help?"

The wind sighed about them, wordless and weary now the storm had passed entirely and the sky was clear.

With a short intake of breath, Gawen pushed himself upright. "I can."

Rowenna took most of his weight as they traveled the few steps to the cottage door. On the threshold, the boy went dead white for a moment. His eyes rolled back, and cold fear shot through Rowenna at the thought that he might fall and further harm himself.

"That's enough," she snapped in a panic. "None of that. If you faint, you won't need the floor to break the rest of your bones—I'll do it myself."

With a jolt, Gawen came round. His dark eyes fixed on hers, clearing as they did.

"You're a right scold, aren't you?" he grumbled, but there was relief behind the words, and more than a hint of gratitude.

"I may be, but it's my scolding that's got you here. I expect you to remember that," Rowenna retorted.

And then they'd made it. Gawen half lowered himself, half fell onto the pallet by the hearth, with Rowenna helping as best she could.

"There's whiskey in the flask," Rowenna said, rocking back on her heels when the boy was settled.

He took a long draft and shut his eyes briefly before looking up at her. "Thank you."

"Don't be ridiculous," Rowenna answered with a wave of her hand. "I'll go and see if I can find my brother Liam. He knows a bit of medicine—the most of anyone within twenty miles of here, besides Father Osric. He'll be able to sort you out, I hope."

"Girl." Gawen's words were already slurring and his eyelids growing heavy. "Sit down for a moment before you go. You look dead on your feet."

Rowenna shook her head. "I can't, I—"

"Please."

Dropping into her father's chair, Rowenna bit back a belea-guered sigh. Athair, *where are you?* "There. Happy now?"

"Yes."

Gawen fell silent. Rowenna gave in to temptation and rested her elbows on the table. Even worry could not hold out against her exhaustion any longer. Without meaning to, she slipped for-ward, already asleep before her head met the pillow of her own arms.

"Rowenna."

Slowly Rowenna came awake, the sick feeling of having slept

far less than was needed lodged in her belly, and a wicked knot sending pain up and down her neck.

"Who's that by the hearth, Enna?" Liam stood peering at her, confusion and concern in his gray eyes.

Rowenna straightened stiffly.

"A stranger," she answered. "I found him shipwrecked, washed up on shore at the bottom of Iteag Burn. I was looking for *Athair* and Duncan, but I found him, instead. Is there any news?"

Rowenna scrupulously avoided mentioning what Gawen had told her at the bottom of the cliff—that he'd come for her, and for her craft. It seemed best not to say anything about it given Liam's disapproval of her work. And it made Rowenna feel weighted down and useless, remembering how she'd failed once again to channel her power.

Liam let out a slow breath and squared his shoulders. "Rowenna, here it is—I don't exactly know how to go about telling you this, but we found *Athair* and Duncan and . . ."

Liam's voice trailed off, and Rowenna balled her hands into fists, hiding them under the table.

"*What* did you find?" she asked. "You've got to tell me. Are *Athair* and Duncan dead?"

At that moment the door swung open, letting in a shaft of thin spring sunshine.

"If we're dead, it's news to me," Duncan said with a grin.

Rowenna left her seat so quickly the chair clattered over. She was across the cot in an instant and threw her arms around Duncan, who hugged her back fiercely. But before he could speak again, Rowenna pulled away with a scowl.

"You worthless, reckless, sheep-brained boy," she scolded. "What were you thinking, keeping the boat out in a storm like that, when everyone else had come in?"

"We're both to blame for being stubborn fools," Cam's booming voice said, and Rowenna felt dizzy for a moment as her father appeared behind Duncan. "Neither of us are much for thinking—we're more for doing. I'm sorry we worried you, Enna."

Rowenna put her hands on her hips and looked her father up and down. He seemed to be all in one piece, and no worse for a stormy night at sea. No, it was more than that—Cam looked *happy*. Happier than Rowenna had seen him since he'd returned home only to find his beloved wife gone.

"Well, I'm glad you're back," she admitted. "Both of you. I've taken too much trouble over this family for any Winthrop to be allowed to come to harm. Oh, hold still."

She elbowed Duncan in the ribs. He stood next to her, beaming and fidgeting like he'd done as a child.

"Come on, *Athair*," Duncan begged. "Tell her, why don't you?"

Cam beamed back at Duncan, and Rowenna could feel herself growing more annoyed by the instant. It was one thing for her family to be happy, quite another for them to act as if they'd taken leave of their senses.

"Rowenna," Cam said. "We found something, Duncan and I, while we were out at sea."

Rowenna frowned suspiciously. "Well, I found something while you were away too. What did *you* find?"

"Something you've been missing."

"I haven't been—" Rowenna began, and then a woman stepped into view at Cam's side.

Golden hair. Sky-blue eyes. A face Rowenna knew better than her own.

Mairead Winthrop hadn't changed the slightest bit. Or rather, she'd changed in one regard. Where before, she'd always had a soft and wary look about her, now Rowenna's mother gave off an air of contentment. Satisfaction, even.

"Hello, Rowenna," Mairead said. "I hear you've been looking after things while I was away."

For a moment, Rowenna stood motionless. The walls of the cot felt unbearably close, tightening around her like a snare. Rowenna knew it should be relief rising up in her and not fear, yet there it was, keen and wild and breathtaking. All because suddenly, somehow, through miracle or magic—and Rowenna wasn't sure which—she'd been granted her dearest and most impossible desire.

"Well then," Mairead said. "Won't you give your own mother a kiss?"

Rowenna drew closer, eyes fixed uncertainly on Mairead. She'd never seen her mother stand so tall before, or seem so sure of herself. When she came within reach, Mairead drew her along the rest of the way, with hands that looked gentle but bit into the soft skin on the inside of Rowenna's upper arms.

"Say something," Mairead murmured, as she swathed Rowenna in an embrace that felt like drowning.

"Welcome home, *Màthair*," Rowenna said mechanically.

Mairead's golden hair was soft against the side of her face, but it smelled of brine and cold stone and the blood of small, frightened things. And Rowenna could not help but notice that in spite of the show of affection, Mairead kept her at a slight distance and refused to allow Rowenna to touch her skin.

Deep within the girl, an instinctive knowing awakened. Whatever her eyes saw, her heart knew better.

This is not my own mother. This is something else. This is something dangerous. This is something wrong.

"That's enough," Mairead said, and Rowenna stepped quickly away. "Now where's my little Finn?"

He'd come in with the others but stood lingering by the door, looking young and fragile and every bit as uncertain as Rowenna felt. She fought back an urge to stop her youngest brother in his tracks, to tell him *No, Finn, don't touch her.*

But with Cam and Duncan and Liam all standing by, no harm could come to Finn, no matter who stood in Mairead's place. Sick shock was lancing through Rowenna, and until she could sort out what was happening, she refused to let it show.

Turning on her heel, she crossed the cot to the hearth and dropped to her knees at Gawen MacArthur's side. He was awake now, quietly watching everything happening in the Winthrop cottage.

"Liam," Rowenna called, her voice fraying a little. "Look over this boy I found, won't you? He's a mess after the wreck, and I want to know if you think he'll live, or if he'll die."

Gawen managed a weak scowl. "It's been a rough night, but I'm not in my grave yet."

Behind her, Rowenna could hear Mairead speaking, her voice golden and sweet, and Finn answering hesitantly. The sound set tendrils of fear to slithering up and down Rowenna's spine, and she wanted nothing more than a moment to think. To be entirely, uninterruptably alone. But Rowenna knew she could not allow herself to seem unhappy or unwelcoming. *Rowenna the witch,* the gossips of Neadeala would say. *Who was given a miracle and took offense at the wonders of God.*

At last Cam and Liam both joined her. Liam knelt at Rowenna's side and glanced at Gawen.

"We'll need some salve for your face to start with," Liam said. "You're half raw meat, aren't you?"

"I've felt and seen worse." Gawen gasped as Liam reached out and kneaded his ribs. Then the boy turned his attention to Cam. "Sir, if you're the Cam Winthrop who fought with Hugh MacArthur at Culloden, I came to tell you Hugh's gone the way of everyone else who died on that field. Or he's as good as gone—Torr Pendragon took him prisoner after the battle. No one's heard a word of his fate since."

Cam frowned. "That's grave news, boy. You're his youngest, aye?"

"Yes, sir."

"And are you all that's left of the MacArthurs now?"

For a moment, Rowenna thought Gawen wouldn't answer. A shadow crossed his face. Rowenna recognized the soul-deep extent of it at once—she felt the same acute and all-consuming despair herself, whenever she thought of her last night with Mairead on the cliff top and the things she'd seen there.

As the darkness swept over him, Rowenna knew the strange

boy was balancing on a knife's edge. That a heartbeat at most stood between him and the sort of collapse that would heap shame upon his despair.

So when his hesitation grew into a fraught silence, Rowenna snapped.

"I want all of you gone," she said, her voice sharp and relentless as she took the risk of clearing the cottage upon herself. "Only Liam stays. It's too much, too fast—first *Athair* and Duncan being lost, then *Màthair* coming home. Give me a moment to breathe."

"Enna, mind your tone," Cam warned, but at a little urging from Duncan, even he went. The cot was left emptier and quieter, with only Rowenna and Liam kneeling beside the stray boy.

"He was right," Gawen MacArthur said quietly. The moment of despair was gone, staved off by the sudden force of Rowenna's displeasure, and only weariness seemed to remain in its wake. "When my father dies—if he's not gone already—I'm . . . I'm the last of us."

As he spoke, Rowenna held his gaze and refused to quail, and so Gawen, propped up by her attention, could not falter again.

Liam cut in, putting pressure on Gawen's stomach. "Does this hurt?"

The boy shook his head.

"Now your leg," Liam said. "Rowenna, fetch some bandages and arnica for a poultice. You know where I keep everything—I've had to patch Duncan up often enough."

Rowenna did as she was told, drawing aside the curtain to the sleeping area of the cot and crouching before a wooden chest pushed up against one of the walls. It was the work of a moment for her to find what she needed, but she paused briefly and silently berated herself.

Maybe Liam's right, and there's something wicked in you, Rowenna thought fiercely. *Seeing a monster first. Now being given the one thing you wanted too much even to wish for, and thinking it's a curse, rather than a miracle.*

But all she could remember, over and over, was that night at Iteag Burn—the creature she'd seen and the sound of her mother's breaking neck. Trying and failing to shut it all out—her guilt and worry and fear—Rowenna slipped past the curtain again and knelt once more at Gawen's side.

"Take Rowenna's hands," Liam ordered the boy. When Gawen hesitated, Liam rolled his eyes. "You're not going to break her—she's made of stone and salt water."

Gawen looked at Rowenna, his dark eyes fixing on hers once more. She nodded and held out her hands. Gawen gripped them hard, and then his grasp tightened until Rowenna knew his touch would bruise. He let out a strangled yelp as Liam felt over his leg, fingers kneading deep to test the soundness of the bone.

Gawen's eyes never left Rowenna's, and hers never left his. *I hurt,* his gaze said to her. *I hurt,* hers said back, because hard as she fought, she couldn't keep her shock and concern over Mairead's impossible homecoming at bay.

At last it was done. Liam rocked back on his heels, and Gawen's grip slackened. Rowenna pulled her hands from the boy's and rubbed at the sore places where Gawen had held too tight.

"Well, you broke some ribs, which'll have to knit on their own," Liam said. "The good news is, your insides seem all right, and I doubt your leg's broken, or at least not badly. Just swollen and bruised. It'll likely all have gone black and blue by day's end. I'm off to old Molly McIntyre's to fetch some salve for that face. Give him more whiskey if he wants, Enna, but make sure he drinks plenty of water, too. I won't be long, and I'll make up the poultice when I get back."

Don't go, Rowenna wanted to beg Liam. *Don't leave me alone without saying something to explain how all this can be, when you know what I saw on the rocks that night. Tell me it's all right, and that I haven't taken leave of my senses.*

Instead, she stayed in her place at Gawen's side and spoke gently to him as Liam left the cot.

"You never told my father it was me you came here for," Rowenna murmured as she propped the boy's head up and held a tin cup to his lips. He was sweating and white-faced after Liam's ministrations, smelling of salt and peat and damp wool. It softened Rowenna's sharp edges to have a boy so helpless before her, his damp hair tangled between her fingers. "Why not?"

"You said you couldn't help," Gawen answered bleakly as Rowenna took the cup away. "If you can't, then it doesn't matter. Nothing matters at all."

He shut his eyes resolutely, and Rowenna sighed. Behind her, the latch to the cottage door lifted with a wooden scrape. An achingly familiar tread sounded on the earth floor.

Rowenna gathered together every tattered scrap of courage she possessed and turned to her mother.

Mairead stood with a graceful hand resting on one of the pegs by the door, head tilted to one side, staring intently at Gawen. An eager smile turned up her cherry red lips, and something terribly like hunger lurked in her expression.

Rowenna had felt many things in the past two days. Grief, despair, determination, fear. But the look on Mairead's face kindled an instinctive protectiveness inside her chest and fury in her bones.

"What're you looking at?" she snapped. Even as she spoke, Rowenna's heart sank—she'd been harsh with many people before, but her mother was the great exception. Until that last night on the cliff, Rowenna had never once shown Mairead her temper.

Mairead blinked. At once she was all serenity and placid good nature, as if Rowenna had dreamed the eagerness and appetite on her face.

"Nothing," Mairead said sweetly. Without another word to Rowenna, she took a cloak from its place by the door, draped it around her pretty shoulders, and followed after the rest of the Winthrops, heading toward Neadeala with an assured sway to her walk that had never been there before.

Chapter Five

"It's too cold, Rowenna," Mairead said in a honeyed voice at breakfast the following morning as she handed her bowl of porridge back to the girl. "You'll have to heat it longer."

"Yes, *Màthair*," Rowenna answered dutifully, taking the bowl and setting it down among the coals on the hearth.

From where he sat at the table, Duncan tried to catch Rowenna's eye, but she staunchly refused to look at her brother. She knew what she'd find in his gaze—pity, commiseration, a spark of humor. And Rowenna could not bear to see any of it. Not when she knew in her bones that this wasn't Mairead, but some wicked thing come to claim her place.

Never in her life had Rowenna felt so useless and helpless. Danger now lurked at the heart of her household, but what could she do? Tell her father that this woman, who looked and sounded exactly as Mairead had, was an imposter? And that Rowenna had lied to him about the circumstances surrounding Mairead's death? It would seem like bitterness or malice or madness, not truth.

Nearly tripping over Gawen MacArthur, who still lay on his pallet by the hearth, Rowenna bit her lip to keep from muttering a curse.

"Sorry," Gawen said under his breath so that only she could hear.

"Don't apologize for getting kicked," Rowenna shot back, but quietly too. "You know it's my fault."

The boy who'd washed up on her shores had his nose buried in one of Liam's few books and a half-empty flask of whiskey sitting at his side—one for the boredom and one for the pain, and that was all the Winthrops could offer for either. But at Rowenna's admission of guilt, he glanced up quickly.

"We're all waiting on you, Rowenna," Mairead said. "I hope you're about finished there."

"Is *everything* your fault?" Gawen asked as Rowenna leaned over him again to take her mother's bowl back out from among the coals. Pointedly, Rowenna refused to answer.

"Won't you sit, En?" Cam said from his place at the head of the table when the girl set her mother's breakfast down. There was a wistfulness in his voice that tore at Rowenna. "I can't remember the last time we all had a meal together."

The only vacant seat was next to Mairead, and Rowenna fought back a wince. But for Cam, she went to her place and pulled out the chair. As she set Mairead's bowl down, the back of her hand brushed one of her mother's fingers, and Mairead drew back with a pained gasp.

"You've burned me—the bowl's scalding hot," Mairead said.

Rowenna only stood, rooted to the floor, swallowing and swallowing at a sour taste in the back of her throat. She'd felt something, just then. A flash of craft. Of power. But such a twisted and malevolent magic that it had pierced Rowenna like knives and set a sensation of rot in her bones.

Across the table Duncan ducked his head, gone pale and unhappy. Finn fidgeted and stared down at his bowl. Only Liam and Cam stolidly ate their breakfast, as if this were an ordinary morning.

"It'll need more milk," Mairead said pointedly. She pushed the porridge bowl to the side, so that it rested in front of Rowenna, and for a moment the girl stared at it. Then she went wordlessly back to the hearth and poured a bit of milk into the porridge from a pitcher on the hutch. She took her time stirring it in, and when she returned to the table, her father's attention was already elsewhere, as he and the boys talked over the day to come. Rowenna felt reduced to a shadow as, yet again, she set the bowl in front of her mother.

Mairead spooned up a minute amount of porridge, touched it to her lips, frowned, and pushed the offering away.

"I think I'll take a walk this morning," Mairead announced sunnily to Cam and the boys. "Reacquaint myself with the villagers, while you're all busy during the day."

"Bring Rowenna with you if you go," Cam said. "She could use a morning out."

Mairead's smile never slipped. "I wouldn't want to take her away from the cot. She's got so much to do."

"Aye," Cam answered. He met Mairead's cheer with an implacable good humor of his own. "All the more reason for the two of you to share the visiting *and* the work, like you once did. We're not a family that can afford to keep anyone who's not pulling their weight, if you recall."

Rowenna glanced instinctively at Gawen. Though the reminder had not been meant for him, his jaw was tense, and he kept his gaze fixed on the pages of the book in his hand.

"All right," Mairead said, giving in to Cam without argument. "If that's what you want, I'll do it, though I expect having her with me will make for a bit of awkwardness with some of the villagers. They think—"

"I don't care what they think," Cam answered firmly. "I didn't when their spite and their gossip was about you, and I don't now that it's about our daughter. Duncan, we're off. Liam and Finn, you'd best be going too."

There was a small commotion as Cam and the boys got themselves ready. When they'd gone, the cottage felt flat and empty, as if all the life had left it. Mairead waited a few minutes and then, with a slow smile at Rowenna but not a word spoken by way of invitation, she took her cloak off the peg, slipped it on, and followed in their wake.

"This miraculous homecoming seems to be going rather well for you," Gawen said darkly as the door shut behind Mairead. "It's almost enough to reconcile me to having watched my whole family die and stay dead, seeing how yours behaves after coming back from the grave."

It was gallows humor—a knife-twist of a joke meant to hurt both the one who spoke it and the one who heard. Gawen's words found their mark, and before she could stop herself, Rowenna snapped at him, letting loose the truth she'd kept unspoken until now.

"That's *not* my mother," she said, bristling. "I don't know who or what it is, but it's not her."

Surprise and fascination wrote themselves across the strange boy's face. Stifling a groan, he propped himself up on his elbows and fixed his eyes on Rowenna. Reluctantly she met his gaze.

"What do you mean that's not your mother?" Gawen pressed. "Everyone else in this house has no doubts it's her, and you haven't let on for a moment that you think otherwise."

"Aye, I know that." Rowenna gathered up an armful of dirty breakfast dishes and dropped them into the washbasin in frustration. "But what am I going to say? *I know you're all happy, and yes, whoever that is, she's the spitting image of Mairead Winthrop, but I, the family's uncanny witch-daughter, say she's something else entirely?* They'd never believe me. They'd think I've run mad."

"I believe you," Gawen said solemnly.

Rowenna narrowed her eyes. "Why?"

The boy shrugged. "Because I want your help. I'll believe anything you tell me, if you just agree to do what I asked, and help me with your craft."

Hot anger surged in Rowenna at his pragmatism.

"Do you know why you're here?" she told him, her sharpness honed to a cutting edge. "Do you know why *she's* here? Because I went looking for my father with my craft and couldn't find him, despite the blood that binds us. Instead, I made a mess of it all and ended up with a half-broken stranger and an imposter in my house, and no idea what to do about either of them."

"But your father and your brother are back, safe and well, just like you intended." Gawen settled himself down again with great care, putting his arms behind his head and staring at the ceiling. "As far as I'm concerned, scold, that means you succeeded."

Rowenna scrubbed angrily at the porridge pot. "Then you've got seawater for brains. My craft brought me to you, and opened the way for whoever that is calling herself my mother to steal her way into the heart of this family, and that's all. The rest is just . . . something wicked at work and toying with me, and I've been a fool to think I could pit myself against it."

"Something wicked?" Gawen asked. "As in . . ."

But Rowenna kept stubbornly silent.

"Couldn't you be wrong, though?" the boy said after a moment. "I asked Liam last night, and he told me your mother was lost after falling in a storm. Perhaps she lived, in spite of it."

Rowenna rounded on him. *"I saw her die."*

"Maybe you only thought—"

"So help me God, if you'd seen what I did, you wouldn't doubt any of this," Rowenna answered fiercely, frustration churning inside her.

But Gawen only grew mild in the face of her temper.

"Come here to me," he said.

Reluctantly Rowenna went, drying her hands on her apron as she knelt at his side. Once more, the boy propped himself up, and though he winced, this time he did it in silence.

"What did you see?" Gawen asked, his voice soft. "Whatever it is you tell me, I swear I'll believe you. Not because I want your help, but because I've seen things too. Terrible things. Powerful things. Things another person might not think possible."

"No one will believe me," Rowenna whispered, but she couldn't look away from his dark eyes.

Reaching out, Gawen took one of her raw, work-hardened hands in his own. Rowenna drew in a shallow breath but did not pull away.

"Tell me your truth, Rowenna Winthrop," Gawen said.

Swallowing, Rowenna shut her eyes.

"I saw my mother die." In the labyrinth of her mind, it happened all over again. "It was storming. We were together on the north cliffs and setting out for home, when something crawled up the burn and dragged her back down with it. A creature—a monster—some wicked thing from the deep, worse than any nightmare you could ever dream. She begged for help, and there was nothing I could do. It broke her neck while I stood watching. I saw the life leave her, and it pulled her body out to sea."

Gawen was quiet for a moment. Then,

"I saw my mother die too. Torr Pendragon brought her to Inverness and burned her at a stake along with my sister, not four weeks back. My older brother was already dead, having been killed at Drumossie, and my father a prisoner. There was only me left to look after the family, and I failed."

Rowenna opened her eyes. Darkness and despair met her gaze, in the person of Gawen MacArthur.

"There was only me left who could have looked after my mother, and I failed too," she said, echoing his words.

"Then what will you do," Gawen asked, "now your failure's come back to haunt you?"

Rowenna turned away, slipping her hand out of his, though it felt like coming unmoored.

"I don't know," she said. "Perhaps nothing. I'm not enough for this sort of trouble."

"Are you sure about that?"

"Sure as I am of anything."

Silence fell between them. Gawen spoke not a word as Rowenna finished clearing off the table and washed the last of the dishes in water gone cold and gray as the coast. The boy sat and drank and made a show of reading, though he never turned a page, and there was something pained in the set of his jaw.

Letting out a sigh as she put the last dish away in the hutch, Rowenna hefted the basin of wash water and hauled it over to the door, struggling a little, as she always did, with the clumsy weight of it. She stepped out into the chilly morning, thick with fog, and startled as a sudden gust of wind slammed the cottage door shut behind her.

Beware, the wind breathed, speaking for the first time that morning. *Beware.*

Ignoring it, Rowenna went around the side of the cottage to dump the filthy water and froze. Nailed to the wall of the cot, framed between two storm-shuttered windows, was a warning in the shape of a gutted swan.

I know you know, it said, plain as day. *And you and your family are as much in my power now as you were that night.*

64

The wretched swan had not been killed cleanly—the creature's head lolled, its eyes were filmed over, and it looked to have been torn open while still alive. For a moment, Rowenna could not draw breath. But the insistent weight of the washbasin brought her back to herself. Glancing across the heath, she dumped the water and hurried back inside the cot.

"Wait a moment now," Gawen said as Rowenna replaced the basin with hands that shook and pulled on the oldest, most worn woolen sweater she could find. He was too observant, even while nursing a near-finished flask of whiskey. His eyes on Rowenna set her to sweating. "Is something wrong? You look rattled."

"Nothing's wrong," Rowenna managed to get out. "Or at least nothing you can help with. I just want some air. Don't know when I'll be back."

Only when she was out in the fog once more did Rowenna realize she'd brought nothing with her to pry the nail from the cottage wall. But she couldn't go in again—it would put the lie to her excuse, and Gawen would be sure to ask more questions. She couldn't bear that—yet another confidence, and him perhaps prodding her to do more than hide the truth and keep her secrets close. So instead, she stopped before the desecrated body of the swan, took a trembling breath, and began to work at the nail with her own fingers.

It was the closest Rowenna Winthrop had ever been to a thing killed by violence and malice. The unnatural angle of the creature's neck reminded her of Mairead on the shingle. Of how she'd seen her mother die. By the time the nail came free, Rowenna was sobbing for air, her throat closing in on itself. But she had no time for panic—if one of the villagers were to see this thing, this witch sign, this abomination, pinned to the very walls of her cottage, it would go badly indeed. She'd find herself hauled off to Inverness, with a stake and a torch waiting at the end of that journey, just as it had done for Gawen MacArthur's mother and sister.

Gathering the body of the swan up into her arms, Rowenna hurried away across the moorland, reluctant even to drop it over the cliffs so near her home, where the sea might wash it back to shore. Instead she went north, toward Iteag Burn and the sad, tumbledown remains of her mother's broken wards.

When she reached the cliffs, Rowenna let the swan go. It felt like an echo of the night Mairead died two months back as the broken white shape of the bird fell and fell before being swallowed by the sea.

For a time, Rowenna lingered at the edge of the land. She stood and watched the vast expanse of restless water and the over-arching dome of cold sky. Offshore, a few porpoises broke free of the waves, arching through the air in an exultation of silver skin and shed water that gleamed like diamonds.

What must it feel like, Rowenna wondered, to be that unfet-tered and carefree? To be unbound by cliffs or rocky beach or life-less moorland in every direction? To live without being chained by duty and worry to a place that held no future for her?

"What is it you see when you look at me?" a sweet voice said from behind Rowenna. "What is it you notice that no one else does?"

Fear clawed its way up Rowenna's spine even as resignation caused her to slowly turn.

"*Màthair,*" Rowenna answered, struggling to keep her voice even when fear was already slicking her palms with sweat. "I thought you'd gone into the village."

"I thought about it." Mairead's voice was light, and she stepped forward, reaching out to run a finger along the line of Rowenna's jaw. "But then I realized your *athair* was right, and that you and I should get reacquainted instead. So I came back to have a word with you. I'm asking again, what is it you see when you look at me? The truth, mind. I'll know if you lie."

Rowenna clutched at her skirts, balling her hands up around fistfuls of fabric.

"I see my mother," she breathed. But this close, the things she'd smelled when she first embraced Mairead—seawater and cold rock and the gunmetal tang of blood—were overpowering. The scent made her head swim, and as her vision wavered, so did Mairead before her. Now it was cornflower-blue eyes that looked out from Mairead's fair face, but a moment before they'd been staring, deepwater orbs. And here was her charming, cherry-lipped smile, but Rowenna was sure that behind those lips she'd caught a flash of curving, fishhook teeth.

"Wrong," Mairead said, shaking her head in something like disappointment. Her slim finger rested on the hollow of Rowenna's throat now, gentle, but a reminder. "Try again, and this time, speak the truth."

"I don't know the truth," Rowenna managed at last. "Not about you, not about myself. You—she—my mother, the one from before—wouldn't teach me. I loved her, but we were at odds, and she never let me learn to be more than I am."

"Is that so?" It was no longer Mairead's finger resting around Rowenna's throat but her entire hand cupping it, her touch soft but the gesture itself an unspoken threat. "Clever of her, to make things so easy for me."

"You're not her, then." Though she was trembling, it was an unspeakable relief to Rowenna, to banish the last of her doubts and hear that she hadn't taken leave of her senses. That if there was a monster in her household, it existed in truth, and not just in her own tortured imaginings.

"Of course not, witchling." The creature in Mairead's skin drew closer yet, until her lips brushed Rowenna's ear. "And now you know it, are you afraid? The truth again, tell me no lies."

"Yes," Rowenna whispered. "I'm afraid."

"Then this is what I want you to do. I want you to run. Now. Take nothing with you. Go, and leave me be, and I promise to pay you the same courtesy. You'll never see me again, unless it be in your dreams."

Finn's face flashed through Rowenna's mind, young and innocent. And Cam's, older and careworn, but unspeakably dear. Duncan, with his wild heart, and even Liam, with whom she could never find peace, and Gawen, who she'd only just met.

"What will happen to my family if I leave?" Rowenna asked.

In answer Mairead smiled, and nothing, not even the moment of her mother's death, had ever chilled Rowenna so before.

"Don't fret over them. *You'll* be safe," Mairead purred. "Whereas if you stay, I'll see you're put through agonies before the end."

Rowenna hesitated.

"Run away, little witch," Mairead urged. "Run for your life, and run for freedom."

Part of Rowenna wanted to go. Part of her wanted to flee this horror she'd never asked for and refuse to look back. But she summoned all the things Mairead had seen as unfit or dangerous in her—her sharpness, her anger, her unwillingness to yield when pushed. She stepped away and turned her back to this thing that was not her mother. Then she began walking, with slow, decided steps.

"Where are you going?" Mairead called out. "I had thought to see you make a little more haste, while running from me."

"I'm going home," Rowenna shot back, and though her voice shook, there was steel behind the words. "You can come if you like. But I can't stay away for too long—I've got people to look after. People I won't leave behind."

"It'll end in heartbreak," Mairead warned. "It'll end in blood and death and tears."

It already has, Rowenna thought as she walked steadily on. *You're a devil and a fool, and I've weathered each one of those already. I know the shape and the feel of them, and I may be afraid, but I will not flee.*

Chapter Six

For all her tongue could be sharp and her temper quick, there was no true violence in Rowenna Winthrop. If a cockerel wanted butchering, she had Duncan undertake the killing. If any small and ailing thing crossed her path and seemed unlikely to recover, she asked Liam to do what was merciful.

But that night when she took to her narrow pallet in the lee of the cottage's front door, she slipped a keen-bladed gutting knife beneath her pillow. Her heart and mind were in turmoil. She hadn't the craft necessary to set herself against such a creature. And she hadn't the proof required to expose the monster that lurked beneath Mairead's skin. All Rowenna knew was that if the beast so much as laid a finger on any of her family with intent to harm, she'd cut its throat herself, even if it was her mother's face staring back at her as she did.

For hours, Rowenna lay awake, her fingertips brushing the smooth handle of the knife, the gentle sounds of sleepers' breathing filling the cot. She'd insisted that Cam leave the curtain open that night, that partitioned her parents' bed and the boys' sleeping pallets off from the rest of the living space. From where she lay, she could see the shadowy shape of the four-poster bed that Cam and Mairead shared and the huddle of blankets that marked each of her brothers on the floor. For a long, long while, nothing happened.

And then Mairead sat up. She positioned herself on the edge of the bed but made no move to touch Cam or any of the boys. Instead, she smiled and began to hum. It was a soft, eerie sound, wild like the water of the Atlantic. The music Mairead made filled the air, and Rowenna swallowed back nerves, listening as the cot seemed to grow colder with each passing note.

By the time she realized her head was filling with cobwebs and that she was losing her grip on consciousness, it was too late. Mairead's smile widened, her lips parting to reveal a mouth over-full with needle-sharp teeth. Her eyes glinted like small moons, and that was the last thing Rowenna Winthrop saw as she fell into a sleep that felt like drowning.

❧

It was cold as bones and old graves inside the cot.

That was the first thought that crossed Rowenna's mind as she struggled toward wakefulness. She felt sluggish and sick, unable to fully cast off the dreams still clinging to her. The wind was no help—it gusted around the eaves and set the fire to smoking as it moaned her name senselessly.

Rowenna rowennarowennarowenna.

With a supreme effort, she opened her eyes. Everything seemed dim and foggy, as if the doors had been left open and the mist that often shrouded the land had crept into the cot. The wind was still fretting, soughing and sighing to her.

Rowenna. Rowenna Winthrop. Awake, arise, away.

Shaking her head in a vain attempt to clear it, Rowenna moved to slide out from under her blanket, but an odd weight pinned her down. Still in a muddle, she sat up, only to find a heap of gory white feathers resting on her lap, blood staining the thin wool blanket. With a ragged gasp, Rowenna scrambled away, heart throbbing in her chest as she realized the thing was yet another gutted swan, laid spread-winged across her while she slept. Its beak gaped, and Rowenna saw, to her horror, that the tongue had been cut out of its mouth.

Snatching the knife from beneath her pillow, Rowenna found it, too, was slick with blood, a few downy feathers sticking to the blade. But it felt like safety, so she clung to it as she glanced instinctively across the cot. The curtain separating the rest of the family from her was drawn shut now, blocking them from view. Gawen lay by the hearth, though, worried lines creasing his face as he slept. Another swan lay atop him, black this time, its wings pinioning him in a stomach-turning embrace.

Knife in hand, Rowenna hurried over and shoved the dead thing aside.

"Stray," she said, reaching out to shake the boy. "Stray, wake up. Wake up."

She spoke so quickly the words tumbled over one another, but hard as she shook him, Gawen MacArthur slept on. Rowenna had begun to tremble, and she saw, for the first time, that both doors were open and the fire burned down to nothing but ash, which accounted for the life-sapping cold in the Winthrop cot.

Awake, arise, away, the wind continued to sing. Rowenna

steeled her nerves and pushed through the curtain behind which her family slept.

The boys lay strewn about the floor, around the bed reserved for Cam and Mairead. The bed itself stood empty, the covers pushed back, and resting upon each of her brothers was another broken swan, leaving it hard to tell where bloody feathers ended and boy began. Rowenna knelt at Finn's side, for it was his small childish face that cut her deepest.

"Finn," she begged through tears. "Finny. Get up."

But he could not be wakened.

Panic clawed at the inside of Rowenna's chest. *Awake, arise, away,* the wind called out to her, but she could not. She would not. Perhaps it would be the death of her, but she'd stand by her family till the end.

Reaching out, Rowenna took the swan that lay across Finn by its snapped neck. She dragged its dead weight across the cot and out through the open front door, never letting go of her fear or the gore-spattered gutting knife.

No sooner was she through the door than she found Cam and Mairead coming up the worn path from the village. Mairead caught sight of her first, and startled at the spectacle of Rowenna, weighted down by a dead swan and a knife. But she hid her surprise swiftly, replacing it with a calculated look of heartbreak.

The gray, predawn light was more than enough to see by, and there was no hiding. All Rowenna could do was stand motionless as Cam strode over to her, confusion and disbelief etched across his face.

"What's going on here?" Cam said. "What's happened?"

"I don't know," Rowenna choked, and then Cam was past her, pushing through the doorway to her sleeping brothers beyond. Once it would have reassured Rowenna to have him back, but now she felt entirely lost. She only stood where she was as Mairead surveyed the scene with quiet satisfaction.

"I told you to go, witchling," Mairead murmured. "I told you to go, or it would end in agony."

As she spoke, a wave of dizziness washed over Rowenna. Mairead's face swam, growing indistinct, until Rowenna caught yet another monstrous glimpse of her true form.

She pressed a hand to her forehead, desperately fighting for clarity, and the moment passed. There was only Mairead before her, sadly shaking her golden head as Cam reappeared, the last four swans held firm in his bearlike grip.

"Athair," Rowenna pleaded. Her own voice sounded small and afraid, and when Cam fixed his eyes on her, she wanted nothing more than to sink into the ground or melt away like frost. Because her father's face was a mask of suspicion and anger and revulsion. He pointed a finger at Rowenna and shook his head.

"What have you done, girl? So help me God, if you've hurt the boys . . ."

"They're sleeping," Rowenna hurried to confess, though unshed tears clouded the words. "I can't get them to wake. I don't know what's happened. I swear to you, *Athair,* I had no part of this."

"No?" he growled. "And I suppose you've no idea where these dead things came from either?"

Rowenna shook her head.

"Your *màthair*," Cam began impatiently. He took a breath to steady himself and carried on, fixing his eyes on Mairead as if for reassurance. "Your *màthair* here used swans in her work before the sea took her, though now she's given up her old ways. But even before, Enna, it was never like this. What in the devil's hell were you about? This is foul witchery, not innocent craft."

Mairead nodded, looking anxious and penitent, and Rowenna turned to Cam, dropping the knife she held and clasping her hands together.

"*Athair*, I'm begging you," she pleaded. "You've always believed me. Always believed in me. And I swear this wasn't—"

But as she spoke, the eastern sky grew golden with the first flush of dawn. Somewhere out at sea, a gull called mournfully as light crept over the horizon. The sun's earliest warmth brushed Rowenna's face. Then her hands flew to her lips of their own accord, and she let out a wordless cry. It felt as if there was a knife in her mouth—a heated blade viciously cutting at her tongue. The sensation came on so sharp and sudden, it drove her to her knees, but as quickly as it came, it subsided. With tears smarting at her eyes—not of fear or anger but of pain this time—Rowenna got shakily to her feet.

Disgust and pity showed in Cam's gaze as he shook his head.

"Liam had his concerns," Cam said. "I should have listened. I should have kept a closer eye on you, after coming home."

It wasn't me, Rowenna tried to protest. *None of it was me.*

But she could not get the words out. Even as she tried to give voice to them, the pain rose up in her mouth again and constricted around her throat, like coiled iron. Badly as she wanted to speak, something had muzzled her. She stood mute, unable to make a sound even to save her own life.

In her mind, she could still hear the words she'd spoken to Mairead during her mother's last living moments.

They call me a witch, though I've none of the craft of one. I bear all the blame, and none of the power.

Behind the house, past the rise of the cliff tops and across the sea, the inexorable sun was still rising. A first sliver of intolerable brightness slid above the horizon, and true morning light flooded the Winthrop cot through its open doors. Squinting and with her eyes watering, Rowenna caught a sudden scent, of brine and wood-smoke, open air and good, rich peat sodden with rain. It smelled of home, distilled into a single potent breath.

Then came a thunderous rushing noise from within the cot and a clamorous trumpeting. Wind beat at Rowenna. There was a confusion of sunlight and gale and feathers, and when it cleared, a swan stood where each of her brothers and Gawen had lain sleeping. They arched their long necks and stretched their wide wings and called out their displeasure in loud, brassy voices.

Not a trace of who the swans had been was left. They were reduced to something rampant and unknowable, and if the pain of Rowenna's own curse had come as a shock, it was nothing compared to the breathless hurt of seeing boys she'd cared for and tended turned witless and wild.

"God in heaven," Mairead murmured from behind Rowenna,

her dismay sounding almost genuine. "She's laid a curse on every one of them."

Mairead's hands snaked out and held Rowenna fast by the arms as Cam turned away from the cot and his sons in a daze.

"Enna?" he asked, his voice breaking. "Why would you do it?"

But Rowenna could not answer. All she could do was stand silent before the ruins of her family, with tears tracking down her face.

Chapter Seven

"It's my fault," Mairead said, standing before Rowenna and the swans and matching Cam's sorrow with her own. "If I hadn't been lost for so long . . . if I'd managed to find a way back sooner, or if I'd understood her true nature better . . ."

Though grief clouded Mairead's voice, she still held fast to Rowenna. Her fingers dug sharp into the girl's arms through her sleeves, setting fear coursing through her. Cam fixed his eyes on Rowenna, and she could see in his face that he was remembering every word she'd ever snapped, every bitter sigh that had ever escaped her, every halfhearted complaint that had fallen from her lips. All of her flaws, and none of her virtues.

"How could you, Enna?" Cam asked. Behind him, the swans that were Rowenna's brothers staggered and stretched, vainly trying to learn the trick of moving in their new forms. "How could you, when we've always taken your side?"

"What will we do with her?" Mairead pressed. "What will we do with the boys? I'm afraid, Cam."

"Can you right this?" Cam asked Mairead. "With your old craft? Bring the boys back to who they were?"

Mairead shook her head sadly. "I'm afraid not. This is beyond me. There's a wickedness in it I can't undo."

Slowly the anguish and despair in Cam's eyes faded, replaced by wrath.

"Say something at least," he growled at Rowenna. "Speak a word in your own defense. Tell me this wasn't you, or that there was some reason behind it."

Rowenna pressed her hands together in silent petition, but words were beyond her. The cursed silence that had fallen over her could not be cast off.

"I want you out, then," Cam said. "Rowenna Winthrop, you're no longer welcome under my roof. You've broken my heart and been the downfall of this family. I hope to God I never see your face again."

Seizing Mairead by the hand, he drew her into the cot after him and slammed the door. Rowenna could hear the dim sound of wings beating and swans trumpeting from within the cot, followed by curses from Cam and a deep sob.

That last undid her. Gathering up her skirts, Rowenna turned and fled, hardly knowing where she was going. But at last a shock of purpose ran through her—a boat. She should find a boat and take to the sea, leaving the Highlands and her shame behind forever. Then she could drift, and if the deeps and their monsters made an end of her, so be it.

Her feet led her down a familiar path, along the outskirts of Neadeala and toward the harbor where the fishing fleet was kept.

But stumbling with grief and blinded by tears, Rowenna's progress had been nowhere near as quick as Mairead's, who'd left the cot and Cam behind. By the time Rowenna reached the harbor, the creature in her mother's skin stood waiting on the shingle. A small cluster of villagers hung back at the beach's far edge.

Rowenna, Rowenna, the wind sobbed, whipping at her skirts. *What to do, dark-hearted girl?*

Grass and earth gave way to shifting pebbles as Rowenna walked on, because she'd come this far and would keep moving until the end. The tide was in, and frothing waves beat endlessly against the shore. Mairead stepped aside with a mocking curtsy as Rowenna carried on into the surf, where water nipped cold around her ankles. Only when she stood with the sea foaming around her did she turn inland and find Mairead mere inches away.

"Rowenna Winthrop," the thing that was not her mother said slyly. "Didn't I tell you this would end in agony? And it's not over yet—each night your brothers will regain their true forms. But the time as their full selves will fade, night by night, until at the last they're left wholly animal and other and cursed."

Unreasoning fury filled Rowenna. She wanted to rant and rage, to tear into the creature with her words, because they were the only power she'd ever been able to wield rightly.

But she had no voice. She struggled mutely as Mairead took her by the arm and by the back of the neck with preternaturally strong hands. In that moment, caught between death and life, Rowenna could hardly focus on her mother, her image flashed and wavered so. Back and forth, from winsome woman to a wretched creature, all hollows and hunger and fishbones, with wide glassy eyes made for catching scant light in the deeps, and with teeth like a hundred curving needles.

A shocked murmur rose up from the villagers as Mairead spun Rowenna about and shoved her forward, on into the foaming sea.

"Won't someone stop her?" Alice Sutherland's soft voice called out, pleading with the people of Neadeala.

Frigid water climbed to Rowenna's knees, and her waist, and then without warning, she was plunged beneath the surface.

In the few moments before breathlessness truly took over, memory flooded Rowenna. She recalled in perfect detail the clear summer sky above the cove near home the day Cam taught her to swim long ago. How he'd held her up, ensuring none of the breakers caught her off guard or carried her away. And after, when she'd learned the trick of moving her arms and legs just so while the sea did the rest, Cam wrapped her in a wool blanket and took her back to the cot on his shoulders, and it had felt to Rowenna as if she could see the whole world from that height. She remembered her brothers, too—how they would all play together by the fretful shores of the sea, and how the boys each cared for her in their own particular way.

Lastly, Rowenna remembered her mother, not as she'd come back, but as she was before—how kind and cautious and gentle Mairead had been. How her instinct was always to protect Rowenna, even from herself.

Everything was a chaos of froth and bubbles and seaweed. Rowenna felt the pain of Mairead's grip on the back of her arm and her neck for one last instant before the need for air grew all consuming. She jerked and thrashed, and then salt water burned its way in through her nose and mouth.

Rowenna, our heart, our dark-hearted girl, the wind howled mournfully from above, audible even below the waves as Rowenna felt herself going limp. The seething water began to fade as her vision blurred.

But before her last thread of consciousness snapped, Mairead's hands left her. Something unfamiliar scrabbled at the back of Rowenna's head, tugging at her hair, and without thinking, she burst upward, choking and gasping. A wild, ear-splitting trumpeting filled the air, and as Rowenna found her feet and coughed up seawater, she saw a bevy of swans driving Mairead back to shore with battering wings and snakelike, outstretched necks. Two of them were snow white, the third smaller, with a few remaining patches of fledgling gray.

The gathered villagers had erupted into chaotic argument, and Rowenna could hear Father Osric's voice rising above the others.

"... do not care *what* you think. There should be a proper trial first—otherwise we're no better than ..."

A pull at the back of Rowenna's soaked kirtle urged her eastward, toward the place where half a dozen fishing boats were drawn up on shore. She hardly had time to register the black swan before he was pushing at her and snapping with his long red bill. With the black swan at her side and the remaining three still hissing at Mairead, she made for the boats.

Throwing her weight against the nearest yoal, Rowenna

shoved desperately. A clamor rose up from the villagers as it became clear that Rowenna meant to steal a boat, and a few of the bravest began to hurry in her direction. At first the boat hardly budged, but Rowenna dug her feet into the loose stone and put all her rage, all her powerlessness and frustration, into her arms and legs and desperate pushing. With a thunderclap of wing-beats and feathers, the three white swans left their guard posts and alighted beside her. The added force of their heavy, feathered bodies tipped the scales, and the yoal picked up momentum, slid-ing down the beach to the water's edge.

Still, Rowenna kept on shoving it away, as clear of the breakers as she could get, until she had no choice but to fling an arm over the gunwale and haul herself aboard. The white swans carried on pushing at the boat as Rowenna settled herself and slid a pair of oars into the water. With everything in her, she began to row.

A startled cry sounded from not far behind. Rowenna twisted her neck to glance back and saw her father up to his waist in the surf, regret and heartbreak written across his face.

"Rowenna!" he called, his voice echoing from the cliffs. "Come back. I shouldn't have spoken so harshly to you. I'm sure there's a reason for all this, and we'll find a way to make things right."

"No." Mairead's voice was a command, and Cam swayed on his feet, battered by her certainty. "Let them go. She's no more concern to us, and the boys were lost as soon as she cursed them."

Though part of Rowenna ached to turn back, all four of the swans were around her, hurrying the boat along its way, and the tide pulled at it too, drawing her out to sea. But the last thing she saw as her boat cleared the harbor was her father standing at the water's edge. None of the anger Mairead had stirred up in him remained.

All Rowenna could see as she drifted away was despair in Cam Winthrop's eyes and defeat in the slump of his shoulders—a mirror image of her own heartbreak.

Chapter Eight

Rowenna wasn't sure which family's yoal she'd stolen, but whoever they were, they seemed a slipshod and careless lot. The bottom of the boat was littered with cast-off belongings—a torn pullover and spare oilskin Rowenna put to good use immediately, skinning out of her sodden nightclothes and laying them down to dry in the stiff, frigid wind.

The swans bobbed about the prow at first, but once the single sail was up, it became apparent that they would not be able to keep pace in the water. Finn lagged behind, as did Gawen, the bad-tempered bird in black feathers. He listed to one side, dragging his injured leg and panting through his fierce red beak. Even Duncan and Liam, all but indistinguishable with their white wings and slim black bills, struggled to keep up with the yoal.

With a sigh, Rowenna lowered the sail and beckoned to the swans.

They floated near the bow as the boat dipped and rolled. Rowenna lifted each one of them up and out of the sea, and it gave her chills to hold them close, feeling the uncanny shape of them and the rapid beating of their birds' hearts. At last only one white swan was left, his head tilted skeptically to the side.

Duncan, Rowenna thought. Duncan judging her sailing, no doubt.

The swan ruffled his feathers and beat his wings, so that salt spray dampened Rowenna. But at last, with a cantankerous honk, the swan that was Duncan shot over to her and let himself be lifted clumsily into the boat, though he hissed a little as Rowenna bumped him against the gunwale.

She dropped back breathlessly into the bottom of the yoal, causing a confusion of wing flapping and trumpeting and general displeasure as the swans shoved at one another to make room for her. One of them reached out and nipped, not enough to hurt, but enough to warn. It was the tallest and slenderest of the lot, with a long, graceful bill, and Rowenna shook her head. There was no mistaking Liam, even in this new shape.

Liam shook his head and entire body in a disgruntled ruffle of feathers. Rowenna let out a silent laugh that turned into a gasp as panic rose up to choke her. She could feel Mairead's hands holding her under the waves again and the rush of water entering her lungs. Putting her head down on her knees, she focused on her breath.

In and out. In and out. In and out.

All is well, all is well, all is well, the wind whispered across the waves. *We have you now, we'll keep you safe, our love, our light, our dark-hearted girl.*

At last, Rowenna scrambled to her feet. Perhaps her life had been ripped out from under her, but the sail needed to be put up, and with nothing to eat or drink, she'd better make landfall soon. Not too soon, though—not before she'd put some distance between herself and Neadeala and Mairead's baleful influence.

As best she could, Rowenna kept the yoal hugging the coast, so that land stayed on the western horizon as the sun dipped low. But away to the east, only waves and wind stretched to the sky, whispering quiet and wordless reassurances. Thick golden light slicked the surface of the water as the sun began to sink and vanish. Rowenna had seen many a sunset at home, but never one quite like this. Though thirst nagged at her, a creeping sense of doom she'd lived with in the months following Mairead's death had gone, jettisoned like so much unwanted ballast. The worst had already happened—what else could possibly come?

She felt only quiet and empty and sad now, with Cam's face and his last words etched indelibly into her mind. If the sea were to try to claim Rowenna and her brothers in their cursed forms, she wasn't sure she'd fight it. There was no spark left in her for that—she'd been hollowed out by all that had happened, reduced to a mere shell of a girl.

The light grew dim, and a thousand stars sprang to life. Rowenna watched silently as the last of the sun slipped below the horizon. And then her breath caught as a smell rose up around her, of damp peat and woodsmoke and home, entirely incongruous out on the all-encompassing sea. She startled, heart pounding in her chest as the swans grew restless, a flurry of beating wings and outstretched necks and clamorous trumpeting filling the yoal.

But as the last blinding sliver of sun sank, relief and awe surged through Rowenna. The swans rose up as one, and in a sudden chaos of outcry and shed feathers, became boys as daylight left the sky.

The relief was short lived, though, for Rowenna remembered Mairead's words on the beach.

Each night your brothers will regain their true forms. But the time as their full selves will fade, night by night, until at the last they're left wholly animal and other and cursed.

With a stifled sob, Rowenna pulled Finn to herself and hugged him close, pressing kiss after kiss to the top of his golden head.

"Enna, you're squashing," he complained, voice muffled against the wool of the stolen pullover she wore.

"You blessed boys," Rowenna said, and her voice was back again, for now at least, her own familiar voice, clear and joyous, without pain or obstruction. She kissed each of her brothers' foreheads as if they were all small children, but stopped suddenly, just shy of Gawen. He flushed and looked down at the bottom of the boat.

"I'm glad to have you all back, even if it's just for now," Rowenna said, to hide her awkwardness.

"For now? Do you mean this won't keep? That whatever craft you wrought, it'll go on changing us?" Liam asked. He was still gentle, always gentle. But sometimes there was an edge to his gentleness, and when Rowenna stepped back and truly looked at her brothers, she found reproach in every one of their faces.

Cold dread settled within her.

"You'll only have your human shapes by night. She said—" Rowenna began, only to have Duncan cut her off.

"Whatever it is you meant to do, Enna, it was beyond you, and nothing you should have put your hand to. Look what it's done."

Barely restrained anger laced his words, and Rowenna swallowed around a tightening in her throat.

"This wasn't me," she whispered, twining her hands together. "I swear it by anything. I swear it on our *màthair*'s grave."

For a moment they only looked at her. It was Finn who spoke at last, in his high, childish voice.

"But she's not dead, Enna."

Duncan turned away, shaking his head in disgust. "We deserve the truth. You at least owe us that, considering what you've done."

When Rowenna opened her mouth to speak again, he cut her off. "I don't care what your intention was. Everything went wrong, and we're paying the price for it. That's not fair, and it's not right. And who's to fix it now? You? Whatever this was you were doing, you couldn't even manage that. So what the hell comes next?"

Rowenna's stomach dropped out of her. She had no idea what they should do. She'd only been glad, for a single fleeting moment, to see her brothers in their human shapes. But that gladness had burned clear away, replaced by nausea and guilt. In a way it was her fault, that they'd come to this. If she'd warned them about Mairead, perhaps none of it would have happened. If she'd been truthful from the start, they'd have been better prepared. And if she'd been able to do anything but stand helplessly by the night Mairead died . . . but that line of thinking led only to despair. With a wrench, Rowenna brought her mind back to the present.

"I'll mind the sail and the stern oars," Duncan muttered, and pushed past her to the back of the yoal. Liam and Finn huddled together in the center of the small boat. Gawen had retreated to the bow at its front, as far away from the family squabble as he could get, and sat hunched over, a pained and brooding figure. Rowenna could not bear the way Duncan and Liam and even little Finn looked at her, so she went hesitantly to Gawen instead.

"Can I sit?" she asked softly.

In answer, he shifted on the taft—one of three board seats running across the width of the yoal. Gawen's breath caught as he moved, and Rowenna glanced at him. He was pale, sweat beading on his forehead, and his hands shook ever so slightly.

Rowenna bit her lip. "God in heaven, stray, I'm sorry about all this. Are you going to be all right?"

"Well, I was recently a bird, and I've never had that happen before, so I'm not entirely sure." There was no accusation behind the words, only mild humor, and Rowenna went weak with relief.

"Not that," she said. "The rest of you. You were a heap of broken pieces at the base of a cliff only days ago."

"Truth be told, it feels like I'm dying," Gawen confessed. "But I'm not, and sooner or later I'll mend, so there's no need to fuss. Are *you* all right?"

Rowenna looked away, fixing her eyes on the last of the fading evening light. "I'm not the one who's cursed now."

"Aren't you? You couldn't speak when we were swans, could you?"

"No," Rowenna admitted reluctantly.

"That's a curse."

"It's not the same," Rowenna said.

"Still."

She stole a glance at Gawen. Now that he was sitting quietly, he seemed a little better, one hand resting on the gunwale, his gaze on the horizon.

"It wasn't me," she said suddenly, her voice low and desperate. "Tell me you believe me. I need *someone* to believe me."

"You know, I drowned once," Gawen told her instead. "My family's land is all the way across the country, on the western coast. Our keep was in view of the sea, and on fine days in summer, the village boys and I lived in the water.

"The summer I was nine I swam out past the breakers. We'd been told not to, but someone had set it as a dare, and I've never had much sense. I went out to where the seabed dropped away underneath me into endless black. It felt like flying at first, or like being reborn as a star, hanging above that bottomless water. And I wasn't so far that I couldn't swim back to shore, or call out to my friends and be heard.

"So I stayed there to show off. Floated about and taunted them for not having the nerve to follow where I'd gone. I was shouting my fool head off when something grabbed me by the ankles and pulled me under."

Everything in Rowenna went tense. They were forced to sit so close together on the taft, Gawen felt her stiffen. He gave her the ghost of a smile and shook his head. "I'm here aren't I, scold? You know this story comes out all right in the end.

"Of course I fought, though I couldn't see what it was that had hold of me at first. My lungs were filling with water, and everything was going dark by the time I got a glimpse of it. And it was *me.* My own face staring back at me, with wicked satisfaction written across it.

"I suppose I'm luckier than most. Another moment or two and I'd have been finished, dragged down and hidden somewhere for the fish to gnaw at, until finally even my bones were gone. But my sister, Sibyl, was like you—a *cailleach.* A wise woman, who can hear some part of the earth or the water, and speak to it in turn. The sea had been speaking to her since she was just a babe in arms, and at only thirteen my mother had been schooling her in craft for years.

"She was on the shore when I went under and told me later that the waves cried out to her, as if some great pain had wakened in them. The outcry was so sudden and so dreadful that Sibyl sent out all of her power and split the sea apart, water hurrying away to the north and south, leaving a long rocky swath of dry land where only ocean bed had been.

"The path she made cut straight to the place where the water spirit and I were locked in a death struggle. We were dropped onto a shelf of rock jutting out into the abyss, and Sibyl came at us in a fury. She could see well enough which of us was me and which was the creature—*fuathan*, they're called, sly, evil-natured things that can change their skin and lay a curse and drown a grown man. Though the rest of the village children standing on the shore could see no difference between me and the creature, Sibyl knew. She gathered up sea earth and cut open her hand with a shard of coral and laid a work of earth and bone and blood so powerful on the *fuath* that it was driven back out to sea, and never troubled our shore again."

Rowenna felt hollowed out by her own ignorance and gutted by her longing to be as capable as Gawen's sister once was—to be enough for whatever came her way.

"How could she be so strong and yet still die?" Rowenna murmured.

Gawen raised one shoulder, in a careful, emotionless gesture. "We were rebels, all. My whole family and me. And some monsters you can't fight, Rowenna, no matter how strong you become. Torr Pendragon held my own life and my father's over my mother and Sibyl like a threat, and at the end, both of them walked to a witch's stake without hesitation."

He recounted that last without inflection, as if it had happened to someone else. As if it had been years ago, instead of mere weeks. For a long while, Gawen and Rowenna sat in silence, the yoal going up and down beneath them, the waves breaking ceaselessly against its sides.

"You ask me if I believe you, that you didn't make this curse," Gawen said finally. "Aye, I do. I've known despots and monsters and what some would call witches, and there's more to this world than most care to see. But I've seen it, and I believe you."

Silence fell between them, and for a long while there was only the lapping of the waves and the wordless singing of the wind.

Chapter Nine

At dawn, the maddening scent of peat and rain and smoke descended on them once more, and with a rush of wings, the boys became swans. None of them besides Gawen had spoken to Rowenna since they'd cast the blame for their curse on her, and she watched their transformation numbly. She tested her silence, too, trying to murmur a word and finding herself voiceless again.

The swans dozed, but not long after their change, clouds began to build on the northern horizon. They grew more threatening by the minute, until finally the first drops of cold, stinging rain hit Rowenna. She wrapped the oilskin tighter about herself and wished fiercely that Duncan was in his human form. Whatever the tension between them, he was better with a boat than most, and she knew precious little.

But she did know enough to trim the sail, ship the oars, and hold tight as the first gust of wind hit.

It lashed against the yoal, ruffling the swans' feathers as they huddled together in the bottom of the boat amid growing puddles of bilge water. The waves roared against the hull, battering the little craft and threatening to swamp it. The fear in Rowenna was a wild thing, raging at the encompassing walls of her rib cage.

And then, through the wind's furious howling, she caught

the sound of its voice. Never had Rowenna welcomed that sound before, but here, far from home and caught on the storm-tossed sea, it was as welcome and beloved as reassurance from an old friend.

Rowenna, the wind wailed. *Our love, our light, our dark-hearted girl.*

At the sound, Rowenna's fear subsided a little, and though she was still forced to cling to the gunwales to avoid being dashed from the yoal, the storm no longer seemed quite as terrible.

After what seemed like an eternity, her trust in the harrying wind was rewarded, for it drove the yoal on, and with a sudden sickening jolt, dashed it against the shore. Rowenna was thrown in among the swans, and then they were all tumbling out of the boat, onto unfamiliar earth.

Even through the driving rain, Rowenna caught sight of a world entirely different from the one she'd known all her life. Where the cliffs around Neadeala were craggy and the coves and harbors rock strewn, here a long, straight spit of sand stretched as far as the eye could see from one direction to another. There was something strange away inland, too—a dark, uneven *thing* hanging over the flat countryside like a shadow, hugging the horizon but keeping away from the coast.

Having lived all her life in a place surrounded by treeless heath, it took Rowenna a moment to realize that what she saw was a forest. Without hesitation, she started across the sand for the strange and looming wood. The rain was frigid, and the night before, her brothers and Gawen had come back to their human forms in the nightshirts and breeches they'd transformed in.

They'd need shelter if they shed their feathers and wings again. Rowenna had every intention of finding it for them before the change occurred.

It took far longer to reach the trees than she'd expected, and when she made it to the eaves of the forest, she couldn't help but stare up, awestruck by their height. There was a pungent tang to the air too, and dead needles crunched beneath her feet. But before long, Rowenna's attention was drawn back to earth as she realized the black swan was lagging behind. His gait was awkward and unsteady, and Rowenna went to the creature, dropping to her knees at his side.

Wordlessly she opened her arms in an invitation, and though the swan's fierce red eyes were undaunted and prideful, nevertheless he came to her. She settled the creature in against her chest, his bird heart beating rapidly, and they carried on.

It had come into Rowenna's mind that perhaps if she could only keep walking, eventually, by the time her legs gave way, things might be better. She might have outstripped all the troubles that had descended upon her like carrion crows. And while she knew the idea to be untrue, still she could not shake the compulsion. It at least felt like progress, to put one foot endlessly in front of the other. So she continued on through the pine forest, until the trees gave way a little and she found herself on a woodland path scored by the imprint of cart wheels.

But all along the cart road, shadowy shapes hung from the trees. As Rowenna drew up alongside the first, she stopped short, eyes widening in horror.

It was a body, clothes in tatters, flesh decaying and bones showing stark through ruined skin. Whoever it had been, their face was unrecognizable, having been picked at by birds. Rowenna peered down the path and realized that other bodies lined the road, stretching as far she could see. There were men and women and the smaller shapes of children. She looked and looked and could not tear her gaze from the tragic sight—not until the black swan in her arms raised a wing and shielded her face.

These must have been rebels and their families, Rowenna realized. Those who'd stood against Torr Pendragon and paid for it with their lives. But she could not stay and mourn them indefinitely—not if they were to find more shelter than the pine wood could afford. Carrying on, Rowenna fixed her eyes on the path, until the trees thinned out and gave way and she walked across open heath once more.

The storm clouds of morning had broken up, drifting in great banks across the sky, and the sun hung low ahead of Rowenna, dipping down to brush the horizon. Crimson light still bathed the moors, and Rowenna ceased walking. She set Gawen down and held her breath, waiting for her swans to change.

The sun sank and set, and darkness fell. Stars pricked to life across the indigo sky, and tears pricked behind Rowenna's eyes. Perhaps the monster in her mother's skin had lied. Perhaps the night before had been the single chance for her to reconcile with her brothers, and now the curse had taken hold of them irrevocably.

But then the earthy scent of home filled the air. Feathers were shaken off. Boys stood where birds had been a moment ago.

Anxiousness turned Rowenna's palms clammy as she looked at them. Their change had come later tonight. And if Mairead had spoken the truth, it would come still later tomorrow, until their time in human form dwindled away entirely and left them swans forever.

She wasn't the only one who'd noticed. Duncan, with his sailor's eye for wind and weather, glanced sharply up at the sky.

"It's late," he said. "Yesterday there was still a bit of light left after we changed. What is this, Enna? Are we going to run out of time?"

"I don't . . . I don't know for sure," Rowenna answered, faltering on the words. Her voice, stolen by day, came out unsteady at first, and then gained power. But she had no will to protest yet again that the curse was not of her making. "I'm afraid you might."

"You can fix it, though, can't you?" Finn asked, fear setting his child's voice to wavering. "You did it, so you can fix it."

All three of her brothers looked expectantly at her, Duncan and Liam with bitterness and reproach in their eyes as well. But it was Finn's desperate trust that hurt Rowenna worst.

That and the memory of Cam standing brokenhearted on the shore, not knowing the creature beside him was a monster rather than his beloved wife. Without her swift return, what would become of him? Yet even if she went back, what could she possibly do? And how could she begin to go about unraveling her brothers' curse before they were bound to their swan shapes forever?

In spite of her doubts, she could not bear to see Finn looking so—as if all the world had been proved wicked, when before he'd believed it to be good.

"Yes," she found herself saying, though the lie burned at her throat like a brand. "Of course I can fix this, Finny. It might take some time and some work, but I promise you—I *promise* you—that I'll right what's gone wrong."

"You can't right wrong with yet more wrong," Liam warned, long shadows making his thin face seem ghostly. "We don't want anything else wicked or unnatural done to us or for us."

Rowenna was trying to be forbearing. But her patience was worn down to dust by carrying the weight of truth and the responsibility for resolving all the misfortune that had befallen them.

"Then you'll have to keep your curse," she snapped at Liam. "Though I doubt even *your* righteousness will be enough to rid you of it without help."

Her breath was coming quick and hard, and she could feel herself edging toward some shameful loss of composure. It was Duncan who saved her, despite the tension between them.

"We can't stay out here all night," he grumbled, shivering in his nightclothes. "Wherever here is. We'll have to carry on, until we find somewhere with enough shelter to keep us from freezing before dawn."

"I know where we are."

It was the first time Gawen had spoken since they'd resumed their human forms and Rowenna's voice had returned. There was something in his words, some warning or trouble, that made all of them turn to look at him.

But all he said when faced with the Winthrops' attention was "There's a place we can shelter not far from here."

It was slow going, following in Gawen's wake as he limped doggedly on across the moorland. Once they crossed paths with a wizened old farmer leading a shaggy red bullock across the heath, and Gawen drew him aside. A few hushed words and some token or currency passed between the two.

"We're nearly there" was all Gawen said as the farmer carried on.

At last he stopped them at the edge of a vast, fog-draped field. The mist parted for brief moments, then closed again, allowing only an occasional glimpse of the wide expanse of heather-clad flat land. Something woke in Rowenna's bones as they approached the place—an ache and an itch and a wrongness, rising up from the land itself. The wind that pushed at the shreds of fog keened in the hollows and cried among the branches of the occasional twisted pines that dotted the field, but its voice was wordless.

No one spoke. The desolate air of the open land ahead of them was so pervasive, even Rowenna's brothers seemed to sense it. Gawen stood a little apart from the rest of them, his jaw tense and his eyes fixed on something Rowenna could not see.

"We'll have to cross it," Gawen said presently. "There's an empty church we can spend the night in on the other side."

"I don't like it," Finn confessed, drawing closer to Liam. "It doesn't feel right."

"It's Drumossie Moor," Gawen said. "Your father and I were both here, only a month ago. This is where the Highlands uprising against Torr Pendragon finally died. Thousands of men met their end on this field, including my own brother."

Finn shivered, eyes owl wide in his small, pale face.

"The dead can't hurt you, Finn," Liam said reassuringly.

"And I won't let anything happen to you," Rowenna promised. "I swear I'll keep you safe."

But when she moved toward him, her youngest brother shied away. "I don't believe you. We had to leave home, didn't we? And there's something wrong with all of us now. I don't like changing, Enna. It hurts my head, and it makes me forget things I wish I could remember."

Stung by Finn's words, Rowenna stepped back.

"We'll all keep together while we cross," Liam said. "So as not to get lost in the fog. Gawen, you'd best lead, since you know where we're headed."

Rowenna bit back a swift retort. She didn't want Gawen in front of them. She wanted him beside her or behind her, in this place where the end of his old life had begun, when his brother was killed and his father captured and the Highland uprising put down. But if he'd been here before it only made sense for him to guide them, so she held her tongue.

One by one, they stepped out into the fog, Gawen in front and Rowenna coming last. Nothing was said to sort out the order in which they proceeded, but a look passed between Rowenna and Gawen as they flanked the rest of the boys, as if to protect them from what lay ahead and what might follow along from behind.

Somewhere above, the moon was surely shining. It would have been impossible to see, otherwise. But the occasional lonely tree cast long shadows, and when the breeze managed to tear a rent in the fog, Rowenna could see her brothers walking along before her, no more than five paces between any of them for fear of losing one another in the mist. The moonlight made them over into haunted versions of themselves, and a sudden, creeping chill washed over Rowenna. It felt like a glimpse of the future—of what might happen if she failed to break Mairead's curse, and the boys were left to languish in the inhuman forms they'd been bound to.

Voices whispered in the fog, and Rowenna couldn't be sure if it was the wind or others out wandering the moor at night, or if the souls of the restless dead were speaking. But she didn't dare ask her brothers if they heard it too. Finn was already on edge, and she would not say anything that might push him further into fear.

At last the fog broke, and they found themselves coming out on the moor's opposite side, near an ivy-clad and tumbledown church.

"Where's Gawen?" Rowenna asked sharply, glancing at her brothers and finding him missing.

Duncan and Liam cast about themselves.

"He was just here," Duncan said in bewilderment. "I followed him all the way. Didn't take my eyes from him once until I heard Finn come up behind me. Perhaps he needed to use the bushes?"

"Don't move," Rowenna warned. Something had begun to tug at her, like that night she'd searched for Cam and Duncan. It pulled insistently, drawing her back toward the mist. "Every one of you, stay just where you are until I get back. I'm going to find my stray."

Before any of them could speak, she plunged into the fog, following that familiar pull. Rowenna did not call out—she had no need of her voice when her craft led her so. Instead she stumbled over hummocks of land, bypassing clumps of heather and trying her best to keep a straight course as she followed the invisible, ineffable sense that drew her along.

Beware, behold, be still, the wind sighed, as it ran mournfully across Drumossie. *Here is your lost one, your missing piece, the wayward soul we brought to you.*

The fog cleared for a moment, driven before the breeze, and Rowenna caught sight of Gawen on his knees among the heather.

"You are not allowed to be lost," she said, closing the little distance between them and dropping down at his side. "I forbid it. I found you once. Now's a second time. And I will keep on finding you, if need be, because you seem to be the one thing I *can* find."

"It's not me who's lost, though." Gawen's voice was a cold, dead thing, as lifeless and dreary as the draping fog. "It's him. It's all of them, sinking under the earth here, with no markers to show where they fell. They'd no peace in their lives, or in their dying, and they have none now in their decay."

Rowenna looked down and saw that before them, some creature had been scrabbling at the earth. On the newly turned soil there rested the leathery remains of a human hand and a riven skull, yellowed bone showing through tatters of old flesh.

"This is haunted land," Rowenna said with a shudder. "And you're still living. Leave the dead to themselves. Come away with me."

"I will." Gawen sounded far away as he spoke, and he kept his eyes fixed on the sad, lonely bones before them. "But we've got caught up in each other's troubles, scold, like moths tangled in webs that weren't of their making. Drumossie casts a shadow over you now too—sure as your monster casts a shadow over me."

Together, they got up from the damp earth. Rowenna kept near enough to Gawen that their arms nearly touched, as if she could bind him to her by that closeness.

"How are all your broken bits?" she asked as they made for the edge of the moor, where the rest of the boys were waiting.

"Better than my spirits," Gawen said, but dark humor lurked behind the words, and Rowenna knew that for the moment, whatever despair had come over him was once again past.

Chapter Ten

The church at the edge of Drumossie Moor had been half ruined by cannon fire. Its vestry lay in a crumble of stone, revealing an interior door that led to the nave. Thick ivy ran over the cracking walls, and shards of tinted glass still gleamed from where the mullioned windows had blown out.

Rowenna stood poised on the doorstep as her brothers hung back, but Gawen stopped her with a hand on her arm.

"Wait," he said. "Let me go in first."

Rowenna stepped aside. As Gawen opened the door, the decaying wood around its hinges finally gave way, and it fell inward with a hollow thud. Half a dozen pigeons burst into flight from within the nave, winging their way skyward in a flurry of feathers and soft, disconcerted sounds. For the first time Rowenna realized that much of the church's roof had collapsed, leaving only the outer walls.

"You said you knew a church we could shelter in," Liam said doubtfully. He had his hands in the pockets of his breeches and his shoulders hunched. "This is a ruin—just an empty shell."

The breeze kicked up, bringing a gust of dank air from the back of the churchyard.

"No use fussing," Duncan said. "If it's as good as we can get, we'll make do."

He strode into the open, roofless sanctuary and paused in a pool of moonlight. Something in Rowenna twisted as she watched him—all tussled hair and sea-glass eyes and anger. There'd never been much closeness between Rowenna and Liam, but she and Duncan were always on each other's side.

Or they had been, until now.

"Wait," she said softly, going after him as Liam and Finn settled in the vestibule, where there was still enough roof to keep off rain. "Duncan, can I speak to you?"

But he rounded on her, harsh and furious.

"No, Enna. You can't. In fact, I don't want a word with you until all of this is over. Until this curse, or whatever it is you've done to us, is *undone*. So don't try to make things better when you're the one who broke them in the first place."

"It wasn't me," Rowenna insisted, balling her hands into fists until her nails dug into her palms. "By God in heaven, I didn't do this. It was—"

She stopped abruptly.

"Who, Enna?" Duncan said belligerently, his words a challenge. "Who else could possibly have done this?"

"It was *Màthair*," Rowenna blurted out before she could stop herself. "She did it."

And in that instant, the disappointment and reproach she'd seen in her brothers turned to disgust.

"*Màthair* knew what she was doing with her craft. She never had to be kept ignorant because of her temper, like you," Duncan shot back, at the same time as Liam drew himself up to his full height.

"What reason," Liam said, "could *Màthair* possibly have to do such a thing? When she'd just come home to us? It makes no sense, Enna. Speak the truth and we'll think better of you for it."

"She'd have no reason to do this if it was really her who'd come home," Rowenna insisted. Speak the truth she would, though she knew Liam's promise to be a lie—they would not think better of her for it. "But I saw her die. And that thing that's come back in her body? That's not Mairead Winthrop. It's something else. Something monstrous."

"Is she mad?" Duncan asked, looking past Rowenna at Liam.

Liam shook his head. "I don't know. After what happened to *Màthair*, she said something similar. Something about a monster. I thought it was just grief then, and needing to lay blame. But *Màthair* coming back clearly made things worse, and set her off again."

For the first time since leaving home, Duncan looked at Rowenna with something like pity.

"Were you trying to protect us then, Enna? From this monster you think you saw?"

Rowenna shut her eyes. Tears tracked down her face as she thought of how she might answer.

No. It wasn't my doing. And while you're losing time under this curse, Athair's *been left behind with that creature.*

But it would only sound like madness to the two of them. Further proof that her grasp on reality was slipping.

"Yes," Rowenna lied, her voice breaking on the word. "I was

trying to keep you safe, and I never meant for any of this to happen. But I'll see it set right, I promise."

With that, she hurried out of the ruined church. She could not bear to have her brothers or Gawen see her cry—not when they were the cause of it. So she skirted the edge of the church and, finding an overgrown tangle of a graveyard at its rear, let herself in through the rusted gate. It wailed mournfully on its hinges, but then Rowenna was past and into the tall grasses, where headstones listed at odd angles or lay shattered upon the earth.

Seating herself with her back to one such stone, Rowenna drew her knees up to her chest and buried her face in her arms. She took in breath after sobbing breath, trying to imagine that the grave marker behind her was one of Mairead's wards and that none of this had happened. That they were all, even her mother, home and safe and well. That uncanny creatures existed only in fairy stories and legend, and the world was kind and straightforward and good.

The worst of her grief had passed by the time she became aware of a rhythmic sound coming from the far end of the graveyard. Drying her eyes on one sleeve of the fraying pullover she wore, Rowenna got to her feet and cast about herself.

There, in the shadows of a little copse that grew right up to the edge of the graveyard's dry stone wall, was a stranger. He was towheaded and freckled, on the cusp of adulthood, and behind him a tethered horse pulled contentedly at the long grass. It was the serene sound of the horse at its dinner that had caught her attention. The boy himself was eating an apple with evident enjoyment, and as Rowenna's gaze met his, he smiled. It was an honest, disarming sort of smile—a farm boy's smile, and in spite of everything, Rowenna couldn't help but feel a little warmed by it.

"I didn't like to interrupt," the boy said in the broader, flatter accent of the hill country away south. "You obviously needed a bit of time. Better now?"

Rowenna sniffed. She felt wrung out and abominably tired after everything that had happened over the past days. But as she opened her mouth to answer the stranger, a sudden realization dawned on her—without a voice by daylight, perhaps it would be best to keep silent. If she could not convince her own brothers that she hadn't been the source of this curse, how would she convince others if they discovered her peculiar daytime affliction?

So rather than speak, Rowenna only nodded.

"Come and sit," the farm boy offered, patting the space on the wall next to him.

Reluctantly Rowenna drew closer.

"Apple?" the boy offered, pulling one from a satchel. "You look as if you could use it."

After two days without food, Rowenna's mouth set to watering just at the thought. She took the proffered apple and settled down on the wall, carefully keeping space between herself and the boy.

As she bit into the fruit, the tart flavor of it filled her mouth, and she sighed.

"What is it that's bothered you so?" the boy asked. "Can I help at all?"

He had a straightforward and reassuring way about him. Though the horse cropping the grass was a fine one, the boy wore loose, belted trousers and a homespun woolen shirt, and up close Rowenna could see the flecks of green in his hazel eyes.

Rowenna shook her head, taking another bite of apple.

"What's your name?" the boy asked. "No one should be out on their own when they feel so low."

Helplessly Rowenna shrugged.

"Are you mute, then?"

A nod.

"Were you born that way?" He certainly was one for questions. Rowenna shook her head.

"Did it happen in an accident? Or through some illness?" No again.

The boy's voice went very soft. "Is it a curse?"

Rowenna stiffened and sprang from the wall, ready to flee from him if need be.

"Don't be afraid." The boy hurried to reassure her, holding both hands up disarmingly. "It's only, my mother had a bit of craft. It runs in my family, and I spent enough time around those with power to learn the look of someone under a curse."

Rowenna shivered. It had never occurred to her that the curse might be apparent to some, just as Mairead's true nature was apparent to her when most did not perceive it.

"Are you wanting help? Because I know someone who might be able to put an end to your troubles," the boy offered. "She's not far from here either, just in Inverness. Her name's Elspeth Crannach and she is—was—a *cailleach*. Someone wise, someone with power. If anyone can tell you how to get your voice back, it'll be her."

A surge of hope flooded through Rowenna.

"Here," the boy offered. "Take this."

He reached into his satchel and pulled out a round silver medallion, with swirling circles and spirals etched onto its tarnished surface.

"If you give that to Elspeth, she'll know I'm the one who sent you, and she'll be sure to help. She's close to me and I to her. And perhaps if you're in Inverness for a time, I'll see you there too. I've been away, but it's where I'm headed now."

Rowenna clutched the medallion and nodded, wide-eyed. After the anger she'd met with from her brothers lately, she'd not expected to find compassion in a stranger.

"Do you have people nearby, and will you be all right if I go?" the boy asked, concern written across his simple face. "I don't like to leave you otherwise."

Rowenna managed a reassuring smile and gestured to the church. The boy got to his feet and slipped the reins back over his fine horse's head. Then, with an ease born of practice, he swung himself up into the saddle.

"Elspeth Crannach," he reminded Rowenna. "I'm sure she can help you, and you'll be glad to have met her. Just follow the road west, and you'll find your way to the city."

The horse chafed at its bit, and the boy patted the creature's neck. "Well, I hate to go. And I hope from now on life treats you better than it did this night. Till Inverness, if the fates will it."

Rowenna stood and watched him ride away, the horse's movement light and fluid, the boy sure in the saddle. At last the night swallowed them up. She wrapped her arms around herself, feeling suddenly bereft. There was only her family now, and Gawen with his grief, all of them bound together by this curse and dependent upon Rowenna to find a way to break it.

Wearily she turned back to the church.

Within its shadowed interior, the Winthrop boys were sleeping. They'd found a pair of torn altar cloths somewhere, and clearly Liam had deemed it acceptable in the eyes of God to make use of them in a time of need. Duncan lay huddled beneath one, Liam and Finn beneath the other.

At first, Rowenna saw no sign of Gawen, but as she reached the center of the church and glanced back at the doorway, there he was in the gloom beside the entrance. It reminded her palpably of the night she'd found him, cast up into the darkness at the base of the cliffs beyond Neadeala.

Sitting forward, Gawen fixed Rowenna with his dark eyes.

"It's not safe to go off on your own this close to Torr Pendragon's court," he warned. "Take care, Rowenna Winthrop, and stay close to the rest of us from now on."

"Odd you should care about my well-being, all of a sudden," Rowenna said, her words holding an edge, "as you couldn't be bothered to say anything when my brothers called me a liar and you knew better."

"They'd hardly believe me when they don't believe their own kin," Gawen pointed out.

"Then you're a coward," Rowenna shot back. "Not speaking the truth just because it wouldn't be heard the way it ought."

"Did you speak your own truth before you were forced into it, though?" Gawen asked, his composure slipping. "Or did you hold it close until you couldn't any longer? And aren't you lying even now, letting your brothers believe this curse was your work?"

Rowenna took the few steps back to the door in an instant and sank to her knees before Gawen, everything in her on fire.

"What I do is my own business, Gawen MacArthur," she said, low and fierce. "It's not me who came begging for *your* help."

Immediately he curbed his own sharpness, though she could still feel it in him. He might play at penitence, but Rowenna suspected neither of them were ever entirely without anger.

"I'm sorry." The words came out mild, Gawen's face schooled into a careful blank. "You're right, and I'm sure you know what you're about."

Rowenna leaned forward, still blazing, until she was mere inches from him. Until she could smell him—sweat and salt and grave earth.

"Don't lie to me when you've just been scolding me for deceit," she said, tension singing through her and him and the very air. "I'd rather the truth from you than false kindness."

Rowenna watched Gawen struggle. For a moment, he warred within himself, knowing he ought to maintain his feigned humility. But it was against his nature. Rowenna knew that already, and watching him give in to fire that answered her own felt like triumph.

"You want truth from me?" Gawen said. "Then here's the truth for you. I'm not on your side, Rowenna Winthrop. Perhaps I'll take your part when it suits, and perhaps I know more of who you are than some others do, but I'm on my own side, now and always. You're working on behalf of your kin, and I'm working on behalf of myself and my own ends, and if either of us has to break with the other because of that, we'll do it in a heartbeat."

"What exactly *are* your own ends?" Rowenna asked for the first time, eyes narrowing as she looked him up and down. "You said you want me to find something for you, with my craft. What is it?"

Gawen hesitated.

"If you lie to me now, I'll never forgive you." Rowenna watched his throat work as he swallowed. Gawen's gaze faltered, and he looked down.

"I want you to help me find my father," he said. "The one rebel Torr Pendragon hasn't killed outright yet. I've tried bribing guards, tried getting into the Inverness dungeons on false pretenses, but I can never sort out where he's being kept. I need you and your craft for that. I've been failing at every turn, and it's not something I can manage without help."

Rowenna could see that the admission had cost him. Reaching out, she took one of his hands in her own, and a look of pure misery crossed the boy's face.

"If I can get this curse sorted and learn to manage a little of my own power, I'll help you," Rowenna promised. "But there's my own father to get back to as well—the work can't take too long."

"It won't," Gawen said swiftly. "Just one night's use of your craft. That's all I need."

"Done," Rowenna answered.

Gawen drew his hand away, and Rowenna retreated, settling herself into a patch of long grass growing against the church wall. Wind played wordlessly about, skittering here and there and making soft, comforting sounds. Cold stars burned across the spring sky, visible beyond the gaping holes in the church roof.

Rowenna had thought Gawen long asleep when his voice came out of the shadows again.

"You remind me of them, scold," he said. "Perhaps you've not come into your power yet, but you're just like they were. Full of spite and pride and fire."

By the time Rowenna realized he must mean his mother and sister, who'd gone to the stake for their craft and their rebellion, Gawen had silently gotten up and slipped out into the night.

Chapter Eleven

In sleep, Rowenna found her dreaming self surrounded by fog and greeted by the voice of the sea. Waves bit cold at her ankles, and loose stones turned over treacherously beneath her feet.

Even before a gust of wind cleared the fog, Rowenna knew where she was. There was no mistaking the ghostly, metallic clank of rigging being moved by the breeze. She stood at the fishing harbor, where she'd fled Neadeala and last seen Cam. Waiting in the fog was the village's fleet of yoals, the boats that kept the people of those parts alive and fed.

The mist scudded away, and the boats appeared around Rowenna, their masts like a small winter forest on that shore where no trees grew. The sails had been lowered and tied down overnight, and each boat safely drawn onto the shingle. But someone had been among the yoals.

From every mast hung a dead swan, pegged up by its neck and slit open from tail to throat. A mound of viscera lay on the decks beneath each one of them, but not a single seabird had appeared to take advantage of the unexpected feast. Instead, the boats stood lifeless, a strange timber-wrought graveyard marked by witch signs and speaking mutely of evil that now stalked those parts.

Because there was evil in this work that had been done—

Rowenna could feel it, even in dream. Whatever her mother's wards had been, with their sense of protection and care, this was the opposite. It gave her an impression of binding, and holding, and drowning. Of chains and hopelessness in a night with no end.

As Rowenna stood watching, a small group of villagers appeared at the head of the beach—fishermen, carrying their meals for the day in tin buckets. The comfortable sound of them talking among themselves cut off abruptly as they saw the boats and stopped short.

"What is this witchcraft?" one of the men muttered.

Cam turned to him slowly, and Rowenna could read a world of regret and pain on her father's face. "Whatever it is, who'll we blame? Who'll we blame, now my Enna is gone?"

The villager spat. "She's cursed us. Cursed us because you drove her out."

Cam only shook his head and started for the boats. "If she has, we deserve it. I deserve it, for the things I said to her."

Swinging himself into the Winthrop yoal, Cam wordlessly cut down the swan's corpse. He tossed it out to sea and shoveled the pile of viscera after it. By the time he hauled in a bucket of seawater to rinse the hold, the rest of the fishermen had followed suit. But none of them spoke. They did the work silently, each alone with their thoughts and their suspicions.

Rowenna felt something ice cold touch her shoulder and turned to find Mairead at her back once more. A small smile turned up the corners of her mother's sweet mouth, but when Mairead raised a hand, it was stained with blood to the wrist. Nevertheless, she pressed one finger to Rowenna's lips and murmured to her.

"Hush, saltwater girl."

It was dark still. Something tasted of iron, and Gawen MacArthur crouched over Rowenna in the shadows.

"You were talking," he said quietly. "Something about blood and earth and seawater. Do you dream, scold?"

"Aye." Rowenna sat up. "I do."

"Will you tell me what about?"

Rowenna peered at the moon, which hung low over the church's west end. She could not speak of what she saw in her sleep—it filled her with slow horror even to think of what she was shown.

"About home" was all she could offer.

But when Rowenna got to her feet, Gawen was up and at her side in a moment.

"What's that? Have you hurt yourself?" he pressed. Rowenna looked at him in bewilderment, until he raised a hand and held one finger to her mouth.

It came away slick with blood.

Rowenna felt as if she might choke. So she scrubbed at her mouth with one sleeve and forced rising panic away, striding across the sanctuary of the ruined church.

"Get up," Rowenna snapped at her brothers, still sleeping in the dark. Dawn was perhaps an hour away, but if their time in human form was waning, as Mairead had suggested, she'd have to speak to them early if she wished to speak to them at all.

Liam rose at once, a question written across his face. Finn yawned and stretched, trying valiantly to wake after so little sleep. But Duncan only grunted sulkily and rolled over.

Rowenna nudged him with her foot. "Duncan, don't be like this."

"Go away, Enna," he muttered.

"Finn's behaving himself better than you are, and he's a *child*," Rowenna pointed out. "We're going to Inverness, and I want to get moving. There's someone in the city who might be able to help with the curse."

"Then go ahead. I won't stop you."

"Duncan!" Frustration set the edges of Rowenna's words to fraying. "I'm trying to help you all. Could you at least *pretend* to cooperate?"

Duncan sat up suddenly, his face flushed and unhappy. "God in heaven, Enna, do I have to say it right out? I don't want to be awake for the change. It feels like living death, being made less. Being made small, and stupid, and wild."

Rowenna pressed a hand to her mouth. Liam said nothing, but as she glanced his way, she could see it in him, too. Weariness and pained resignation over what was to come. Finn sniffed, and there were tears shining in his eyes, though he tried to hide them.

"I'm sorry," Rowenna breathed. "I hadn't realized it was as bad as all that."

"Well, it is." Duncan glared up at Rowenna, and a sharp pang of fear shot through her, at the thought that perhaps the easiness and camaraderie that existed between them was now ruined forever. "Whether you meant it to be or not, that's the way of it."

"I'll leave you, then," Rowenna said, stumbling over her words in her haste. "I don't want to make things worse."

But as she hurried out of the church, the heartbreaking scent of peat and woodsmoke enfolded her as the wind surged up around them. She couldn't help but look back, and for an instant, her gaze met Duncan's. Then she shut her eyes tight, because she could not bear to see the dread in him as the wind grew louder and resolved into wingbeats.

When she looked again, there were only swans where her brothers had been, and the sky had not yet grown gray with the first hint of dawn.

Gawen in his black swan guise rejoined them as they left the church and started down the road to Inverness. It irked Rowenna that she could not mutter curses to express her displeasure with the entire situation—traipsing down a strange road in her night-gown and a stolen pullover, with a gaggle of swans trailing along behind her. She tried pressing her lips together in a thin, tight line. She tried scowling. None of it helped.

Slowly the landscape changed. The moors gave way to farm-land. An occasional crofter passed by but chose not to offer a greeting after seeing the dark look on Rowenna's face. The wind, seeming bent on putting Rowenna in better spirits, played about constantly, rustling the grasses on the verge and ruffling the swans' feathers. It chuckled about Rowenna's ankles and purred as it brushed her face.

Carry on, carry on, our love, our light. Carry on, carry on, our salt-water girl.

With a shake of her head, Rowenna did as the wind bid her.

Intermittent clusters of buildings cropped up among the farmland—little groupings of farriers and tinsmiths and wheelwrights. Rowenna ducked her head when met with groups of the villagers, and when anyone drew too near, the swans stretched out their necks and hissed a warning, so she passed by unbothered. The land began to rise gradually upward. The road grew wider and more worn. At last, Rowenna crested a hill and stopped short at the sight that met her.

Spread out below and before them lay what could only be the city of Inverness. It sprang up on either side of a broad river, the water of which was a cold, indigo blue beneath the thin spring sun. There were houses and shops and pubs and workhouses all crammed together, more than Rowenna had ever imagined possible to see in one place. Ships with masts as tall as trees lay moored in the deep river, and a castle with high curtain walls crouched to the south of the city proper, guarding it all like a forbidding dragon. Even from the hilltop where she stood, Rowenna could smell the smoke and pitch and sewage, and hear the clatter of hammers and tongs and cart wheels.

Surely, if the cure for a curse could be found anywhere, it would be in such a place. Yet Rowenna stayed rooted to the spot. The sight of so many buildings and so many people unnerved her in a way she'd never felt before. She wished, fiercely, that her brothers and Gawen were not in their swan forms. That they were their tall, human selves, who would gather round her and make her forget her fear.

Gawen in his black swan shape carried on a few steps and looked back over his shoulder expectantly. When Rowenna made no move toward him, he returned and nibbled at the hem of her skirt. The rest of the swans huddled close about her, the tension between them forgotten now that they were in feathered form, and an infusion of new courage flooded Rowenna.

She wanted her family back, which meant there was work to be done. Without allowing herself a chance to falter again, Rowenna started down the hill.

The city was a labyrinth of overhanging buildings, the laneways filled with a miasma of overpowering and unpleasant smells. Rowenna wound down alleys and pushed through crowded squares, until at last she came to a busy riverside market, where vendors spread their stalls and carts along the quay and shouted raucously to anyone who passed by. Smells of fish and seaweed and spices choked the air, and Rowenna lost no time finding herself a small open space and settling down to watch. The swans surrounded her, and several of them tucked their heads beneath their wings.

She could not ask after Elspeth Crannach until night fell and her voice returned. Thinking of it, Rowenna pulled the medallion on its leather braid out from under the neck of her pullover and idly ran her thumb along the sigil's silver edge. For now, at least, she could try to orient herself in this strange and overwhelming place.

Rowenna had never seen so many people from so many places. There was an odd boat in the river, with papery folding sails, crewed by black-haired men in silk and linen who unloaded crate after crate of spices and fruits while speaking to one another in a clipped language Rowenna could not understand. A man and a woman in brightly colored garments walked by, an intricate filigree of designs painted across the woman's brown hands. They had a collared beast at their side like nothing Rowenna had ever heard of—larger than a mastiff, it was shaped like a cat, and its pelt shone ruddy orange in the winter light, riven with black stripes. The great beast pulled back its lips and snarled as its keepers passed by a moored ship with a figurehead like a dragon. The vessel was crewed by pale, tawny-haired folk who laughed loudly, all of them wearing furs and knife belts or swords.

Rowenna shook her head to clear it. None of this would be of help in breaking her curse, or in finding the woman she was searching for.

Instead, she turned her attention to the merchants and vendors along the quay, watching carefully. The fishmonger four carts down sold eels, but for the right price, and if the right words were spoken, had a selection of braided charms and small pocket wards hidden away. The herbwife across the quay kept calling out that her inventory was *for the kitchen, just the kitchen*, but Rowenna saw a woman with a sickly child approach her, and with a glance to the right and left, the herbwife bent and spoke a quick blessing into the child's ear before pressing a vial into the mother's hand.

Better, but still not quite enough.

With a sigh, Rowenna tucked a little of her knotted hair behind one ear and looked out at the river, which slipped silently past.

She hadn't expected that away from her home on the cliffs, she'd constantly miss the sound of the sea. It had been the backdrop to her whole life, and to be in a place where it did not undercut every sound and every thought felt like missing a limb, or some essential function of the mind.

A startled trumpet and small flurry of feathers drew Rowenna's attention back to her immediate surroundings with a snap. Gawen in his black swan form stood before her, neck outstretched, wings spread, hissing like a demon at half a dozen men in scarlet uniforms who were approaching from down the quay.

Anxiously Rowenna got up. She rubbed a finger at the silver medallion around her neck in a nervous gesture. The soldiers stopped a few feet away, and while Rowenna's brothers had gathered uncertainly about her, Gawen still stood his ground, making a racket that drew the attention of anyone within earshot.

"Shut that creature up, girl, or we'll snap its neck," one of the men in uniform growled.

Immediately Rowenna stepped forward and lifted Gawen, who carried on hissing but did not struggle.

"Where did you get that?" the same man asked roughly, pointing to the medallion around Rowenna's neck. "That's the Crannach sigil, don't you know?"

Rowenna nodded warily.

"What's your name, girl?"

Shifting Gawen's weight awkwardly to one arm, Rowenna gestured futilely at her lips.

The man in uniform sighed. His ash-blond hair was beginning

to gray, and there was an air of confidence about him—as if he expected, at all times, to be obeyed.

"You're coming with us," the man said. "I'm Greaves, Torr Pendragon's steward, and anyone bearing that symbol you're wearing is to be brought to the castle."

Rowenna's anxiousness blossomed into full fear. But she could not outrun or resist six men, and now that Gawen had settled, the people milling about the pier were pointedly looking away, intent on not noticing what was unfolding before them. There was a bleak resignation in the air, as if such things happened often—the descent of soldiers and people being escorted away.

So, with her heart beating raggedly in her chest, Rowenna ducked her head in assent.

"Well that's something at least," Greaves said, the words sour. "The last lass we had to escort up the hill tried to slip us. She fell and split her head open in four different places—a terrible thing. Would hate to see the same fate befall someone else."

Rowenna tightened her grip on the black swan. She wasn't sure yet how much the boys understood in their bird forms, but Gawen had certainly caught the threat in Greaves's voice and stiffened in her arms.

Don't you dare, Rowenna thought at him sharply. *Don't you give them an excuse.*

"Right. So long as you cooperate, there's no need to bind your hands," Greaves said. "Let's be on our way, then."

Flanked by three men in front and three behind, Rowenna did as she was told, the white swans that were her brothers following in their wake. As they marched through the city, the tight-packed buildings began to thin and the air to freshen. At last they stepped out into green, open parkland surrounding a forbidding gray castle, which stood on a hill overlooking the river. Jewel-bright peacocks strutted about the lawns, and little copses dotted the park. Greaves took a ring of heavy keys from his pocket and opened a door in the massive curtain wall.

"After you," he said with exaggerated courtesy, and stepped aside to let Rowenna pass by first. That must mean there'd be no easy way for her to escape the curtain wall—he'd not have let her enter first if there was.

Rowenna's fear bit deeper. Once inside these walls, would she ever come out again? She knew nothing about this place, or the people who lived in it, beyond the fact that Torr Pendragon was a tyrant her father had fought against and who'd slaughtered Gawen MacArthur's family.

Seeing her hesitation, Greaves shrugged. "Or we can drag you in, whatever you wish. You're a skittish thing, aren't you?"

Steeling her nerves, Rowenna entered the castle proper.

They'd come up into a bustling side courtyard, full of merchants' and grocers' carts, where servants in livery or voluminous white aprons milled about, shouting to one another. A few nodded to Greaves as they passed by, but he did not deign to return the greeting.

After the kitchen court, they reached a stable yard, where exercise boys led sleek-coated horses about. Past the stables stood a tall box hedge, from behind which strange and unfamiliar noises rose.

"Pendragon's menagerie is back there," Greaves offered with grim satisfaction. "He likes to keep things in cages. Perhaps you're to become one of them. Nearly there now—one more door."

Again, Greaves took the keys from his pocket. But this time, when he pushed open yet another small door in the curtain wall, Rowenna stepped through without hesitation, for she could see green hillside beyond.

They came out on the slope that led to the River Ness. It was wilder and woodsier than the rest of the castle grounds, dotted with tall pines and heather. Greaves led their party down a winding path that meandered along the hill until it reached the river, and Rowenna could do nothing but follow.

Halfway down the hill, a voice called out.

"Robert, what have you got there?"

At once, Greaves's demeanor changed. All the visible harshness left him, smoothing from his face as he straightened and pasted on a pleasant smile.

"Your ladyship. I've brought you something."

For the first time, Rowenna caught sight of a group of young women dallying by the river's edge, looking like butterflies in their fine, jewel-colored gowns. One of them broke away from the group, gathering up her silk skirts and picking her way along the path to the group of guards, where she stopped before Greaves.

They made a stark contrast—the delicate girl radiant in sky blue, with sapphire eyes and a fall of auburn hair, and Greaves, attempting to mask the violent nature Rowenna could feel in him. But it was the girl who took the lead.

"Well that's familiar, isn't it?" she said, her voice sweet and low as she nodded at the medallion. "I wonder what market she found it at. I'm sure it ended up lost, and traders happened upon it somewhere. I've never seen this disheveled creature before—she was certainly no member of my household. Truth be told, when I told you I'd like to see anyone found wearing my family's sigil, I didn't expect you to actually *find* someone."

The silk-clad girl turned to Rowenna and held out a hand.

"I'm Elspeth Crannach," she said warmly. "That piece of silver you found is an heirloom of my family's. I'm happy to see it again— could I pay you for your trouble in bringing it here? Greaves, are you still hovering? Haven't you got better things to do?"

Reluctantly the steward motioned to his men. All six of them trooped up the hill, and Rowenna was left with her swans, in the company of Elspeth and her waiting maids. Slipping the medallion from around her neck, Rowenna held it out. Fate had brought her to precisely the person she'd wanted, and it was a relief to have something, for once, work out in her favor.

Elspeth took the silver piece and looked down at it, her gaze growing soft and distant. But then she brought the full weight of her attention to bear on Rowenna again.

"What beautiful swans," Elspeth said lightly, and there was something calculating in the way she glanced from Rowenna to the swans and back again. "I'd love to have such creatures about, to look down on from the castle while they swam on the river, or to visit with a bit of bread now and then. I don't suppose I could convince you to stay here with them?"

Rowenna frowned. But the boy in the graveyard with his open-hearted smile had promised this Elspeth could help her, so she put her head to one side, to show she was listening.

"Can't you speak?" Elspeth asked. But there was something showy about the question—as if she knew the answer without ever asking.

Rowenna shook her head.

"I see. How sad." Elspeth turned to her companions and gestured to them to wait just a moment more. "If you were to stay, there's a groundskeeper's hut just over there that's been sitting vacant for half a year now. You could look after your swans, and be left to yourself for the most part. So long as you're in my service, I can protect you too. But I'm afraid if you choose to go, you'll be left to the tender mercies of Greaves and his lot. Inverness isn't a kind place to the homeless and friendless, of late."

Her eyes locked on Rowenna's, and there was an indomitable and compelling quality to that clear blue gaze. Rowenna went half-dizzy with it. Yet there was no sense of wrongness, no underlying panic like that she'd felt when faced with the monster in Mairead's skin.

And this girl might be the key to unlocking the curse tying Rowenna's tongue and binding her brothers to swan form.

Slowly Rowenna nodded.

"Wonderful!" Elspeth's smile was enough to dazzle, and she beckoned to the finely dressed girls on the riverbank.

"Come, my loves," she called to them. "We'd better get in to dress for tonight. Swan maiden, I'll let the keepers know you're staying. You can help yourself to the hut in the meantime—you won't find the door locked. And I'll send down something suitable for you to wear—Torr wouldn't like it, having someone wandering about the grounds in rags."

The courtiers in their gossamer gowns approached, and Elspeth motioned to them to carry on without her. Soon the hillside was quiet and empty, with only Rowenna and this bright, rigidly controlled girl left facing each other.

"I can *see* the curse on you," Elspeth murmured. "Like a shadow. That's what stilled your tongue, isn't it?"

Swallowing, Rowenna nodded. Elspeth stepped forward, until she was too close for comfort. She looked Rowenna up and down, a thoughtful frown creasing the space between her eyes. "Yet you've got a spark of your own craft. Wild and untouched to be sure, but it ought to have been enough to protect you. Don't you know how to wield your own magic?"

As Rowenna shook her head, Elspeth sighed. "That's a pity. Would you like to learn?"

This time, Rowenna nodded eagerly, pride giving way to need. The beautiful girl glanced up the hill, in the direction the courtiers had gone.

"I'll come back tomorrow morning," she said decidedly. "On my own. We'll see if we can sort out your curse, and perhaps teach you a little of what you should know along the way."

It was a generous offer, made to a perfect stranger. Rowenna bowed her head in thanks but couldn't help noticing the troubled look on Elspeth's face as she walked off, rubbing her thumb against the cool silver of the medallion.

Be cautious with that one, whatever kindness she offers, Rowenna warned herself. *There's more to her than she lets anyone see.*

Chapter Twelve

The swans took to the river with an eagerness Rowenna had not expected. She stood for a while, fretting over them. They were growing more and more comfortable in their feathered shapes and becoming truly birdlike in their mannerisms. Finn was paddling about in fledgling gray, upending himself now and then to find weeds below the water. Liam and Duncan stayed nearer the shore, nibbling at cattails, and Gawen dozed in the sun on the bank, head tucked under one of his black wings.

Worry wouldn't save them, though. Reluctantly Rowenna turned aside and ducked into the run-down hut Elspeth had given her the use of. Inside was a single windowless room. Ashes choked the narrow hearth, and the leaky south end was cluttered with a jumble of shovels and shears and broken furniture. But to the north there was a cot with a musty straw-tick mattress and a threadbare blanket. Next to it stood an upturned crate with a lamp and a tinderbox set upon it.

The place was dank and cheerless, and a sudden wave of exhaustion swept over Rowenna. She let herself down onto the cot and lay on her side, face to the wall, with her eyes shut tight.

After a moment, the thin door squealed on rusty hinges. Rowenna glanced over one shoulder and felt the cot shift as

Gawen hopped up beside her in his clumsy bird form. He was still unsteady, favoring his injured side, but the warmth and weight of him against the small of her back was like an anchor. It held her to the world, a keystone that kept her from falling entirely apart, so she turned and curled herself around Gawen, one arm draping over his broad black wings. Everything felt insurmountably difficult—the separation from Cam, the unfathomable task of freeing her brothers from their curse, the idea that even if she broke the curse, there would still be Mairead left unchallenged at the end of it.

The black swan stayed motionless but for the rise and fall of his breath, and at some point, though she could not say when, Rowenna fell into a bitter and restless sleep.

Hushed voices drifted into the hut from outside. Rowenna sat bolt upright as she realized it was fully dark—she'd slept far longer than she'd meant to, and there was no sign of the boys. But two people were speaking in tense whispers beyond the hut's thin door.

With her heart in her throat, Rowenna swung the door open, only to find Gawen and Elspeth Crannach on the threshold and clearly in the middle of a fraught conversation. His hand was on her arm, and they both looked up the moment Rowenna appeared, Elspeth's bright eyes going wide and Gawen clearly holding back anger.

At the sight of Rowenna, Gawen turned and gave Elspeth a long, fathomless look. Then he limped off into the night without another word. Elspeth stayed, and Rowenna saw a flash of despair in the beautiful girl's face before she hid it expertly.

"I know you're Rowenna," she said at once. "And I know you can speak by nights. More than that, I've been mulling over your curse—I could feel it on Gawen, and on you as you slept, even from out here."

"You and Gawen have met before?" Rowenna asked doggedly, ignoring what Elspeth had said.

"Yes," she said. "But I don't want to discuss it right now. Who or what is it that cursed you?"

There was something indomitable about Elspeth as she stood there, straight-backed and lovely in the moonlight. She wore a different gown now than she had earlier that afternoon. This time she was all in midnight-blue velvet, with silver embroidery spangling her skirt and bodice. The medallion Rowenna had given to her rested at the hollow of her throat, and it was as if a piece of the night had taken human form.

With a pang, Rowenna realized that this was what Mairead must have hoped for from her. This serene, perfect control. The discipline she could sense in Elspeth, just as Elspeth sensed the curse on her. But Rowenna had never been such a person, and never would. She'd always harbor darkness and temper, though compassion and loyalty often kept them in check.

"Not to be discourteous, mind, but even if Gawen knows you, I don't," Rowenna pointed out, struggling to hide the bitterness her realization had dredged up. "I met a boy on the road who said you could help me and gave me that trinket you're wearing. Then I was accosted by your steward and brought here. That's all I know. Would you be very trusting in my place?"

"I suppose not," Elspeth answered. She looked Rowenna up and down, taking a measure of her, and for a moment it seemed as if Elspeth was rummaging about in the dusty corners of Rowenna's very soul. "But I'll tell you who I am. Do you know what a doxy is, Rowenna Winthrop, with your village manners?"

"A whore," Rowenna said bluntly. "Or a mistress. Whichever word you'd like to use."

Elspeth smiled, though there was something cool and remote about the expression. "That's who I am, then. I'm Torr Pendragon's doxy. Do you still want my help?"

Rowenna shifted. In spite of herself, she liked Elspeth better for her bluntness. And then it occurred to her that Elspeth must know just that. That the girl, with her calculated looks and her carefully hidden feelings, had taken a measure of Rowenna in truth, and sorted out with perfect ease how to lower her guard.

Out of your depth, Rowenna warned herself. *You're out of your depth with this one, and yet you need her.*

"Why shouldn't I take your help?" Rowenna asked carelessly. "If you're willing and able to give it? You're not Torr Pendragon himself, and anyway, I've suffered no loss at the tyrant's hand."

But memories surged up in her. Of the redcoat she'd tried to curse years ago. The abject loneliness she'd felt when Mairead died and Cam had not been there to lean on. The stories Gawen had told her, of his family and their tragic ends. The way the pine woods along the road to Drumossie looked, with bodies hanging from their branches. Rowenna's breath quickened, and she could not keep from clenching her hands into fists at her sides.

Elspeth frowned, ever so slightly—the first uncertain manner-ism she'd shown. "There's no one in the Highlands who hasn't suf-fered somehow because of Torr Pendragon and his presence here. I doubt you're the exception to that rule."

She regarded Rowenna in the dim, silver light, and briefly seemed displeased. But the moment passed, and her face settled into a mask of untouchable calm once more.

"Tell me about this curse on you," Elspeth said. "It's not only yours and Gawen's, is it? I can feel that there are others caught in its web—there're gossamer strands, running from you out to them. It'll make the unbinding difficult. You'll all have to be freed at once for it to take."

"My brothers," Rowenna answered cautiously. "They're in the city, and they've been cursed as well. There are three others, besides me and Gawen. The curse on the boys isn't like mine, though. They're all bound to another shape by daylight. Some-thing inhuman."

To Rowenna's surprise, Elspeth sat down on the grass, show-ing no care for her fine gown. She patted the place on the turf before her, and Rowenna lowered herself down too.

"Give me your hands," Elspeth said. "Let me see what I can make of this."

With reluctance, Rowenna held out her hands and allowed Elspeth to take them in her own. The girl let out a faint sigh, and Rowenna fought back a sarcastic expression.

"There's . . . there's a *ward* on you," Elspeth said after a moment, her brows drawing together in surprise. "It's faint and weak, and already failing, but it kept the curse from taking full effect. I think that's why you hold your true form, when your brothers don't. You were protected."

Rowenna blinked, unable to hide her own astonishment. "By who?"

"You don't know?"

Shaking her head, Rowenna swallowed back frustration.

"You laid it yourself," Elspeth said. "*You* made the ward, Rowenna."

"*What?*" The word came out all sharp edges and disbelief. "That's not possible. I don't know how. My mother never taught me that. I don't know the first thing about craft, because she was afraid I'd misuse it."

Elspeth's answer was mild and controlled by comparison to Rowenna's. "Well, however you did it, it happened. Whether you intended to or not, you marred this curse from the outset. And you've bought yourself time by doing it. Time in your own shape, to unravel the craft that's been laid on you and yours."

"But I don't understand," Rowenna insisted, even as she recalled Mairead's initial look of bitter surprise upon catching sight of her in the doorway to the Winthrop cot. "I've never even tried to make a ward."

"Well you must have," Elspeth said. "Blood willingly given is what's needed for warding work—either the making or the breaking of one."

Rowenna saw the deeps of the Atlantic before her. The sea's dark emissary, undulating on the current. Herself, offering blood on behalf of her family and herself. She'd only meant to find her kin, not make a ward. Yet she'd done true craft without knowing it. An unfamiliar sense of wonder swept over her.

Even unschooled and ignorant, she'd managed to channel her power. And it had not been a sharp or petty magic as her mother had feared, but one made to protect and safeguard.

"Tell me what else must be done to unbind this curse," Rowenna said decidedly. "Whatever it is, I'll do what's needed."

"It'll be difficult," Elspeth warned. "To undo craft is harder than to make it. As for your curse, it was wrought through suffering and death, and made with the help of salt water and blood, and it won't be easy to undo. It'll mean pain for you, I'm afraid."

"*I'm* not afraid," Rowenna told her.

Elspeth got to her feet. "Walk with me, then. I have something to show you."

Rowenna followed Elspeth out into the dark. She glanced about, hoping for a glimpse of her brothers, but they were nowhere to be seen.

Here in the sheltered lee of the castle, the spring air felt cool rather than cold. Flowers bloomed like jewels beneath the pines, and owls murmured in the treetops. Rowenna trailed along behind Elspeth as the girl led her half a mile down the river, to an open meadow of tall grasses. In the midst of it, Elspeth stopped.

"Do you see this plant?" she asked, gesturing to a patch of stalks that grew up among the grass, green and vibrant, and with saw-toothed leaves. "It's called witchnettle. Someone brought it to Inverness from the south ages ago, and it's grown here ever since, but nowhere else in the Highlands. Have you worked with it before?"

Rowenna shook her head, ashamed of her own ignorance. "I've never even heard of it."

"It's good for unbinding things," Elspeth explained. "For pulling things apart, and undoing curses. But what you've told me about your brothers—that's difficult. Changing their skins. That's intricate work, and to undo it will require yet more."

"Just tell me what to do," Rowenna begged. "Whatever it is, I'll see it done."

Elspeth's face was drawn in the moonlight. "All right. To change your brothers' shapes, you must give them something else to wear. But it must not give them an entirely new form, as you want to restore those they had before. Since witchnettle unbinds, if you weave a shirt of nettles for each of your swans and place it upon them, it should undo this curse, once every one of them has been clothed thus. And as your curse is lesser and bound up with theirs, if you free them, it should also loose your tongue."

Rowenna nodded, unspeakably relieved to hear this was all that would be required to free her brothers and Gawen—a bit of weaving. That she could do.

But as she stepped toward the tall plants with an outstretched hand, Elspeth stopped her.

"Wait. There's . . . there's a reason this is called witchnettle."

Rowenna waited.

"They have a saying in the markets," Elspeth told her slowly.

"That it stings like the devil, and if you duck it once, it shows its heart, but if you duck it twice it drowns."

The two of them fell silent at that. Rowenna thought of how it had felt to be held beneath the waves of the Atlantic by Mairead— to lose her breath and at last gasp for air, only to have seawater rush in. She thought too of how she'd heard stories of women being ducked for working craft. It had not been done for a generation in her own village of Neadeala, for Father Osric, whatever his failings, was not a cruel man. But elsewhere, such things still happened. And certainly they did here in Inverness.

"What that means," Elspeth said at last, "is that witchnettle burns to the touch. You will do injury to yourself in undertaking this work. But it will be part and parcel of the curse's unbinding— this work was made with blood and suffering, so it must be undone with the same. You must not wear gloves when you pull up your nettles, nor stockings when you tread out the stalks for their fiber."

Before Elspeth had even finished speaking, Rowenna reached out and tore up a great handful of witchnettle by the roots. Elspeth let out a pained gasp, but for the span of a heartbeat, Rowenna felt nothing. And then it began. The sudden shock, as if she'd pricked herself with a needle, but more than one, a hundred of them. A creeping burn, as if she'd put her hand against a pot fresh from the fire. The sting and the heat grew and grew, and Rowenna dropped the witchnettle, staring down at her palm as it flushed red and small round blisters sprang up on her skin.

"You can stop still," Elspeth offered, the words coming out

strained. "It was just one handful, the work's not yet well under-way, but once you've truly set yourself to it—"

Rowenna reached out again. With her jaw set, she pulled up fistful after fistful of witchnettle, until she'd cleared every bit within her reach. And when she finished, she bound the stalks into a bundle tied off neatly with a twist of long meadow grass.

"There." Rowenna straightened up as the burning in her hands grew near unbearable. "I've chosen my path. There'll be no straying from it now."

"Are you sure?" Elspeth breathed.

Refusing to show how the spreading burns pained her, Rowenna nodded. "Never surer."

"I'll leave you to your work then," Elspeth said. But at the edge of the meadow, she paused.

"Rowenna," the girl offered. "I'll come to you tomorrow morn-ing, when the rest of the court is still abed. It's past time someone taught you how to properly work your craft."

"I'd take it as a kindness," Rowenna said absently. She did not look up, though—all her attention was bent on pulling as many of the wicked nettles as she could. Elspeth drifted away, and Rowenna was left alone, to work until she could endure the touch of the nettles no longer. Then she lifted the bundles she'd gathered and heaved them back to the hut. By the time she reached it, the weight of the sheaves had her gasping.

Letting the bundles fall, Rowenna flexed her ruined hands and hissed in pain. But a noise startled her, and when she glanced up, Gawen had stepped out from the shadows within the open doorway.

"You spend a great deal of your time lurking," Rowenna said, but there was no bite to the accusation.

"I know Elspeth from before," Gawen told her at once. "Our families were on good terms. But we're all that's left now."

"You looked very familiar with each other," Rowenna said as she dragged the first of her sheaves of witchnettle the few feet to the riverside. "Glad to see it wasn't just your families on good terms."

With a fierce pull at the meadow grass tying it together, she unbound the first sheaf of nettles. The twist of grass cut at her blistered palm and drew blood, but Rowenna welcomed the sting of it. Some dark, unhappy thing had lodged inside her at the memory of how Gawen and Elspeth looked standing so close together, with his hand resting on her arm.

"Are you sore at me for some reason?" Gawen asked, stepping forward. He stopped abruptly upon reaching the remainder of Rowenna's nettle sheaves and crouched beside them, peering at the leaves in the moonlight. Disbelief laced Gawen's voice as he spoke again. "God in heaven, scold, is this *witchnettle*? What can you be thinking?"

Up to her ankles in water, Rowenna spread nettle stalks in the shallows and weighted them down with stones, so that they might soak and soften before she trod out the linen fibers.

"I am thinking," she said, a little breathless with the work, "that someone has to break our curse. And since neither you nor my brothers have the craft for it, it falls to me."

"But not like this. This is—"

142

Whatever Gawen had been about to say, Rowenna straightened and set her hands on her hips, cutting him off.

"Do you trust Elspeth Crannach, who you're so familiar with?"

"Yes," Gawen answered unhesitatingly. "I don't always agree with her, but I trust her. Why?"

"Because she's the one who told me how to go about this work," Rowenna said. Frustration frayed the edges of her words. She was tired and her hands burned like hellfire and she already hated this task though she'd only just begun. "Maybe there'd be an easier way to manage the curse breaking if I were less ignorant, but I am as I am, and this is what's needed. An unbinding made of nettle linen, for you and each of my brothers to wear, crafted through pain freely offered. Unless you think your Elspeth would find it amusing to toy with a girl under a curse and bid her to suffer when it's not required?"

"She wouldn't," Gawen said. "And she's not my Elspeth. Can I help, at least?"

His hand hovered over one of the bundles, but Rowenna stilled him with a word as she gathered up her sopping skirts and climbed the riverbank to where he stood.

"No. I think . . . I think it must be me who does this. She was clear on that, your Elspeth—that I could not wear gloves nor stockings to safeguard against the pain. So I don't think it would be all right for someone else to help, and I can't risk anything marring this work. I won't fail my family again."

"She's not my Elspeth," Gawen repeated. They were close now, only an arm's length apart, with a sheaf of wicked nettle serving as a barrier between them. "Never has been, never will."

"She's very beautiful," Rowenna pointed out.

"Aye," Gawen admitted. "And cold, and always in control. But I like a lass who's a little more trouble, Rowenna Winthrop. If I ever fall for someone, she'll be half thorns and stings, and sharp enough for me to cut myself upon."

"But you won't fall for someone, because you've got your own worries and your own work to be done, as you told me in the church at Drumossie," Rowenna pointed out, ducking to lift another sheaf of nettles and to hide the way her face heated.

"That's so," Gawen said, but there was a moment's pause before his agreement came.

Rowenna laid out the rest of the nettles to soak, but before she'd finished with the last bundle, footsteps sounded on the hill path and her brothers appeared. Finn was flushed with some sort of excitement, and Liam looked serene as always, but Duncan had clearly met with trouble. His bottom lip was split, and his left eye swollen shut, yet he grinned in his old, easy way, as Rowenna had not seen him do since the curse began.

"Where have you been all night?" Rowenna asked as the boys came up to the hut, bringing an atmosphere of high spirits with them.

"Down at the docks," Duncan said, and none of the bitterness he'd shown toward Rowenna over the last few days was present in the words. "They may be bringing enough bread down here to keep you fed, Enna, but the rest of us are going to have to fend for ourselves, or live on duckweed and corn. I found a tavern that'll pay any man willing to fight with his fists, and I made more tonight than *Athair* and I would in a month on the boat."

"Oh, Duncan," Rowenna chided. "I don't like the risk."

And though she'd been gentler than was her habit, at once his anger returned.

"You don't get to say a thing about risk," he said, pointing a finger in her direction. "I'll do what I like with whatever time I have left, before I'm turned into something less forever. There were other things I'd rather have taken a chance on, Rowenna. Alice Sutherland, for one. But all that's lost for now, isn't it? So I'll gamble as I wish, and don't you *dare* speak a word to me about it."

Rowenna fell silent. Swallowing her words felt familiar now, with the curse stilling her tongue by day. Along with the burning of her hands, it seemed like penance for a sin not of her making, but for which she must nevertheless pay the price.

Duncan brushed past her and into the hut, where he shut the door firmly behind him.

"Go on inside and get settled, Finn," Liam said quietly. "I'll be there in a minute."

With a reluctant glance at Rowenna, little Finn followed too. But Liam stayed, lingering in the dark.

"What happened to your hands, Rowenna?" he asked. Even in the shadows, nothing escaped his notice. Stung by the attention and the question, Rowenna put her hands behind her back.

"Very well," Liam said with a sigh. "If you want your secrets, you can keep them."

Then it was only her and Gawen left, to wait for the moment when the curse would descend and change them both.

"You could have told them," Gawen said. He'd settled down

on the riverbank, and Rowenna went to sit at his side, resting her hands gingerly on her lap. "Maybe they'd think more kindly of you, if they knew what you're doing."

"No," Rowenna told him. "It'd only make them feel badly. I don't want that. And in a way, they're right. Perhaps I didn't make this curse, but none of these troubles would have come about if I'd been the sort of person my mother thought trustworthy enough to teach our craft. I failed my family, so now I'll pay the price."

"That's not—" Gawen began, but the smell of peat and smoke surrounded them.

Rowenna fixed her eyes on the river and reached out with one blistered hand. Ever so carefully, Gawen took it in his own. For a moment they sat like that, until the pain in Rowenna's hands was briefly eclipsed by pain in her throat and mouth, and the touch of Gawen's skin turned to feathers.

She stayed on the riverbank with the black swan until sunrise, and it was a full hour from their change until dawn.

Chapter Thirteen

Home pulled at Rowenna as she dozed in the cool, bright hours between dawn and midmorning. She found herself wandering the pale, ghostly version of Neadeala that came to her in sleep. Fog scudded across the lonely moorland, and her bones ached intolerably with a lostness seeping up from the cliff top earth.

It was quiet. Far too quiet. The near silence sent a shudder coursing through Rowenna. She could hear the pulse of the surf, but just barely. It was somehow muffled, as if coming from a greater distance than that which the cliffs afforded.

Not a single seabird called. No silvery wyverns wheeled overhead or squabbled at the cliff's edge. There was no bleating of sheep or occasional bark from an attentive sheepdog.

And when the mist cleared, Rowenna could see why.

She was out on a wide, open expanse of meadow that ran down to the sea, not far from the village of Neadeala itself. Mairead stood a dozen yards off, with her back to Rowenna, facing the Atlantic. And all around them, strewn across the earth, lay dead things.

Wyverns and gulls and albatross, lambs and ewes and tricolored dogs littered the ground in every direction, as far as Rowenna could see. She could smell their dying on the air—the heavy, metallic scent of blood and the insidious, choking odor of decay.

As Rowenna watched, Mairead turned. Her arms were slick with gore to the elbows, and her mouth rimmed with thick scarlet blood. At the sight of Rowenna, Mairead's eyes lit with recognition, and her face arranged itself into a vicious smile. As always, it set a sickness in Rowenna, to see the shape and form of the woman she remembered so well now inhabited by some desperate and hungry thing.

But that sick feeling turned to ice and panic as Mairead stepped aside, and Rowenna saw what it was she'd been looking at so intently.

There, not ten feet from Mairead, glassy eyed and haggard, was Cam, staring out at the sea.

⚬⚬

Rowenna and Elspeth stood together in the nettle field. True to her word, Elspeth had appeared at midmorning, fresh and radiant in a yellow brocade gown. Rowenna herself felt pale and drawn with lack of sleep and, though she'd washed at a hidden spot in the river, still had nothing to wear besides her torn and stained nightgown and the ragged pullover she'd found in the yoal that had brought her to Inverness.

"You look tired," Elspeth said entirely unhelpfully. "And like a vagrant, or a very underwhelming tart. I forgot about clothes, but I'll have them sent down today, and you'll have to wear them if you want to stay on."

I have nowhere else to go, Rowenna thought sullenly. *So I suppose you can dress me however you like.*

Elspeth nodded, as if that was decided. While she chose to

comment on Rowenna's clothes, she seemed to be able to look everywhere but at the girl's fiercely blistered hands, and a little twinge of triumph woke in Rowenna. Managing to make even the smallest crack in Elspeth's armor felt like a victory.

"I've never done this before," Elspeth admitted. "Taught someone about craft, I mean. My *màthair* taught me, but we started when I was barely walking. I'm not—I'm not sure where to begin."

Rowenna remained stony and blank faced, hating to hear how Elspeth had learned her craft, even as the other girl took in a long breath to steady herself.

"The first thing I learned is that every *cailleach* has something that speaks to her," Elspeth explained. "For me it is—I'm sorry, it was—the earth itself. For Gawen MacArthur's sister, Sibyl, who was one of my dearest friends, it was the sea. For my *màthair*, it's the wood we live near the edge of. It's not ours to choose what speaks to us—this happens on its own. We're not born or made so much as called, in that way. What is it that speaks to you, Rowenna Winthrop?"

Elspeth waited expectantly. Rowenna pantomimed the wind blowing about and pointed to the swaying tree branches above them.

"The wind?" Elspeth asked. "Well, that's where your craft begins then. You can try to work with other elements, but you'll always be strongest when you work with the wind. Can you call it to yourself?"

Rowenna gave Elspeth a bewildered look and gestured to her mouth.

"Not like that," Elspeth explained. "It doesn't have to be with your voice. Just . . . bid it come to you, and see if it will."

Rowenna glanced up doubtfully at the pines surrounding the meadow and the way their tops swayed in the breeze. The wind had been quiet today, simply scudding about wordlessly without trying to gain Rowenna's attention.

Come here to me, Rowenna thought at the wind.

Nothing.

She turned to Elspeth, the sort of look on her face that said *I told you so.* That said *I've been kept ignorant for too long—this world is beyond my grasp now.*

"Try again," Elspeth urged.

Come here to me.

The treetops shook in a sudden gust, but that was all.

"Can't you do better?" Elspeth needled, cool disapproval in her voice.

Seething, Rowenna turned inward. She went down to the very core of herself, where all her darkness and bitterness dwelled, like an endless churning sea. And on its wild shores, she called the wind.

Come. Here. This time Rowenna snapped the words, as she might have done if she were able to speak and had lost her forever-fraying temper.

In a jubilant surge, the wind came down. It swept over from among the trees, rippling the meadow grass like waves and swirling about Rowenna's legs. It purred and fawned and whispered for all the world like an eager cat, and if she'd had the voice for it, she would have laughed. Up the wind leaped and twined itself about her hands, a fresh stir of air that soothed the constant sting of her nettle burns.

Our love, the wind sang sweetly, as if it had been waiting for this moment since the day the world was founded. *Our light. Our saltwater girl.*

And Rowenna, who could not recall the last time she'd been greeted with such pure joy, found herself entirely undone. She hid her face in her blistered hands and sobbed, falling to her knees in the meadow as the wind murmured and fawned about her.

Be still

Be well

Be loved

Our own

Our choice

Our light

When at last Rowenna looked up, Elspeth had gone. Left alone with the wind, Rowenna stayed on her knees in the meadow for a long time, listening to its idle words, watching as it gamboled through the grass. When it strayed too far, Rowenna called it back to herself. Each time it came, and each time its return brought new tears to her eyes.

After a lifetime of fear and resistance, she had not expected this—that allowing herself to finally reach for her power would feel like being made whole.

Rowenna had not even known she was broken before. But it pained her greatly to realize that this was what Mairead had kept her from, all for fear of Rowenna's temper. She'd known this relief, this wholeness, but not found Rowenna fit for it.

That mistrust had cost her everything in the end.

Much as she hated to lose time, Rowenna waited until dark to dredge her nettle stalks up from the river and begin the task of treading them out and separating the linen fiber. The idea of someone less sympathetic than Elspeth coming across her as she did the work was an unnerving one, and she'd have brought the stalks into the hut if she could. But there was no room to spread them out indoors, so she was forced to scatter them across the open ground along the river. When she finished with that, she herded the swans inside, to ensure no one saw them when the change occurred.

True to her word, Elspeth had sent down a set of clothes for Rowenna that afternoon. Before beginning her work, Rowenna slipped off her loose shoes and stockings and tucked the hem of her plain brown overskirt into the band of a wide apron. Then, with measured steps, she trod back and forth, back and forth, across the swollen and softened stalks. It was at once better and worse, now that she knew what to expect from the touch of the witchnettle. It helped that she could steel herself against the sudden pain and the way it only grew and intensified as she continued her work. It did *not* help that she could anticipate beforehand just how it would feel—nothing at first, and then a thousand fiery needles.

As the scent of smoke and peat descended, Rowenna carried on doggedly treading out the stalks. A few moments later her brothers appeared in the doorway.

"You don't need to do that, En," Duncan said brusquely. "We

don't need your linen-work to support us. I earned enough last night to buy us all something to wear and enough to eat. Not the stray, though—he'll have to fend for himself."

"The stray can look after himself just fine, thank you very much," Gawen said. He edged through the small crowd of boys in the doorway and went to sit on the riverbank, just as he'd done the night before.

Rowenna said nothing to any of them. She kept on with her work, and only Finn looked back as her brothers set off, heading away from the castle and toward the busy heart of Inverness.

"You can go with them, if you like," Rowenna said when it was only Gawen left. "There's nothing to keep you here."

"I'll stay, just for a while," Gawen answered. He lowered himself down onto the soft riverside turf and put his hands behind his head, staring up at the star-strewn night sky. Rowenna finished treading out the nettle stalks and knelt next to them, pulling fibrous strands free for her linen-work. It was difficult, working by hand rather than with a wooden-toothed comb, but she didn't dare risk a tool. All her heart and intent went into the task, and the wind ducked low to flit about her as she worked.

"You should sleep tonight too, scold," Gawen said presently, and it was not what Rowenna had expected.

"I'll sleep when we're free, or when time's run out and we're all cursed for good," she answered. Her blistered hands were clumsy, the ferocious burning turned to pins and needles. But the moon overhead was near to full, and she hated to waste the light, so she worked on.

Down by the riverbank, Gawen began to sing, low and tuneful, and that was not what Rowenna had expected either.

> *Now as I roved out one summer's day,*
> *Among lofty hills, moorland, and mountain,*
> *It was there I spied a fine young maid,*
> *While I with others was out a-hunting.*

> *No shoes nor stockings did she wear,*
> *Neither had she hat nor had she feathers.*
> *But her black hair hung in ringlets there,*
> *And the gentle breeze played round her shoulders.*

> *Now I said, "Fair lass, why roam the lane,*
> *why roam the lane among the heather?"*
> *She said, "My father's away from home,*
> *And I'm a-herding his ewes together."*

> *I said, "Fair lass, if you'll be mine,*
> *You'll lie on a bed of feathers.*
> *In silks and satins you will shine,*
> *And you'll be my queen among the heather."*

> *She said, "Kind sir, your offer's good,*
> *But I'm afraid 'twas meant for laughter.*
> *For I know you are a rich lord's son,*
> *And I'm but a poor shepherd's daughter.*

"Oh but had you been a shepherd lad,
A-herding ewes in yonder valley,
Or had you been a plowman's son,
With all my heart, I would have loved you."

Now I've been to halls and I've been to balls,
And I've been to London and Balquhidder.
But the fairest lass that ever I've seen,
She was herding ewes among the heather.

So we both sat down upon the plain,
We sat awhile and talked together.
And we left the ewes to stray along the lane,
till I loved my queen among the heather.

"Anytime I've heard that sung, the girl has golden hair," Rowenna said sternly, tugging at a stubborn strand of nettle fiber. "Don't you have anywhere else to be? Or do you plan to spend your whole night mooning about on that riverbank?"

Gawen got to his feet, and at once Rowenna regretted chiding him. She hadn't truly wanted him to go—it kept her mind off the pain in her hands and feet to have him there.

"I can go try to find my father again, I suppose," Gawen said. "Though it'll do no good. I need a *cailleach*'s help for that."

"This one's busy," Rowenna answered. "You'll have to ask another if you need help with your searching tonight. Perhaps Elspeth's not occupied."

She didn't mean any of it. She didn't want him to leave, and she certainly didn't want him seeking out Elspeth's company, whether he said the beautiful girl was a temptation or not. But it was as if something in Rowenna compelled her to say such things and be harsh when her heart bent toward softness.

"Did Elspeth not tell you?" Gawen asked, his eyes narrowing. "She has no more craft. She can sense it in others still, but not work it herself. The day after Drumossie, she tried to undertake a thing that shattered her power. Torr Pendragon was not pleased with that, and she's little more than a prisoner here now, no matter how it might look."

Rowenna faltered. "I didn't . . . I didn't know you could lose your craft, or break it."

"Well, you can. And she did."

Gawen was already past the hut on his way up the hill path when Rowenna stopped him with a word. "Wait."

He did as he was told at once, turning to look back at her.

"I don't mean to be sharp with you," Rowenna offered. "You mustn't mind me."

Gawen gave her a crooked smile, and it was the first time Rowenna had seen him wear the expression. "I don't mind, scold. I don't mind at all."

"Wherever you're off to, just . . . promise me you'll come back before the change," Rowenna said. "For all our sakes, I'd rather no one see it happen."

Gawen nodded. "I promise. And what's more, I'll find your brothers and get them back before it happens too."

"Thank you," Rowenna said, and managed, this time, to say the words gently.

"No, Rowenna." Gawen frowned, his dark eyes fixed on her, seated among the witchnettle with her blistered hands and feet. "Thank *you*."

Rowenna waited till he'd gone, and only then did she set her work aside for a few moments, keeping her hands and feet immobile while she tried vainly to breathe through the pain. The wind frisked about her, and she shook her head at it.

"I might run mad before this is over," she admitted. "The work's worse than I thought it would be."

Our thanks, our thanks, our thanks, the wind sang back sweetly, as if to echo Gawen's words.

Chapter Fourteen

Sometimes, by day or by night, Rowenna could hear the sounds of life in Inverness Castle. The shouting of servants, music drifting from hidden courtyards of an evening, laughter as courtiers spilled out across the hillside. But she kept to herself, bent upon her work. Her brothers came and went by cover of darkness, and though Gawen made a habit of lingering for longer, she spent most evenings alone, focused on her curse breaking. Only Elspeth seemed able to bridge the gap between Rowenna and the castle, appearing at midmorning every day to instruct the girl in her craft.

She came down the hill in her gossamer gowns, and to Rowenna, bound to the pain of her work and to haunted dreams of Mairead, it felt as if Elspeth were a denizen of an entirely different world. From Elspeth she learned to guide and direct the wind—to instruct it to go here or there across the riverside meadow, to lift handfuls of leaves, or to climb up and sway among the treetops. None of it seemed like the sort of work that might be of much use, but it was what Elspeth offered, and there was a certain joy about it.

One night after her brothers and Gawen took their leave, Rowenna went out to the meadow on the banks of the Ness only to find she'd pulled every last stalk of witchnettle. Experience told her that she'd nowhere near the quantity of flax she needed to piece together four linen shirts for four cursed swans, and she stood in the moonlight for a long while, racked by indecision.

It felt safe down here, in her strange solitary world beside the river. But to carry on her work, she'd have to risk searching elsewhere for a fresh crop of nettles.

"Come with me," Rowenna called to the wind. "I want your company, beloved."

Eagerly the wind did as she'd asked, circling about Rowenna's ankles and roaming through the grass as she climbed the hillside. At the curtain wall, a guard stood aside to let Rowenna in, recognizing the mute swan maiden who'd taken up residence on the castle grounds.

It was the first time since her arrival in Inverness that Rowenna had been within the walls of the castle proper. It was all a maze—alleyways and courtyards and dead ends, and everywhere signs of more walls being built, more expansion undertaken. She wandered here and there, avoiding any doorway that looked as if it might lead to an interior passage, and finally found herself up against the tall hedge she'd seen upon arriving. It stretched from side to side as far as the eye could see, and Rowenna sighed.

But the wind rushed ahead of her and swept creeping vines from a door that stood ajar. Hesitating for a moment on the threshold, Rowenna stepped inside.

Beyond the box hedge lay a vast open space, dotted by large iron cages on pedestals of stone. Ivy ran up and around the bars, softening their outline and making it seem as if the cages had grown out of the earth itself. Within each of them was a creature like nothing Rowenna had ever seen before. There was a doglike beast, larger than even Laird Sutherland's hounds, which had thick fur the color of new fallen snow and startling yellow eyes. Beyond it was some manner of horse, dun colored and thick bodied, with a brush of black mane that stood on end. Inside one cage, a brazier filled with hot coals glowed bright. At first Rowenna thought there was no animal there, but then what she'd taken to be a pile of leaves stirred, and she realized there was a vast, speckled snake coiled up upon itself near the heat.

There were apes and oryxes, tigers and tarsiers, jackals and jaguars, though Rowenna did not know their names and could not read the small brass plaques in front of each enclosure. At the center of the menagerie, she came to a cage set apart from all the others and stopped short, heart beating wildly in her chest.

Inside stood Mairead. With one pale hand, she clasped the bars of the cage, and with the other she reached out for Rowenna.

"Enna," Mairead called, in a voice like heartbreak, "come here to me!"

Not stopping to think, Rowenna went. She gathered up her skirts and bolted across the gravel of the menagerie, but when she was nearly within arm's reach of her beloved mother, the wind stopped her. It roared up in a gale, pushing at Rowenna and keening wordlessly.

Only a week ago, Rowenna would have dismissed it. But now she listened, coming to an abrupt halt and casting a cautious eye over Mairead. As she did, Mairead's face wavered, and there beneath it were the familiar incandescent eyes, the jagged needle-thin teeth. Shedding its disguise, the *fuath* in the cage grinned wickedly at Rowenna. She'd not seen such a creature without at least some glamour on it since Mairead's death, and the sight came like a blow to the stomach. Its mottled skin and unnatural limbs, its elongated and webbed fingers made for grasping and rending, all reminded her of Mairead's hopeless last moments, and how she'd been unable to help.

Not until the wind subsided, sure of Rowenna's safety, did she hear someone calling out. Turning, Rowenna found a boy running toward her. And not just any boy, but her acquaintance from the churchyard at Drumossie, who'd given her Elspeth Crannach's name.

"Are you all right?" he asked breathlessly, stopping at Rowenna's side. "It's not safe in here sometimes."

Rowenna smiled to show she was well, and the boy's honest face lit up. "I'm glad you made it to Inverness, at any rate. Did you find your way to Elspeth, too?"

Rowenna nodded. There was something about this nameless boy that set her at ease, and she was tempted to speak—to tell him about the curse, and how his help had made a difference. But the wind murmured about her, whispering to itself.

Take care, take care, take care.

Rowenna heeded it and kept silent. Instead, she took a measure of the stranger. His clothes were still simply cut, though the fabric was very fine—finer than anything Rowenna or Mairead had ever woven. And that same sense of trustworthiness emanated from him. Rowenna found herself having to push against it a little, to keep herself from inadvertently speaking and baring more of her soul than was wise. Frowning, she glanced away from him and toward the *fuath*.

"Did you have a look about?" the boy asked eagerly. "I do a bit of work tending the creatures here. There are some curious beasts."

But Rowenna knew she could not stay. The night was wearing on, and every evening that passed brought her brothers closer to a life spent entirely in swan form. She needed more nettles, and plenty of them. Perhaps this boy, who'd helped her once before, could be of help again.

Rowenna reached into her pocket, pulled out a single nettle leaf, and held it on her blistered hand to show him.

"Hellfire, what did you do to your hands?" the boy said at once, but Rowenna shook her head adamantly and pointed to the leaf.

"You . . . you want *more* of those?" he asked. "I suppose—there are more in the old chapel yard. Should I show you?"

Rowenna's eager look was all the answer he needed. Together, they set off through the warren of the castle grounds. Around twists and turns they went, up and down alleys, and past shadowy doors, until they came into a wide, quiet courtyard. Grass and nettles choked it, growing up among old gravestones, and it reminded Rowenna palpably of the place she'd first met the boy guiding her, behind the church at the edge of Drumossie.

"What do you think of that?" the boy said. He settled himself on a broken headstone and watched as Rowenna began to pull up nettles. Though she'd expected him to take his leave of her, he did not—instead, he stayed where he was, silently observing Rowenna at her work. She ignored him after a few moments, focusing on the act of harvesting the witchnettle. As the blisters on her hands split and cracked and her palms began to bleed, she put all her hopes for her brothers into the work. All her love and all her heartbreak over the rift between them.

But when she'd nearly pulled as many nettles as she could carry, stealthy footsteps caught her ear from within the chapel. Rowenna glanced at the boy on the gravestone. He put a finger to his lips and motioned to her to hide herself away, so she dropped her work, shrinking back into the shadows along the wall. From where she stood, she could see in through one of the chapel's low, glassless windows, which let in moonlight and fresh air.

A low groan rose from the chapel's hinges, but no glow from a torch or votive candle showed. There was a long silence, and then a murmur of voices began.

Elspeth Crannach stood in a pool of pale light, which glinted off the gilt threads that embroidered her heavy velvet gown. The deep crimson of her frock stood in stark contrast to the milk-whiteness of her skin and the ruddy sheen of her auburn hair, which she wore long and unbound. She was, now and always, the most beautiful girl Rowenna had ever seen.

Rowenna watched as Elspeth whispered urgently to someone in the gloom. She heard a quiet reply, and then the girl's companion stepped out of the shadows.

Black hair. A feral wariness. And yet the usual surly or sarcastic light was gone from Gawen's eyes. Rowenna could see only

163

eagerness there. Gawen glanced over one shoulder before pressing a note into Elspeth's hand and pulling her into an embrace.

Something in Rowenna twisted at that. She balled her hands into fists, ignoring the pain the motion brought. Inside the chapel, Elspeth pulled on a long, hooded cloak and hurried away.

Dropping down to sit with her back against the chapel wall, Rowenna hugged her knees to herself and rested her chin atop them. She stared out across the graveyard, at the broken head-stones and choking weeds, and felt as if something on the inside she'd never even known was there had suddenly withered and died.

Rowenna kept still for a long while, until well after she'd heard the chapel hinges whine again and the sound of sly foot-steps retreating down some castle alleyway. She stared blankly up at the moon, until at last the towheaded graveyard boy came and sat himself down at her side.

"One of them played you false, didn't they?" he said, his voice gentle. "I can see it on your face."

Rowenna nodded, and the boy let out a sigh. "You're not the only one. It seems our fates are bound together, lass. And I know I said it when we last met, but I'm sorry for your troubles. I'd make them easier for you, if I could. Do you want me to stay, and see you back to wherever you're lodging, or would you rather be alone?"

Solitude was what Rowenna craved, and though the graveyard boy's company was easy, she motioned to him to go. With a courte-ous bow, he took his leave of her.

"Until our paths cross again, little maid."

Numbly Rowenna got to her feet. She'd believed Gawen when he swore there was nothing between himself and Elspeth. And she'd felt understood by him—he seemed so attuned to the darkness and bitterness she could never manage to keep fully at bay.

At last, with a supreme effort, Rowenna forced herself to lift the thick sheaf of stalks she'd have to carry down to the river. It was slow going, departing the castle—her feet burned fiercely, the shoes and stockings Elspeth had given her chafing terribly. She stopped often to set the nettles down and breathe, but at last the curtain wall appeared and Rowenna was out on the hillside with the River Ness below her. There was the hut that served her as home for now, and here was Gawen, waiting outside the door.

Rowenna let the bundle of nettles fall to the ground, too weary to spread them in the river's shallows just yet. She brushed past Gawen, limped into the hut, and, sitting on the side of her narrow cot, put her head in her hands.

"Scold, what is it?" Gawen asked, and she could hear the consternation in his voice.

But Rowenna did not want to speak. It felt as if the silence she was placed under by day was beginning to leach into her bones and become part of her, and when once she might have snapped, she now found herself wordless. She could not bring herself to move, either. The nettles she'd gathered needed soaking, but it seemed an insurmountable task.

The door creaked open and shut.

Rowenna still sat, her mind a blank, everything in her whispering of exhaustion, when the latch lifted once more and Gawen came back in. Through her ravaged fingers, Rowenna saw he had a wooden bucket half-full of river water, which he set down by the hearth. From it, he filled an iron pot and set it among the coals.

A few minutes passed between them in silence before Gawen retrieved the pot, using the hem of his shirt to keep his hand from burning.

"There's a thing I find myself missing by day, when I'm under the curse," he said, pouring hot water from the pot into the bucket. A cloud of steam rose up as the frigid river water warmed. "The world seems dim and muddled when we're in swan shape. It's hard to think clearly, and it feels like being caught in a snare, wearing that body."

Gawen crouched before Rowenna and rolled up his sleeves. She squinted down at him doubtfully.

"Give me your feet, scold," Gawen said.

Pricked by embarrassment, Rowenna pulled her feet farther back, tucking them under her skirt. She'd taken her shoes off upon entering the hut, and what her walk through the castle had wrought was unsightly—stockings bunched around her shins and adhering to the places where her blistered feet had chafed and bled.

Gawen stayed where he was, waiting patiently, until at last Rowenna relented with a weary sigh. She let him take her feet in his hands and lower them into the bucket of warm water.

At first the touch of the water stung bitterly, but after a moment the stinging subsided, and the edges of Rowenna's pain softened.

"It's not my wits I find myself missing, though," Gawen said.

While he spoke, he worked carefully, easing the stockings inch by slow inch down Rowenna's feet as they soaked. Rowenna's face burned as his fingers coaxed the fabric from her damaged skin. She suspected he was speaking to put her at her ease, but it did little to help, particularly when the image of Elspeth in Gawen's arms circled around and around in her mind.

"It's not my own shape I miss either," Gawen went on. "Nor anything about my own self. But I do find myself wishing to hear your sharp tongue."

Rowenna looked down at the top of Gawen's dark head as he bent over the bucket.

"You told me there's nothing between you and Elspeth," she said, even as she felt him slip the first stocking entirely off her foot, leaving all of her skin finally exposed to the warm water. "Yet I saw you with her tonight."

"Aye, I met with her. We're trying to sort something out that's grating between the two of us. She's afraid, and fear's clouding her judgment. Or at least the way I see it, it is."

"Afraid?" Rowenna asked in disbelief. "You say she's a prisoner, but I've seen little of fear in her. And she seems independent enough."

"That's because you don't know how to look," Gawen said. "Just because you don't notice her guards, doesn't mean they aren't there."

He slid the second stocking from Rowenna's foot and pulled them from the bucket, sodden and dripping.

"I didn't like it," Rowenna said, a little of the sharpness creeping back into her voice. "I didn't like seeing the two of you together like that. Perhaps if I were better, I wouldn't have minded, but I did."

She watched as Gawen wrung the water from her stockings, then spread them out in front of the fire to dry. When he finished, he came back to her, kneeling before her as she sat on the edge of the cot. He rested his arms on her knees, and Rowenna swallowed, vainly trying to still the nervous things that sprang to life in her belly. Even now there was a latent darkness in him that matched her own, and that Rowenna found terribly hard to resist.

"You minded because you don't trust me," Gawen said, speaking each word with a significance that sent unfamiliar thrills running up and down Rowenna's spine. "And I've given you no reason to. You've got no claim to my faithfulness. But what if you had? What if I gave you one?"

Rowenna could not look away from him, so close that she could feel his warmth and reach out to touch him if she had a mind to.

"What sort of claim might you give, that I don't have now?" she asked at last.

Gawen's throat worked, and warm yearning spilled through Rowenna as his gaze dropped to her mouth.

A fist pounding on the door shattered the tension between them.

"Under the bed," Rowenna breathed, hardly daring to speak the words aloud. With no regard for his dignity, Gawen did exactly as he was told and had only just disappeared from view when the door flew open.

Rowenna blinked at the man standing on the threshold. Faded

yellow hair. Impeccable livery. This was Steward Greaves, who'd brought her to the grounds of Inverness Castle so roughly.

"Did I hear voices?" he asked in his clipped accent, putting his head to one side. "I could have sworn I did."

Rowenna shrugged, gesturing to the empty hut.

Greaves eyed her narrowly. "It's my job to keep a watch on everyone in Pendragon's service. To ensure they're upright, and a credit to him, and of good character. Do you understand?"

Rowenna nodded.

"No, I don't think you do." Greaves drew closer. "I have had my fill and more of insolent Highlanders who think they're above the laws my master has set in place and the rule he exercises now that he's settled here. So I will tell you what I tell all new servants at the castle—if I see a single spark of rebellion in you, even so much as a mutinous look, I'll have you hanged or burned."

Rowenna only blinked, glad that maintaining the facade of muteness kept her from having to make a reply.

"Answer me," Greaves barked in frustration. Rowenna pointed to her throat as a reminder and shook her head.

"Of course we've found ourselves a mute swan maiden," Greaves growled. "And a diseased one too."

He gestured at Rowenna's blistered hands and feet. "You're sure you're not infectious? Because I swear to you, if anyone comes down with a malady like that, I'll lock you in this hut and burn it to the ground rather than risk contagion."

Rowenna nodded, and Greaves retreated to the door.

"Right, then," he said. "Just remember what I've told you.

Keep to yourself, make no trouble, and you'll have none from me. I expect to see those swans out on the river every afternoon for Pendragon's witch, as well. For whatever reason, he still wants to see her kept happy, even now she's useless to him."

With that Greaves left the hut, muttering as he went out. "Filthy Highlanders. I've had enough of this place for a lifetime."

Rowenna stood and stepped out of the bucket, where her feet had still rested throughout the exchange. Dripping water, she padded across the packed-earth floor and stood in the doorway, watching him go.

When Greaves was halfway up the hill and well out of earshot, Rowenna felt a stir of air. Gawen's voice sounded from only an inch or two behind her.

"I don't like how he spoke to you. Don't expect you did either. Do you want me to kill him for you, scold?"

There was an undercurrent to the question that told Rowenna it wasn't entirely meant as humor, and she shivered.

"I don't want you to kill anyone," she answered. "In fact, I want all of us to do just as that snake suggested—keep our heads down, mind our own business, and stay out of trouble. Then, when I've broken the curse, I'll try to help you find your father, before getting back home to deal with mine."

Rowenna glanced over one shoulder at him, standing behind her in the shadows. She could hear her brothers now, talking among themselves as they made their way back to the hut before the change occurred.

"I give you my word, and a claim to my help and my craft when all this is done," Rowenna said, her voice low. "But where's the claim you said you'd give to me?"

Gawen gazed out the door at the approaching figures of Rowenna's brothers.

"Tomorrow," he promised. "Come hell or high water, scold, I'll give you a claim over me then."

Chapter Fifteen

"Close your eyes," Elspeth said to Rowenna, as she sat in the middle of the riverside meadow. It was the first truly warm day of spring, and the sun beat down on Rowenna's bare head. She was beginning to sweat, but Elspeth seemed as cool and composed as ever.

Rowenna did as she was told, receding inward, to the dark shore that the sea of her craft beat ceaselessly against.

"Call the wind to you."

It came frisking down from among the pines.

"Now invite it in."

Rowenna opened her eyes, fixing Elspeth with a questioning look.

"Ask it to inhabit you? I'm not—I'm not sure how to explain it." As Elspeth searched for words, Rowenna could see a glimmer of frustration in her face.

"It's like—a partnership." Elspeth tried again. "A working together and being together. I would show you, if I could. My mother showed me. But you'll just . . . you'll have to sort it out yourself."

She pressed a hand to her forehead, and a stab of pity twisted through Rowenna. She made for an ignorant student, and Elspeth was trying to help her in spite of that, all without any obligation to. Obediently Rowenna shut her eyes again.

Come here to me, she thought at the wind.

We're here with you, near with you, the wind sang, stirring the damp hair on Rowenna's forehead.

No, come here, Rowenna tried. *Closer? Nearer? I'm not sure?*

The wind seemed to hesitate. And then: *You wish us to see with you? To be with you?*

Yes, Rowenna thought firmly. *Come in.*

With a sudden gust the wind buffeted her, and an overwhelming vertigo made Rowenna sway. She could see herself, seated in the meadow, and Elspeth at her side, but all from above, as if she hung suspended in the sky like a bird.

Or like the wind.

And the wind itself, which had always spoken in half-understood phrases, was within her. Rowenna stood on the shore of her craft and could feel the wind's wildness, its wideness, as it moved through her and surged over Inverness, jubilant and free. She could understand it without words—with the sort of knowing that came in a flash of intuition.

The wind twisted about Rowenna and sank her into vision, and remembering.

Dimly she saw the River Ness. A woman with a lined face and graying auburn hair stood in the shallows, and a pair of liveried guards had hold of each of her arms. Greaves waited on the riverbank, and at a signal from him, the guards shoved the woman farther into the water and forced her below the surface. The water roiled as she struggled, and then all went still. They pulled the woman up and she choked and gasped, but before she'd fully caught her breath, under she went once more.

Again and again the guards ducked her, until a familiar voice rang out.

"Stop," Elspeth Crannach begged, tears shining in her eyes. She stood in the shade of a nearby pine, at the side of someone in fine broadcloth. But his face was shadowed, and Rowenna could not make it out. "Please. I'll do as you ask. I'll do anything. Just leave her be."

There was anguish in every one of the girl's words, and she dropped to her knees before the shadowy figure, taking his hands in her own.

"Whatever you want," Elspeth swore. "I'm yours."

With a motion, the figure before her stopped the guards. They dragged the woman onto the riverbank and dropped her there, sodden and coughing up fetid water. Elspeth started toward her, but Torr Pendragon—for it must be him—stopped her with a hand on her arm.

"No," he said evenly. "You don't go to her. From now on, you stand at my side. You set yourself apart."

Tears slipped down Elspeth's face as she nodded. But she fixed her gaze on her mother and did not look away, not as the guards hauled the woman to her feet roughly and dragged her off, up toward the castle.

The wind receded from Rowenna. Gently it slipped away, leaving her empty and bereft, and haunted by what she'd seen. She opened her eyes, and Elspeth stood before her, untouchable and beautiful as always, with a look of mild curiosity on her face.

"Did it work?" Elspeth asked.

Rowenna got to her feet. She crossed the small distance between them and wrapped her arms about the other girl. Sharp and proud as Rowenna could be, she was not heartless, and she knew all too well what Elspeth had felt, watching her mother near drown. And though Rowenna did not know the full price Torr Pendragon had exacted from Elspeth in exchange for her mother's life, she'd have done precisely as Elspeth did and given herself up, had their situations been reversed.

"Oh," Elspeth said softly, and hugged Rowenna back.

After a moment Rowenna stepped away and nodded in answer to the question Elspeth had asked.

"Well, good," Elspeth said with a smile. "I wasn't—I wasn't sure I'd made it clear."

⤷⤶

Rowenna had made it her habit to sleep during the afternoons, when there was no darkness to hide her curse-breaking work and when Elspeth was occupied at the castle. But this particular afternoon she found herself restless and unwilling to fall into one of her tortured dreams of home. A bale of nettle-flax fiber sat waiting for her in one corner of the hut, but she could not spin it into yarn without a drop spindle at very least, and there was not enough yet to complete the curse breaking with.

For a short while she sat in the sun outside the hut, watching her brothers and Gawen as they alternately dozed in the warm light and paddled about on the river. The wind's vision of Elspeth haunted her, as did the way she'd lost Mairead. She did not want to lose anyone again. Whatever the cost, she'd not give up on her family when there was the least chance they might be saved.

So despite the bright sun, Rowenna picked herself up and

climbed the hill to the castle. The way to the chapel was gratify-ingly quiet, even as she slipped through the tall boxwood hedge and into the menagerie. The strange creatures there were all nap-ping in the afternoon sun, and Rowenna nearly overlooked the graveyard boy, who sat on the gravel before the *fuath*'s cage, watch-ing the creature at rest.

The *fuath* lay in the cage's sole shady corner, its grasping hand draped into the small bowl of brackish water that was the only moisture afforded it. Every now and then the monster gasped, feathery gills on its neck opening and shutting with a moist, stomach-turning sound. Not a hint of glamour clung to it, at least that Rowenna could see. Under the full sun it seemed pitiful and wretched—a thing cast up on shore to dry out and die. Passing the graveyard boy, Rowenna crouched before the bars of the cage and looked full into the *fuath*'s murderous face.

The creature looked back, regarding her with enormous, pale eyes.

"Put out your hand to it. See what it thinks of you."

There was a hint of eagerness to the graveyard boy's voice, and for the first time in his presence, Rowenna felt a twinge of mis-trust. He gestured to the *fuath*, who'd raised its head as if scenting the air, wide eyes gone lightless and black.

"Go on. Reach through the bars. I'd like to see what it does."

Rowenna hesitated. But the creature looked so weak and des-perate in the sun. And a small, dark part of her found it tempting—the thought of having a monster like the one that had killed her mother within her power.

"You're quite safe," the graveyard boy said. "You've nothing to worry about."

Rowenna glanced anxiously over one shoulder at him, and he smiled. A sudden wave of reassurance swept through her.

The creature rose to its feet in a single, sinuous motion, and, drawing closer to where Rowenna stood, pressed its face to the bars.

"Look," the boy coaxed. "The beast has taken to you. Don't be afraid."

His voice was warm and pleasant, and there was something in the way he watched Rowenna that set the better part of her at ease. To look at, he was honest and open, entirely trustworthy.

But the wind fretted about her, muttering to itself. *Beware, beware, beware.*

Rowenna reached out and brushed the *fuath*'s wicked face with the back of one hand.

Tha mi eòlach ort, a vicious whisper said, cutting into Rowenna's mind. *I know you. I know your kind. Do you think he wouldn't put you in a cage as well? Ask the other one what she thinks of her chains.*

Shocked, Rowenna stepped back.

"I saw its true form," the graveyard boy murmured, reverence in his voice. "I saw it, at your touch. Did you know it holds its glamour for the rest of us even now? Even after three years as a captive? All I see when I look at it is my own face reflected back. But no creature can help showing its truest nature when it falls beneath a witch's hand. I've never seen it unmasked before—it wouldn't suffer Elspeth to come near it, not even when she had her craft."

Rowenna swallowed. She did not want to be here, caught between this disarming boy and the *fuath* in its cage. But the *fuath*, at least, was a known quantity. The boy, however—he looked nearly like a farmhand, in his belted trousers and loose, fine-spun shirt, with a scattering of freckles across his nose. There was something that had begun to nag at her though—his self-assurance, perhaps. Rowenna had begun to have her suspicions.

Steeling her courage, she went to him. The graveyard boy stayed motionless, a slight smile playing at the edges of his mouth, as Rowenna reached out. Just as she'd done with the *fuath*, she brushed the back of her fingers against his jaw.

At once it felt as if a weight had dropped from Rowenna. Until now, she hadn't realized the extent to which she'd had to push against this stranger's aggressive trustworthiness, to keep from revealing more of herself and her truths than she intended. Though the boy's face remained much the same, she caught a glint in his eyes she'd never noticed before. A calculating light—a sharp and predatory wit. And when Rowenna looked down at his hands, they were rimed in blood to the elbows. It dripped from his finger-tips to the ground and pooled there in a crimson puddle.

She removed her touch, and the gory vision vanished. The boy before her smiled, and when he looked so, it was very hard not to believe the best of him. Rowenna realized, finally, that it was *craft* projecting this constant mildness, this easy camaraderie and dependable air.

A ward. A ward of such subtlety and gentleness that she might never have noticed it, had she not laid hands on Torr Pendragon.

God in heaven, Rowenna thought to the wind and the *fuath*. *Elspeth Crannach in her power must have been a force to reckon with, if it was she who made this work for him.*

You can have no idea, the *fuath* rasped back in the mire of Rowenna's mind. *She is a shadow now to what she was, before this tyrant broke her. She burned like the sun. Her very presence brought pain to us. But you, little fish. You're different. There's darkness at your edges, and salt water at your core.*

Torr took a step forward, and Rowenna could not help but flinch.

"Isn't it clever, my ward?" he said. "Elspeth Crannach worked it for me. It doesn't just offer protection—no matter who you are, you'll see me as someone worth confiding in, so long as the ward lasts. Someone worthy of trust. But come now. Don't fret because of who I am and who you are. I'm not unmerciful to those with your . . . talents. It's one thing to *be* a witch, but quite another to use your power to stand against me. And you wouldn't dream of that, would you?"

Rowenna shook her head, her breath coming quick and shallow.

Torr Pendragon made a small chirruping noise at the *fuath*, which bared its nightmare teeth and hissed. Torr laughed softly.

"I didn't think you'd choose to set yourself against me, swan maiden. There's no rebel spark in you. You're a good girl, who wants to be free of her curse and to keep herself safe. The question is, how safe do you wish to be?"

Rowenna stared at him, wide-eyed, and all she felt was a great and terrible weariness at the realization that, once again, she stood before a monster and found herself helpless.

"Come, don't look so panic stricken." Torr Pendragon reached out and ran his thumb along the line of Rowenna's jaw, a mockery of her own touch. "If I didn't want you on my grounds, I wouldn't have sent you here myself, and given you a teacher in Elspeth. I think, though, that you may have learned what you need from her, and that it's time to take your education into my own hands."

Rowenna's silence had never felt more like a refuge. She stood wordless before him, a reed that could be bent in whatever way he desired.

"Meet me here tomorrow morning," Torr Pendragon ordered. "I'll bring a rabbit, and let you feed it to the *fuath*."

Ducking her head in a show of courtesy, Rowenna waited until he'd left before departing from the menagerie herself. It took the silence of the overgrown churchyard and the familiar sting of nettles to still her racing heart.

She could not tell her brothers about this new arrangement with Torr Pendragon, and must certainly not speak of it to Gawen. It would only put them in a panic, and perhaps they'd want to leave Inverness altogether. But Rowenna could not afford the delay. *They* could not afford the delay, not if they were to be restored to their human forms before the curse took hold entirely and became irrevocable.

Rowenna would simply have to weather Torr's attention and hope that he found her wanting in some way.

Chapter Sixteen

By the time Rowenna finished pulling her nettles, the sun had set. From somewhere in the chapel, a match flared, and she quickly gathered her sheaves and left, hoping she hadn't been seen. Torr was no longer in the menagerie, and the *fuath* sat in shadow, only its gleaming eyes visible. Rowenna felt like a ghost as she drifted through the deepening twilight. She was so preoccupied that she failed to notice Gawen at first, still trapped in his black swan guise and barreling toward her as she wandered down the hillside beyond the curtain wall. But then he set up a riotous trumpeting and nearly knocked Rowenna off her feet as he passed. She dropped her nettles and scowled, until a muffled curse sounded from behind her.

Pivoting, Rowenna found Steward Greaves not twenty yards back on the hill path. The black swan was hissing fiercely, snapping and buffeting the steward with his wings. Rowenna gasped as Greaves kicked the swan hard, but she had no time to hurry to Gawen, because Greaves was on her then, grasping the back of her neck with one fist and gripping her arm tight with the other.

Memories of her departure from Neadeala flooded through Rowenna.

Greaves shoved her ahead of him, down to the river, and

Rowenna recalled the hungry light that had shone in his eyes as Elspeth's mother had been ducked. Sure enough, Greaves forced her into the shallows, past where her last gathering of nettles lay soaking, and out to where the water hit her knees.

Rowenna had a moment to notice how the moon shone on the black water of the Ness. She drew in a ragged breath, and then Greaves pushed her under as visions of the monster in Mairead's skin threatened to drown her from the inside out.

The submersion came as a sudden shock, followed by a dim and murky view of weeds and mud. Panic set in as she stayed below, and though she tried to keep still, Rowenna couldn't help but begin to thrash. At last the cold, sick rush of fetid water entered her mouth and nose and lungs and stomach, and she choked, and choked, and choked. The world narrowed itself down to a pinpoint, to the color of the ripples in front of Rowenna, and nothing more.

Greaves pulled her back up. Rowenna stayed bent over the surface of the river, streaming water and retching while the steward still gripped her neck and arm.

"I don't trust you, or anyone like you," he muttered, close beside Rowenna's ear. "Not that frigid bitch Pendragon keeps at his side, nor the witch who came before her, nor the one before that. He means to make you next, but every one of you plays us false somehow in the end, and I mean to ensure we maintain our power in this place. No daughter of the devil will get in the way of that."

The wind was shrieking about them, frantic and wordless as it churned the moonlit river into waves. But Greaves paid it no mind.

Rowenna knew a sharp stab of despair, and then she was under again.

This time, though, she hadn't fully lost her breath before a jolt came, and the steward's hold on her slackened. Rowenna seized her chance and fought free at once, hauling herself out onto the river bank and drawing in a few sobbing breaths. With the last of them she caught a fading scent of smoke and peat, and her vision cleared enough to make out Greaves, on his back in the river mud.

Gawen had shed his swan form and knelt over the steward, pinning him to the ground. He held a wicked, short-bladed knife to Greaves's throat, and there was a tense and coiled grace to his posture that Rowenna had never seen there before. He'd always been more collected in his movement than her brothers, but this was different, and Rowenna realized with a cold thrill that the steward was an instant away from death. That his life was entirely within Gawen's hands, and a single wrong word might be his last.

But even as heady triumph at the thought surged through Rowenna, she understood that they'd been placed in an impossible predicament.

"Stop," she called out desperately, as Gawen's knife broke skin and blood snaked down the steward's neck. Scrambling over to the boy, Rowenna put a hand on his arm. He turned to her, and there was nothing behind his eyes. Not anger nor hatred of any kind. Just a vast and abiding emptiness. But she held his gaze, until at last there came a spark of recognition.

"Gawen, you can't," Rowenna said softly. "Think of what would happen. They'd turn the castle upside down looking for him. I'd never be able to keep on with the curse breaking. And in the end, they'd be sure to find the body. It'd be the ruin of us. The end of you and my brothers."

"So you're the MacArthur whelp who's been nosing about Inverness," Greaves spat. "I told Torr he should've killed you while he had the chance. It was foolish not to track you down and put an end to you, but he's had worse than one snapping cur to deal with."

"I can't let him go," Gawen said to Rowenna, ignoring Greaves. His grip was relentless, and the blade of his knife pricked deeper by the moment. "Do you think he'll let either of us live if I do? He'll have you bound to a stake and me at the end of a rope before sunup if I set him free."

Rowenna rocked back on her heels, soaked to the bone and wracked with indecision.

"I leave it to you, scold," Gawen said. "His fate's in your hands. You saved me once—I owe you as much."

Rowenna shut her eyes.

What to do? she thought, reaching out instinctively to the wind. *What to do?*

Let us in, our love, our light, the wind sang.

Without hesitation, Rowenna did as the wind wished. It rushed into her, just as it had in the meadow, and this time, instead of memory, it brought with it a glimpse of herself, working craft. Working an unbinding, not unlike the one she'd been working for her brothers.

"Tie him up," she ordered Gawen, loosing her hair and giving

184

him the length of faded ribbon with which she'd tied it back. "And be quick about it."

Hurrying up the hill, Rowenna tore a fistful of fresh witchnettle leaves from the stalks she'd gathered. Returning, she found Gawen had bound Greaves's wrists but still kept a wary eye on him as the steward lay glaring in the mud. Rowenna knelt at Greaves's side. Flexing one of her hands so that the blisters cracked and bled for the hundredth time, she crushed her handful of nettle until blood stained them. Then with one finger, she smeared blood from the side of the steward's neck and pasted it across the nettle as well.

And all the while, despite the way her pulse thrummed in her veins, she kept her mind a careful, perfect blank. A void, that the unbinding she was working might take on its character and quality.

"Eat it," Rowenna demanded, holding the bloodstained leaves to Greaves's lips. "Eat it or I let him kill you."

A look of disbelief crossed Greaves's face. "What difference does it make if I have my throat cut or your witchwork rots me from within?"

"It won't," Rowenna said stubbornly. "I'm saving your life, you great fool. Do as you're told."

When he resisted yet again, Gawen knelt too and forced the steward's mouth open. Though Greaves coughed and spit, most of the witchnettle made it down his throat. While the leaves had added fresh and stinging blisters to Rowenna's ravaged hands, not a mark showed on the steward's lips.

"Unbind him," Rowenna told Gawen.

For the first time, Gawen hesitated.

"Stray," Rowenna said. "Trust me."

With a single fluid movement, Gawen cut the ribbon that bound Greaves's wrists together. The steward lay where he was, breathing heavily, with his eyes shut.

"Come with me." Rowenna held out a hand again. Gawen took it, and she drew him into the hut, shutting the door behind them and standing with her back to it.

They waited in silence, face to face. After a few moments, the sound of Greaves's voice drifted in. He was muttering to himself in confusion, bewildered by his own presence on the riverbank.

"What in God's name am I doing down here in the mud? That'll be the last time I touch any of this foul place's Scots whiskey."

Gawen's eyes widened, but Rowenna pressed a finger to his lips, wanting silence until the steward had truly gone. Only once Greaves's booted footsteps retreated up the hill path did Gawen speak.

"What did you do, scold?" Gawen asked, his voice low. He reached out with one hand to lean his weight against the doorpost, and fire spread through Rowenna at his nearness.

"I unbound his memory," she told him. "Just as I'm unbinding our curse."

"You *are*, aren't you," Gawen said. It wasn't a question so much as it was a statement of fact, and there was a warmth behind the words that Rowenna seldom heard from him.

She looked up and waited and, when he did not move, let her face slip into a halfhearted scowl. "You're in my way, and I've got work to do. Shift yourself."

"What if I don't want to?" Gawen asked, raising one dark brow.

Rowenna narrowed her eyes. "Do as you're told."

At once Gawen stepped back, but Rowenna relented.

"No," she said. "I've thought better of that. Come back."

Again Gawen obeyed, the ghost of a smile playing about his mouth as he set one hand on either doorpost.

"Now give me the claim over you that you offered yesterday," Rowenna whispered.

"You're the *cailleach*," Gawen answered, though his voice caught on the word. "Can't you use craft to bind me to yourself, if that's what you want?"

Rowenna shook her head. Carefully she raised one nettle-scarred hand and rested it on Gawen's chest, just above his heart. She felt the rapid-fire beat of it and couldn't help but smile. "No. I won't do the binding here. This work's for you to do, or it'll be left undone."

When Gawen stooped and kissed Rowenna, she knew she'd been waiting for it since that first moment on the beach, when her craft called her to him. Whatever her power, Rowenna had never felt anything to equal Gawen MacArthur's mouth on hers, or the way her lips parted instinctively beneath his. His hands went to her waist and hers tangled in his hair, and together, they were salt water and flame, promises made and curses broken. And though she'd been born by the sea and chosen by the wind, Rowenna held this to be the dearest of her gifts—that without witchwork or cunning, Gawen MacArthur would do her bidding and answer to her touch.

Chapter Seventeen

"Rowenna?" Finn's small, uncertain voice cut through Rowenna's fog of exhaustion as she bent over a pile of soaked nettle stalks, drawing fiber from the pith. It was still late, or getting on toward early—Rowenna could never be sure during the narrow dark hours when she undertook her curse-breaking work.

She glanced up and found Finn standing on the hill path, all on his own.

"Finny?" Rowenna said with a frown. "What are you doing here? Where are Liam and Duncan?"

"They're farther back," Finn said, scuffing at the dirt with one foot. "They don't want you to see Duncan until . . . after the change. Well, Duncan doesn't want you to. He says you'd fuss. Liam's not saying much at all."

Rowenna's heart stopped in her chest at Finn's words.

"What's happened?" she asked, dropping her nettles and scrambling to her feet. "Is everyone all right?"

Finn shook his head miserably. "Not really. Not Duncan. You know he's been fist-fighting for money—Liam's been asking him to stop for days and he wouldn't, and it went badly tonight."

"Show me," Rowenna said, holding out a hand. And though her fingers were blistered and bloody, Finn reached back without hesitation, relief and trust shining from his eyes.

He led Rowenna around the base of the castle hill, toward the city sprawled along its opposite side. Rowenna had never gone this way herself—her work lay along the river, or in the nettle-choked graveyard of Inverness Castle itself. The pines grew thicker here, blotting out the sky and filling the air with their resinous, pungent scent. A carpet of old needles deadened the sound of their footfalls, and after half a mile, Finn veered off the path.

Behind a patch of bracken sat Duncan, with Liam kneeling at his side. Liam was vainly attempting to tend to Duncan, while the boy pushed his hands away.

Rowenna stopped short at the sight of them. Guilt was written across Liam's thin face in deep grooves, in the set of his mouth, in the lightlessness of his gaze. Worse was Duncan, who'd been beaten till he was almost unrecognizable—his nose broken yet again, both lips split and bloody, his eyes nearly swollen shut.

"Liam," Rowenna said, keeping her voice perfectly even. She could not afford to let a trace of bitterness or sharpness enter it, not now, not even with fear and anguish twisting inside her. The slightest hint of darkness might set her brothers against her. "Let me look after Duncan. You take Finn and get him to bed."

She drew Finn close and pressed a kiss to the top of his head.

"I'll fix it, Finny, I promise," she said. And it wasn't just Duncan's hurts she meant—it was all of this, her brothers on edge and falling apart, and their father left behind, his fate still unknown.

"I know you will," Finn whispered, and he hugged her fiercely. Then Liam was at their side. He nodded to Rowenna and beckoned to Finn, and the two of them began their walk back to the hut by the river.

Slowly Rowenna took the remaining steps to where Duncan sat. He refused to look at her as she lowered herself down beside him.

"Duncan, talk to me," Rowenna pleaded. "I'm begging you— we used to be good to each other. We used to be honest. I'd have been lost after *Màthair* died if it wasn't for you, and now you're lost, but you won't let me help. I know I hurt you—I know we're in these troubles on my account—but you can't carry on like this."

Instead of answering, Duncan buried his face in his arms. For a moment, Rowenna thought he would not speak at all. But then came the last words she expected to hear.

"I know it wasn't you, Enna," Duncan said, his voice muffled. "I *saw* her."

"What?" Rowenna breathed.

"I saw her. Back in Neadeala. That day at breakfast, when she was needling you about the porridge. Your hand brushed hers and I saw. I thought—I don't know what I thought. But I knew it couldn't have been real. And when we got here, it was easier to believe you're mad and I'm halfway there myself, because if all of this—the curse, I mean—was your doing, you could fix it. And it would mean *Athair* was fine and *Màthair* was home, not that we'd left our father in the clutches of a monster. How could we, Enna? How could we do such a thing?"

Duncan's voice broke, and without even looking at Rowenna, he began to sob. She'd never heard such a despairing sound—he'd wept a little after Mairead's death, this most willful brother of hers, but it had been a restrained grief by comparison. This was hopelessness, and Rowenna could not bear to hear it.

She wrapped her arms about Duncan and held him close until his tears were spent. When he finished, she tilted his chin up with a finger, until he had to look at her. Her hand on his face was a nettle-wrought ruin, but his face was a ruin too, and once again they were alike, she and Duncan, bound together by their wildness and their failings.

"I will break this curse," Rowenna swore. "Whether I laid it or not. And we will get *Athair* back once that's done."

"How?" Duncan asked. "How, Enna? You can't face a creature like that. It'll be the death of you."

Until now, when confronted by Duncan's grief, Rowenna hadn't considered that she might become strong enough to end the *fuath*. Her only thought was that once the curse on her brothers had been broken, they might spirit away their father, and live the rest of their days in fear, because Rowenna could not possibly have it in her to kill the monster and free herself from the long, long shadow it cast.

But Finn's lostness and his trust, Duncan's sorrow and despair, and Liam's unspoken guilt chafed at her. And Rowenna found herself wondering, as she led Duncan to the river to wash his swollen face with strips torn from her petticoat, if she might not have it in her to kill a monster after all.

❧

Torr Pendragon was waiting in the menagerie at midmorning. Rowenna stood silently before him outside the cage of this other *fuath*, a creature so akin to the one who'd murdered her mother and stolen her old life.

Torr looked as unprepossessing as ever, in his simple clothes with his eager smile. But there was an ornate belt around his waist now, and a scabbard that held a dirk. Guards were visible too, posted at intervals around the menagerie. Rowenna had never noticed them there before. As she approached, Torr reached into a burlap sack and eagerly thrust something at her.

"Here, take it."

Good to his word, he held a live rabbit. When he'd said Rowenna could feed the *fuath*, she'd expected a dead thing, neck snapped by Steward Greaves or one of the groundskeepers. As Rowenna reached out and gripped the creature by the loose fur and skin of its scruff, white rims showed around its black eyes. Everything about it spoke of mindless panic—when Torr first removed it from the sack, it had struggled wildly, but now it stayed motionless, past struggle, past fear, frozen by the sort of terror that consumes the senses.

Rowenna felt fear of her own, standing before this tyrant, but she refused to let it show. Torr watched curiously as Rowenna hefted the rabbit, testing its weight.

"Do you have it in you, little witch?" Torr asked. His ward was less effective, now that Rowenna knew it was there. She could sense the hunger in him, like she'd been able to in the *fuath* back home. "Her ladyship who shares my bed certainly never did. Elspeth is too gentle-hearted for feeding monsters. It grieves her even to hear me speak of it. Yet here is the truth—if this rabbit is not killed, our friend in the cage will starve. Which is crueler, do you think?"

Rowenna, of course, said nothing. She caught her lower lip between her teeth in concentration and thought of Duncan sobbing as she thrust the rabbit between the bars of the *fuath*'s cage.

The creature, which had been curled against the far side of the enclosure, watched everything with its head pillowed on one mottled, misshapen forearm. At Rowenna's nod, the *fuath* got to its feet and flowed across the cage like water.

A single tug and a snap of its jaws, and the rabbit was gone, vanished behind those fishhook teeth.

"Is it not a thing of beauty?" Torr asked, his voice warm with affection. "Thirty men were needed to capture it at sea. Even then, it killed five people before they managed to get it under control. My soldiers would have ended up killing the creature as well, and bringing nothing but its head and scales back to me, if a witch like you hadn't intervened."

Rowenna's full attention was fixed on Torr, and he smiled his easy farm boy's smile. "Got you interested now, have I? Yes, a rebel family was hiding out in those parts. I doubt we would have found them, if it weren't for the witch coming out to calm my lovely monster here. And once we had the witch, the rest of the rebels just . . . gave themselves up. They're all dead now, even the witch herself. She served me for a short while, but turned on me in the end. You can't let vermin live, and that's what these rebels are—just pests, in need of putting down, lest they prey upon your flock. And do not doubt that the Highlands is my pasture now, and its people my flock. I will make a kingdom in the north to rival my brother's, and when

I've finished, I'll go south and take *his* throne as well."

Rowenna said nothing in reply. She stood impassively at his side, watching the *fuath* lick blood and fur from its lips.

"Do you know what the difference is between a witch and a saint?" Torr asked. He seemed to take great pleasure in speaking to Rowenna, who could not answer or argue. She made no motion to indicate that she'd heard him, or that she wished for him to go on. She only stayed as she was and, on impulse, reached one hand through the bars of the cage before them.

Tentatively the *fuath* drew near and pressed its monstrous face to her palm with fathomless sorrow in its eyes.

What had she seen in it that was worth saving, Rowenna wondered? That other girl, with her wisdom and her craft, who'd traded her life for this beast's?

"There's very little difference between a witch and a saint on the outside," Torr said. His smile brightened, and his clever eyes fixed on Rowenna's. "A saint is only a witch who does as she's told. And a witch, by contrast, is just a saint with a rebel's heart. Yet how different their fates. One we canonize—the other we burn. That's something to think about, isn't it, swan maiden?"

Rowenna nodded, because she knew it was expected of her, and that it would be a danger not to.

"Show me something you can do," Torr commanded. "Something that I can't."

Reaching farther between the bars of the *fuath*'s cage, Rowenna caressed its face. The monster let out a keening noise and leaned into her touch.

Salt water, its vicious voice said. *You smell of it yet, little fish. Of waves and freedom.*

"Something I haven't seen," Torr pressed.

Rowenna bit her lip and thought. Nothing she could do was visible or showy—not her slow and painful work with the nettles, nor the way she could bid the wind to come into her. Neither of those were things she could parade about as pretty tricks.

Still, Torr Pendragon stood waiting, and a perverse part of Rowenna hated to disappoint him. She knew him to be a tyrant, but he'd never yet shown that side of himself to her. He was, too, the only person who'd ever asked to see the pieces of her others feared.

The wind skittered about her ankles, muttering to itself.

Rowenna Rowenna Rowenna.

Rowenna pulled her raw and blistered hand away from the *fuath* and held it out to the wind. Immediately it came, wrapping itself around her touch. Rowenna raised her hand and panto-mimed a push in Torr Pendragon's direction.

The wind surged forward in a sudden gust but stopped short of Torr and nervously rushed back to her.

"That'll do you no good," Torr said, his eyes gleaming. "The ward her ladyship put on me is too strong for that. Nothing and no one who means me the slightest harm has been able to come near since she made it. They'd have to possess the craft to shatter her work, and I've met no one who could manage it yet, save perhaps the creature in that cage.

"Something else," Torr commanded. "Something bigger."

The breeze danced happily about Rowenna, always ecstatic to have her full attention. And Rowenna gave in to wicked impulse. To her spite and pride. She turned to the *fuath*'s cage and mimed the turning of a key in a lock.

The wind did as she bid it. There was a metallic clang as the bolt slid back and a sudden shriek of hinges as the wind shoved the door open. Quicker than thought and twice as graceful, the *fuath* flowed toward the cage door. Rowenna caught the briefest glimpse of raw fear on Torr's face before she motioned to the wind to shut and bar the door again. Just as the monster reached the threshold, the door slammed to, and the beast stared at Rowenna with fierce and reproachful full-moon eyes.

When Rowenna turned back to Torr, the fear she'd seen for an instant was gone, carefully hidden away.

"Clever girl," he said coolly. "I won't be toyed with, though— you leave that beast locked up from now on, as it should be."

Reaching into the sack at his feet, Torr pulled out a second rabbit and held it up by the scruff.

"One last little bit of craft," he said, and when he spoke, his voice was soft and reassuring. "Why don't you put this creature out of its misery, before our friend in the cage has its way with it?"

Rowenna froze. It had been one thing to offer a rabbit still alive to the *fuath*, who, after all, needed to eat to live. But it seemed wrong to her, to use her less ordinary capabilities to do harm. To enlist the glad wind to take a life, however small, on her behalf. Mairead would surely not have approved.

Nevertheless, Torr and the *fuath* were watching intently, so

Rowenna reached for the wind. As if it could sense her thoughts, the breeze chuckled across the gravel paths of the menagerie.

Rowenna Rowenna Rowenna, it sang. *Our love, our light, our dark-hearted girl.*

"Go on then," Torr coaxed.

Reluctantly she fixed her attention on the rabbit, which had tucked up its legs and watched her with liquid brown eyes. With her arms at her sides, Rowenna began to slowly close her right hand, miming the act of throttling a creature.

Nothing happened.

The wind stayed where it was, swirling about her.

With a sigh, Rowenna shut her eyes. She went inward, to the sea of her craft, and on those night-dark shores, she called the wind.

Come here to me.

The joyous wind rushed to her.

Outside of herself, away from the salt water within, she panto-mimed a hand around the rabbit's throat again.

Once more, the wind failed to respond. Or at least, from with-out it did. Within, Rowenna could feel it bumping and nudging and coaxing her along the shadowy sand to where the frothing sea of her power churned endlessly.

Cold water swept around her ankles.

A smell of salt water rose up in the menagerie courtyard. Rowenna opened her eyes. She could still feel the bite of frigid waves against her feet as a third time she commanded the wind.

At the motion of her hand, the breeze swept over to Torr. It forced itself down the rabbit's throat, pushing and pushing in little gusts. White showed around the rabbit's eyes, and it began to struggle at the realization that it could no longer draw breath. Still the wind pushed.

Rowenna wanted to relent—to stretch out her hand and send the wind skipping away, so that the vicious *fuath* might finish the rabbit off instead. But Torr stood watching with an expression of keen delight, his grip on the struggling rabbit like iron.

So Rowenna balled her hand into a fist and squeezed, and the wind stuffed more of itself down the rabbit's throat, until the small animal went suddenly limp. Blood flowed from its mouth and dripped down onto the gravel, and Rowenna realized with a jolt that the wind had burst the rabbit's lungs.

The breeze retreated from Torr and twined about Rowenna, ruffling her skirts and purring, for all the world like a contented cat.

Rowenna, it sang, affectionately as ever. *Our love, our light. We are yours, to wish, to will. We shall always do your bidding.*

For the first time, it struck Rowenna that perhaps there was nothing innately good or wicked in what she could do. The wind, after all, was just the wind, even with a voice. It was Rowenna herself who guided her gifts. Who could, it seemed, direct the wind to do this or that, to go here or there. Who might weave wards or curses with her hands, depending on the state of her heart.

It felt like freedom and a shackle, all at once, realizing that cleanness or uncleanness, goodness or wickedness, lay not in the nature of her abilities, but in how she chose to wield them. And that this truth was why Mairead had hesitated to teach her.

"That was most instructive," Torr Pendragon said, voice still soft. His eyes were very far away as he gazed down at the lifeless rabbit in his hand. "I think, swan maiden, that we're going to become quite good friends. And if you're very careful, and make a good friend of me, I'll see to it that you're unassailable. No one will ever call you a witch, because all the world will know you to be a saint."

Rowenna, as ever, said nothing. But she knew she was neither—not a witch nor a saint. Just a girl who sometimes chose rightly and sometimes wrongly, but who wanted nothing more than to be free to make those choices on her own behalf.

Chapter Eighteen

In the dark before dawn, Rowenna knelt over her interminable nettles, pulling out linen fibers with her ravaged hands, and the constant backdrop of pain was enough to make her weep.

But she did not. She remained dry eyed and composed, steadily going about her work. Still, when the serene figure of Elspeth appeared on the hillside, it was a relief to Rowenna. She welcomed any distraction that might send her into a place where her hands moved automatically and her mind became preoccupied with something other than pain.

Like Rowenna herself, Elspeth looked as if she had not been to bed. She wore a creased, wine-colored silk gown, with ivory froths of lace at the neckline and the sleeves. A few strands of Elspeth's auburn hair had escaped the diamond pins they were bound up with. Along with the faint shadows beneath her eyes, it all combined to make her seem softer and more fragile than was her usual wont.

Elspeth dropped down onto the damp turf across from Rowenna in a billow of wine-dark skirts. As always, she showed no care for her fine clothes. Rather, she sat and watched Rowenna for a few moments, twisting a delicate white handkerchief in her hands.

"There's something I wanted to speak to you about," Elspeth said at last. "And I wanted to do it when you had your voice, and could ask questions, or rail at me if need be."

"Go on," Rowenna answered with a frown, at a loss as to what the girl could mean.

Elspeth looked down. "I knew you were coming here before you arrived."

"Of course you did," Rowenna said. "I met with Torr at Drumossie, though I didn't know it was him at the time. He sent me straight to you. I didn't imagine he'd said nothing of it."

"No," Elspeth said with a shake of her beautiful head. "Rowenna, I knew before then. Gawen and I planned it together, to have him find another girl like me—a *cailleach*, who might use her craft on our behalf. I knew he was going to you, to ask for your help under false pretenses. I knew he'd arrived at Neadeala and suffered a setback when his boat was wrecked. But he sent word that he planned to stay on and try to convince you to come to Inverness by claiming he needed help searching for his father."

"He does want to find his father," Rowenna said stubbornly, even as anxious things woke and began to flutter in the pit of her stomach. "That's what he's always told me. And why else would he want my help, if not for that?"

Elspeth bit at her lip, and her gaze faltered. "We want . . . we want you to help us kill Torr Pendragon. That's why Gawen went after you. That's why we brought you here. Because both of us have tried, and couldn't get past the ward I made. That's how I lost my power—I shattered it, in trying to pull apart my own work. There's nothing left of it now, except that I can feel craft and power in others, and still hear the earth when it speaks. But I can do no more work of my own."

"I don't believe you." Rowenna regarded Elspeth with unveiled suspicion. "You say Gawen kept in touch with you about me, but that's not possible. He never left our cottage from the time I hauled him up the burn. We were never out of each other's company until coming here."

"Your brother Liam helped first," Elspeth said. "While he was at your cot, Gawen gave him a sealed letter that he sent on by courier."

Rowenna's hands had fallen still. She could feel the slow heat of anger building inside her and tried to cool it through an act of will. She would not be the girl Mairead had seen. The spiteful, dangerous minx her mother had expected craft would make her into.

"There's more than that," Elspeth continued reluctantly. "Torr found you at Drumossie because Gawen and I arranged for him to be there."

The heat in Rowenna went entirely cold, and that chill was a greater danger than fire ever could be. "What?"

"While you were on the road, Gawen sent word to me again, by way of a farmer," Elspeth explained. "Torr has been searching for a *cailleach* to replace me since I broke my craft. I paid a scullery maid to tell him where he could find such a girl. I sent him straight to you, to bring you back to Inverness."

"But why bring him into it?" Rowenna asked. "Why go to so

much trouble to arrange a meeting between Torr and me, and to keep us both in the dark as to how we crossed paths?"

"You'd already refused Gawen several times over, when all he'd done was ask if you'd help him find his father. How much less likely would you be to help if we told you we expected you to break a ward and kill a tyrant? But we knew if Torr once laid eyes on you, you'd be within his power. That you'd have to do away with him entirely, if you were ever to be free again. That you *will* have to do away with him, if you mean to leave when your brothers' curse is broken. And I knew too that there were things I wouldn't be able to teach you, if you were to put an end to Torr. Things he might bring out in you instead. Things I was never capable of. It's a rare *cailleach* who can kill with her craft, Rowenna Winthrop. But from the start, Gawen said he thought that might be you."

Rowenna scrambled to her feet, breath coming hard and fast, and looked down at Elspeth. "You don't just want me to help you, or to break a ward. You want me to use my craft to do murder. And you *gave me over to a tyrant* to make sure I would."

"Don't think we haven't tried ourselves," Elspeth said sadly. "We have, and we've kept trying since you came here, but it's beyond us. I made that ward too well."

Elspeth smoothed out her skirts—a small, unconscious gesture. Rowenna hated it. She hated Elspeth's finery and her discipline and the fact that she'd seen fit to meddle in someone else's life for her own ends.

"The truth is, swan maiden, there's no one here in Inverness that hasn't been using you from the start. Torr wants you to use your craft in his defense. Gawen and I want you to use it to kill him."

Rowenna shut her eyes, and the wind, sensing her distress, came to her.

Our love, our light, it murmured.

Our dark-hearted girl, Rowenna finished on its behalf. And dark-hearted she must be in truth, if all she ever seemed to people was a threat, or a knife to be used. Mairead must have known that about her—that her nature and her craft would become a weapon when tempered together.

"Why are you telling me all this now?" Rowenna asked Elspeth. "If there's no way for me to get free of Torr without killing him, why not just keep me in the dark, until I've done what you wanted or failed in the attempt?"

Elspeth looked out at the glimmering surface of the Ness, slipping away not twenty feet from them. Her face, in profile, was pale and drawn. Her shoulders slumped wearily, and when she turned to meet Rowenna's gaze, there was helplessness in her eyes.

"I'm telling you because I've spent two years as a tool in someone else's hands," Elspeth said, "and I am sick to death of it. I know what it is to be used—to be pushed and prodded to do things you'd not have chosen otherwise. From the start, I've wanted you to know the truth. Gawen and I never saw eye to eye on that. But Rowenna, we're not *people* to the likes of Torr with his ambition or Gawen with his blood oath. We're just craft in their eyes—no more than witches or saints, depending on whether we take their part."

Gawen's voice echoed through Rowenna's mind.

I like a lass who's a little more trouble. . . . If I ever fall for someone, she'll be half thorns and stings. . . .

It's not my own shape I miss. . . . Nor anything about my own self. But I do find myself wishing to hear your sharp tongue.

Had he meant any of it? Or was it just a ploy to ensure Rowenna would do as he wished when things came to a head with Torr Pendragon? She'd fallen for it, after all. Let him woo her. Come near to doing violence with him already, that night on the riverbank with Greaves.

And then there was Torr himself. Though he'd kept his identity hidden at first, he'd done little since to hide his true desire, which was to raise Rowenna up and trade protection for her power. He, at least, had been honest about his intentions.

"I'll understand if you hate me now," Elspeth said softly, getting to her feet. "We put you in an untenable position, Gawen and I. It may look like you and I have our freedom, but there's never a moment that Torr's eyes aren't on us. He won't let you go again without a fight."

Rowenna crossed her arms about her middle and tried desperately to do as she ought.

Forgive if you wish to be forgiven, Liam would say. And she did feel badly for Elspeth, who'd endured much and been bound to a life of distrust and constraint.

But the very darkness in Rowenna, that Torr and Gawen and Elspeth all sought to use, kept her from relenting.

"You should leave," she told Elspeth flatly. "I don't want to see you again. But none of this changes my reasons for being here.

I will free my brothers, get out of Inverness by whatever means necessary, and pry my father from our monster's clutches. I want nothing else."

"And after that?" Elspeth pressed, her tone gentle, her lovely face sorrowful. "Can you and your family truly stand to live the rest of your days in a land being ground down beneath the heel of a butcher and a tyrant?"

"Leave," Rowenna snapped. With a nod, Elspeth obeyed. Rowenna was left alone on the hillside, and as Elspeth disappeared behind the curtain wall, the pain in Rowenna's hands seemed to redouble. Bitter tears finally rose up in her eyes, but Rowenna dashed them away, the salt water burning her blisters like fire.

Chapter Nineteen

Rowenna kept herself scrupulously apart from Gawen, unable to bear the thought of speaking to him. Wherever he was, she was not. But she still went to her trysts with Torr Pendragon, for fear of losing his trust before her curse-breaking work was done. And she kept an eye on her brothers, who had only a handful of hours in human form remaining to them each night.

Get us free, get Athair, *and run* was her heartsong now—the length and breadth and depth of her desire.

After the rabbit came a lamb. Rowenna stole its breath, and the *fuath* tore it in two before swallowing each piece. Then came a calf. That required rending into quarters. Rowenna killed them passionlessly, numbing herself to the act of bidding the wind to burst a creature's lungs, and each time, Torr looked briefly disappointed. But Rowenna realized, after what Elspeth had said, that he was taking care with her. Biding his time. Choosing not to push her craft too far, for fear that it would break as Elspeth's had done.

The morning after the calf Torr had nothing with him. No helpless creature, just his own self, standing on the gravel before the *fuath*'s cage.

"Do something to it." Torr pointed at the mottled deepwater

monster hunched miserably in one corner of the iron cage. "Don't kill it, just . . . work it up a little bit."

But Rowenna had no wish to test the tenuous regard the *fuath* seemed to have for her. She'd too much respect for the monster's capabilities—one of its kind had pitted itself against Rowenna already, and she had no intention of making an enemy of another.

So rather than test the *fuath*, she tested Torr. Instead of doing as she was bid, Rowenna crossed her arms and shook her head.

Torr frowned, the line of his shoulders tense. "All right. We'll just have a stroll round the menagerie this morning then. No witchery. No miracles. Will that suit you better?"

When Rowenna nodded, Torr offered his arm, and she took it, fearing to push him too far. They passed by a dozen strange and unfamiliar creatures before coming to a cage that contained a beast Rowenna recognized.

It was an enormous cat, higher than her waist, with a tawny-and-black-striped pelt like that on the creature she'd seen at the wharves, upon first arriving in Inverness. Perhaps it was the same beast, but if so, it was sadly changed. The cat she'd seen had been sleek and well fed, rippling with muscle. Its coat had gleamed, and every movement it made had spoken of restrained power.

But the sad animal before her was skin and bones, pacing end-lessly up and down the length of its small enclosure. At the sight of Rowenna, it snarled and threw itself against the bars of the cage, reaching for her with hooked claws the length of her fingers.

In spite of herself, Rowenna startled. Torr turned to her and, for the first time that morning, gave her a genuine smile. Behind him, the cat paced and paced, its wide eyes gleaming in the mid-morning light.

"This is Neera," Torr said. "She's not like the *fuath*—not willing to bear a witch's touch. I tried her on an old woman like you, and Neera tore her hands off."

Rowenna's stomach dropped out from inside her as she realized what was about to happen. She thought of edging away, and as if he could read her thoughts, Torr shook his head.

"I wouldn't run if I were you," he said. "Move from that spot, and I'll have you tied to a stake and burned."

Rowenna stayed motionless. She kept her face a careful blank, but inside, her mind was a maelstrom of memories. Water, rushing into her mouth and nose. Hands on the back of her head, holding her under—both the steward's, and Mairead's. The thing in Mairead's skin, watching her with its vicious eyes. The sting of nettles, the weight of weariness. Cam, telling Rowenna he wanted her gone. Elspeth, confessing that she and Gawen had only ever wanted Rowenna for her craft.

Torr Pendragon took a long, spiked metal rod out from a mass of bushes at the base of the cat's enclosure. With one hand, he used the spike to fend off the snarling beast. With the other, he drew a skeleton key from his pocket and reached for the lock.

Rowenna shut her eyes. She heard the clang of the bolt being drawn back. The scrape of rusty hinges. The heavy thump of the cat's body, dropping down from its cage, suddenly grown wary and circumspect at the prospect of freedom.

Even those great velvet paws made the smallest of noises as

the creature crept forward across the menagerie's graveled path. A step. Another.

I don't want to hurt you, Rowenna thought at the beast. Everything about this felt different—with the rabbit and the lamb and the calf, she'd just been one way of dying. They'd always have ended up dead, whether she was the agent of it or not. And she'd been in control, able to ease them mercifully out of life, through just a little slip of the wind.

She was not in control now. Every nerve in her burned with fear.

Step. Step. Each one stealthy, as if the creature expected her to bolt.

Please turn around. I'm not who you want. I've never done you wrong.

Step.

Step.

A silence.

Rowenna's eyes flew open. She found the cat crouched not four feet from her, belly to the ground, tail lashing, every muscle in its body taut and ready to spring.

"Show me your mettle, little saint," Torr Pendragon whispered from behind the relative protection of the open cage door.

At the sound of his voice, the creature sprang. It moved like quicksilver, like a storm at sea, like summer lightning, and like regret. But it was not faster than Rowenna Winthrop's blistered hands, which flashed through the air, one strangling, the other pushing.

And neither cat nor girl was as swift as the waiting wind, which slammed the cat aside and to the ground in a spray of blood that burst from both ends of the creature as the wind tore ruthlessly through it from mouth to tail. Crimson drops spattered Rowenna's face and clothing, and the great cat convulsed once before falling still.

Rowenna's fear and her fury flickered and died in the face of what she'd done. She wanted nothing more than to drop onto the gravel and curl into herself. To become small, and less. But Torr Pendragon was watching, so she stood tall and straight-backed and dry-eyed instead.

A force to be reckoned with.

Let me vanish. Let me dwindle into nothing, like a candle burned down and gone out, she thought to the ever-present wind.

Rowenna, the wind sang. *Our love, our light, our dark-hearted girl.*

Above the wind's reassurances, Rowenna heard Torr's bemused voice.

"God be praised," he said. "A miracle indeed. How many uses I shall have for you, my little saint."

The wind played about Rowenna, murmuring and soothing, running gentle fingers through her hair. It smelled of blood and iron and salt, and everything about Rowenna's life she wished could be undone. For whatever Mairead had feared in her, she had become all that and more.

It wasn't clear to Rowenna how much her brothers and Gawen remembered from their time in swan form. They'd told her it felt muddled and had an obvious distaste for the change, and that had been enough to keep her from pushing for particulars.

But as her brothers wandered away several hours after dark, seeking the privacy of some nearby copse for their change, Gawen lingered. He dogged her steps and kept his uncanny gaze on her, and she had a sinking feeling that the moment he shed his feathers, things would come to a head between them.

Rowenna had just hauled a last bundle of softened nettles from the river when the smell of peat and woodsmoke rose up. It was a cool evening, with a thin, misting rain cloaking the pines around the castle hill. Rowenna was damp through, her hem soaked from working in the shallows, raindrops beading on her hair. She blinked yet more rain from her lashes as Gawen stepped out from the shadows around the hut, fully human once more.

"You're angry with me," Gawen said immediately. "And you're trying to fend me off with coldness instead of telling me what's gone wrong. Let's have it out between us instead, so we can get back to the way we were."

Rowenna rolled her eyes. Predictable. He was utterly predictable, and yet she'd fallen for his charms.

"There's no getting back to how we were," Rowenna muttered. She crouched beside her nettles and began splitting the stalks apart, tugging the loosest flax fibers free as she went. "Because there never was a *we*. There's only myself and my brothers and this curse I've got to unbind. You were caught up in it by mistake, and once I've undone it, we can part ways again."

Kneeling before her, Gawen reached out and set one hand on

the nettles to still her work. Rowenna watched his eyes widen and his throat work as the stalks stung at his palm, still wicked to the touch after a night soaking in the Ness.

"Is that what you want?" Gawen asked.

Rowenna looked away at the moonlit river. She would not lie to him, as he'd lied to her. She'd not pay back his sins with a transgression of her own.

"I want the truth," she said at last. "And I told you so at Drumossie, but you didn't give it to me. Elspeth Crannach told me instead."

For a moment, Gawen fell entirely still. Then he got to his feet and walked away, to stand on the hill path that led to the castle and stare up at the shadowy gray shape of it, stark against the night sky.

"I didn't lie," he said at last. "I know that's not enough, but I *do* want your help finding my father. Only thing is, I swore to him I wouldn't even go looking until Torr Pendragon lies dead."

Gawen turned back to Rowenna, and the emptiness she'd seen in him when he'd held a knife to Greaves's throat was back. "When he and I were at Drumossie, he made me promise that I wouldn't come for him or anyone else in our family unless I'd put an end to Torr. We stood over my brother and watched him take his last breaths, and then my father ordered me to run—to leave the battle behind and live, so that there might be someone left who hates the tyrant enough to cut him down. That's why I'm alive today. Because I did as I was told, and ran like a coward. I'd be dead at my brother's side if not for that."

"Everyone ran in the end," Rowenna said, and she could not help but be gentle with him, despite her anger. "My father was part of the rout, once it became clear the uprising was doomed. I overheard him tell Liam so. He said he barely escaped, what with Torr Pendragon's men slaughtering the Highlanders who were retreating."

"But I was already gone by then," Gawen said, running a hand across his face in frustration. "There was no danger of me being caught in the bloodshed during the retreat, because I'd left hours before. And after, when I'd gone home, my mother and my sister made me swear the same to them. Then, when Torr's soldiers came for us, they hid me and let themselves burn to give me another chance at cutting Pendragon's throat."

Rowenna thought of Mairead, and of how very different things had been between them. Her own mother had denied her the least bit of responsibility or power for fear she would wield it amiss.

"Your family would not have sworn you to this path unless they believed in you," Rowenna told Gawen, tension underpinning every word. "Unless they thought you were enough for what they wanted done. That belief is a gift."

"It's not." The denial came out of him raw and half-broken. "You want the truth from me, scold? The truth is that I'd rather be dead than living under the weight of that sort of expectation. Half the Highlands banded together to put an end to Torr Pendragon's rule, and they couldn't. Now I'm meant to succeed in their place, and I keep failing. I fail at every turn, because there's no getting past the work Elspeth did to save her mother's life. It's like we've all got trapped, wandering in a circle trying to keep our families safe and live up to what they wanted from us."

"You could have just *told* me all that," Rowenna said. "Why didn't you?"

Gawen shook his head. "If I'd said to you at the beginning, *Rowenna Winthrop, I mean to give you over to a tyrant, to learn craft from him because he's wicked and will push you like no one else would, and because I need you to become a knife and cut his throat*, what would you have done?"

"I'd have taken my brothers and left you behind without a second thought," Rowenna admitted.

Gawen fixed her with his dark gaze, and for a long moment, they looked at each other.

"I promised them," he told Rowenna after a time, his eyes still on her face. "I swore to do an impossible thing, and my family died to give me a chance at it. But I can't . . . I can't do the impossible. I need you to do it for me. I need you do it for *them*, because I loved them with every bone and every breath, and I don't think they'll rest easy until Torr Pendragon is in his grave and the Highlands are free.

"Scold, please," he begged, all of his darkness and humor stripped away. "I can't do this without you."

"Then ask for my help," Rowenna said. Her voice trembled on the words, because she did not know yet what her answer would be. She'd not know until the moment she gave it.

Gawen cleared his throat and crossed the little distance between them, kneeling on the grass before her once more.

"Rowenna," he said, reaching out and taking her hands in his own, "will you do what I can't? Will you step into your power, and kill a tyrant to avenge my family and free the Highlands?"

"You're asking me to become everything my mother feared I would," Rowenna whispered, cut to the quick. "She saw me as shadowed. Thought I'd use my craft for violence."

"But will you do it?" Gawen asked again.

Squaring her shoulders, Rowenna met his eyes once more.

"Aye," she said. "I will. I'll do the impossible for you, stray."

"And will you do one other impossible thing?"

"What is it?"

Gawen brushed the back of his hand against her cheek, and Rowenna knew how the *fuath* felt, at the power in her touch. She wanted to lean into him, to murmur of salt water and freedom.

"I want you to live," Gawen said. "Through everything that's coming. Through this curse breaking, and Torr, and the creature in your mother's skin. I need you to outlive every monster in your way, Rowenna Winthrop, because to me, you've become the very last straw. Losing you would be the thing that breaks me."

In answer, Rowenna reached out to him. His regard and his belief made her feel as if she might truly do the impossible: might outlive all her monsters and come out whole in the end. So she knelt on the green turf by the River Ness and kissed her stray, with stalks of witchnettle strewn between them. In that moment it felt as if all the world had fallen away—the nagging pain and persistent fear, the anger that sometimes burned like ice at her core. There was only this: Rowenna Winthrop and Gawen MacArthur with their dark and broken hearts, who'd found each other in the teeth of a storm, who'd fled monsters and would yet face tyrants, and who, God willing, would live to tell the tale.

That night, Liam, Duncan, and Finn returned to the hut before their change occurred. Though Duncan's face had turned several horrific shades of black and blue, there were no new injuries, and he held a bulky, burlap-wrapped bundle under one arm.

"What's this?" Rowenna asked from where she sat by the hut's small hearth, sorting out nettle flax fibers into large, soft bales.

In answer, Duncan set the bundle down beside her.

"Gawen told us what you're doing with your craft," he said. "And so I thought soon you'd be needing this."

He removed the burlap, and beneath it sat a worn and scuffed spinning wheel.

Rowenna nodded. Duncan was right—it was time to bring this work to an end.

Chapter Twenty

There was no sign of Torr in the menagerie. Rowenna walked up and down the gravel pathways and peered behind cages, a sinking feeling in the pit of her stomach.

Had he tired of her already? Or had she displeased him in some way?

The *fuath* sat in its iron enclosure, pressing itself into a patch of shade and panting a little in the warm spring sun. Its skin was riddled with sunburned and drying patches that cracked and flaked and bled. Rowenna, with her ruined hands and feet, knew exactly how that must feel.

I'm sorry, she thought to the creature. *Whatever enmity I have with your kind, nothing and no one deserves this fate.*

Take care, little fish, a sibilant whisper said within the mire of Rowenna's mind. *Do you think he won't cage you, too? Perhaps not with iron bars, but before long you will be a captive, as surely as I am.*

The *fuath* drew itself up to its full height and flowed over to where Rowenna stood, its movements fluid and sinuous. For a long while, they stood regarding each other, Rowenna with her sharp black eyes and the *fuath* with its vicious, deepwater gaze.

Then something sang through the air, and the *fuath* fell to the floor of its cage with an eerie cry, the thick shaft of a crossbow bolt protruding from its leg.

The wind roared to life, gusting and scudding about unpredictably to keep any other arrows from flying true. Rowenna dropped to the ground before the *fuath* and crouched to make herself smaller.

From within its cage, the *fuath* fixed its eyes on Rowenna. For the first time, she read something beyond wildness and hunger there. She saw pain and emptiness and despair.

Kill me, little fish, the *fuath* begged, its harsh voice once again invading Rowenna's mind. *I've had enough of this land and its torments. I have seen you end a life with your craft. End mine now.*

But the wind was howling a warning, and as Rowenna turned, she found a stranger striding toward her from across the menagerie, the naked blade of a dirk gleaming in his hand. He held it at the ready and came on without halting, even as Rowenna implored him with her eyes and vainly shook her head.

He will murder you unless you stop him, the *fuath*'s voice said. *Your blood will spill. Don't think I have not witnessed it before. Other girls, other witches. You are not the first to face these tests—only the strongest. Only the one who will live.*

Wield us well, our love, our light, the wind sang.

With a swift, decisive motion, Rowenna shoved the wind at the oncoming man. The force of it knocked him from his feet, and the dirk flew from his hands. He tried to struggle upright but could not, for the wind kept him pinned to the gravel and gasping for breath.

Reluctantly Rowenna approached.

"I will kill you," the man raged. He was lean as a whip and wild-eyed, his clothing ragged. "If you let me loose for so much as a moment, I will kill you."

Slow footsteps sounded on the gravel, and when Rowenna glanced up, she found Torr approaching. He wore that honest, straightforward smile and had his hands tucked in his pockets. But Rowenna no longer needed touch to see who he was or to feel what hid beneath his clever ward. He was merciless and a murderer, and would be the death of any who failed him.

"Well, you heard what he said," Torr told Rowenna easily. "If you don't kill him, he'll kill you. It's your choice, my witchling."

Rowenna took a few steps back. Whatever she'd promised Gawen about Torr, she had no desire to take a life unless there was no other alternative. All she could see when she contemplated such a thing was the reproach in Mairead's eyes as she asked Rowenna about trying to curse a redcoat.

Calling the wind away, Rowenna let the man go.

Immediately he lunged at her with fury in his eyes, but she was ready. Once again her wind slammed him to the ground.

Over and over she released him, waiting for him to realize it was no good, that he could leave, that the only thing stopping him was his own determination to reach her. It went on and on until her arms were shaking and her vision was clouded by tears. The back of the man's head was a bloody mess, and his eyes had begun to lose focus, but still he tried.

Sometimes the greatest mercy is a swift death, the *fuath* pointed out drily.

A voiceless sob escaped Rowenna. She knew the creature to be right. But something dark and lightless was spreading inside her—that fathomless sea of her craft, surging up from its shores in a rising tide. Tendrils of its darkness crept through her limbs, carrying a spreading malaise with them, a cold to counter even the burn of witchnettle. If she kept pushing her work—if she waded knowingly into that sea—Rowenna feared she'd never set foot on land again. Something within her would be irrevocably altered, and she was not sure she wanted such a change.

So she carried on, calling her wind again and again, pushing at the wild-eyed assassin until at last, chest heaving, he did not get up.

Torr's mouth turned down in displeasure. He raised a hand, and an arrow whined through the air from some unseen vantage point. It caught the man on the gravel full in the throat, and Rowenna watched in horror as he bled out before her eyes. There would never be enough air for her to draw a full breath again, she thought, nor would her heart cease its frantic racing. She would die in this moment, gaze fixed on a man who'd been killed to test her power.

You could have done it, the *fuath* said. *Could have shown him your strength. Given him reason to fear you. Don't shy away from the dark and the depths, little fish—you were made to swim in them. I feel that in you.*

There was something unsettling in Torr's face as he approached her. Impatience. Frustration.

Boredom.

That last was most dangerous of all.

"Did you know," he said slowly, "that you, my saint, are not the first witch I've tested here? None of the others had it in them to take a life—some were too weak, some too softhearted, others too rebellious. They all burned sooner or later for their failure, or broke their craft in trying too hard. But you—you will live another day. I can *see* you holding back, and I will find a way to witness your full strength before the end."

What about Elspeth? Rowenna thought. *Did she kill for you? Or was she too weak, too softhearted, too rebellious?*

Torr could not hear her as the wind and the *fuath* could, though.

"I have a job for you," he told her instead. "Tomorrow at midnight, I want you to wait in the chapel. Someone will come to you there. When they do, kill them for me, and I will let you live yet again."

Rowenna nodded her assent, mind racing as she did. She could stage some accident, or warn whoever it was away. Without Torr's supervision, surely she could find a way to avoid this task while remaining blameless.

Why go to so much trouble? The *fuath* asked. *Why not kill him? You have the power. Shatter his ward and put an end to him, here and now.*

I can't, Rowenna confessed, darkness churning within her. If she pushed too hard, that darkness might swallow her up, and she feared there would be no resurfacing. She feared all her good and all her brightness would drown. *Not when he poses no threat to me.*

The *fuath*'s laugh was a grating, unpleasant sound. *Poses no threat? Look at me, girl.*

Rowenna glanced away from Torr and over one shoulder, to where the monster lay in a puddle of its own dark blood, the crossbow bolt still protruding from its leg.

I will mend, the *fuath* said. *But this princeling who poses no threat to you now does to others. And he will kill you in the end if you do not kill him first.*

Still, Rowenna insisted. *I cannot.*

You're a fool, the *fuath* scoffed. *A strong and stubborn one, but a fool nevertheless.*

"Midnight in the chapel," Torr reminded Rowenna. "Don't forget."

He strode off, whistling to himself, hands still in his pockets, his steps free and easy.

Where is the other one? Rowenna asked the *fuath* as they were left alone, with only the wind frisking about them and the gruesome corpse of Rowenna's ill-fated assailant on the ground. *The other witch, with the auburn hair. I haven't seen her in days—where has she gone?*

The *fuath* ducked its head low and licked at its own blood.

Didn't I tell you he'll have you in a cage sooner or later? it said, mouth rimmed with crimson. *He's locked her in his dungeons below the earth, now that he has another witch to toy with. I've seen many of your kind enter this place and die for it, and though that gentle one lasted longest, her time is running short. He's tired of her, and he'll kill her, too, before long.*

Thank you for telling me, Rowenna offered.

The *fuath* stiffened. *Don't give me your gratitude, little fish. Were I free from these bars, I would sup on your flesh and lap up your blood, as I would with any land dweller.*

Nevertheless, Rowenna insisted. *Thank you. And I'm sorry you were hurt.*

The *fuath* turned its back to her and would say no more.

❧

Rowenna spun flax fiber into yarn. She could feel the progress she'd made as the yarn slipped through her fingers—it was yearning to unravel, to unbind, to pull apart. It made the spinning troublesome, but Rowenna was pleased. Her craft was working, and she'd come far enough to be able to sense it.

She sat and let the rhythmic motion of foot on treadle and hand on fiber lull her into something approaching peace. But when the moon sailed high overhead, she remembered her promise to Torr and set her work aside. Gawen had gone hours ago, murmuring something about searching for his father now that Rowenna had agreed to deal with Torr Pendragon. Her brothers were gone too—though Duncan had given up fighting, he was loading and unloading boats on the docks, Liam was hiring himself out to scribe messages, and Finn followed either of them as he fancied.

So Rowenna left the hut by the river behind, pulling a woolen cloak around her shoulders. It had been given to her by Elspeth, and the thought nagged at Rowenna. She hated to think of the other girl behind bars, and if she managed to put an end to Torr Pendragon, she would have to find and free her. But for now, she had other troubles—most immediately that she was meant to go to church and kill someone.

On her way to the chapel, Rowenna kept to the shadows. Music and light poured from the castle as she had not seen happen before, and she felt like a wraith, flitting from place to place in the dark. But the chapel and the overgrown graveyard were as gloomy and silent as ever.

It was not midnight yet—the bells in the city had not chimed the hour. Rowenna pulled herself through one of the glassless chapel windows and took a breath. She'd never been inside the chapel before—no doorway led in from the graveyard, and until now, she'd only come to gather nettles. The air within the stone walls was cold and still, her tread a mere whisper against stone. It felt like a haunted place—not in the despairing, gut-wrenching way of Drumossie Moor, but as if the chapel remembered countless people, countless conversations, all of them over and done with.

At the farthest end of the apse, Rowenna tucked herself into the darkness and waited. Though she hadn't yet decided what she would do when confronted with the individual Torr had sent her to kill, there was something tantalizing about watching and waiting—about being the one with power. So often she felt helpless and useless, but here she had the upper hand.

The dark sea within lapped quietly at her edges, made calm by this sense of being the watcher, of having control.

Rowenna did not have long to wait. Just as the city bells tolled midnight, the door to the chapel creaked open, whining on unoiled hinges, and a figure stepped inside. Rowenna could not make them out in the darkness, but she caught a glint of moonlight on metal—the gleam of a drawn blade in the stranger's hand.

They'd made it to the middle of the chapel's central aisle before Rowenna unleashed her wind. It leaped through the windows with a jubilant roar and knocked the stranger from their feet. They held fast to the knife, though, and Rowenna's wind lifted the stranger's hand, slamming it against the stone floor with a loud crack. The knife went clattering away, and a strained voice called out.

"Hellfire and damnation, Rowenna Winthrop. It's me."

"Gawen?" Rowenna gasped. She was at his side immediately, helping him to sit up and taking his hand in hers. The knuckles were split and bloody, but everything moved as it should. Relief swept over her in a wave, followed by annoyance.

"What are you doing here?" Rowenna asked in confusion. "Torr sent me to the chapel to *kill* whoever walked into it at midnight."

Gawen scrambled away from her at once, and she could feel fear pouring off him.

"Push me out with your craft," Gawen said in a tense half whisper. "Get me right away from this place. Make it look as if you mean to do as he asked."

"But I—" Rowenna began.

"Do you think there's no one watching, to be sure you do what you're told? Get me *out*, and be rough about it."

He sounded desperate, even though Rowenna could not see

his face in the darkness. So she gathered her wind and shoved.

As if it could sense Gawen's panic, the wind rushed at him with more force than Rowenna had intended. He fell and fought his way upright and fell again, and Rowenna was reminded of the dreadful minutes leading up to the death in the menagerie, only that morning. Deep within her, the cold water of her power was lapping at her waist. Outside, the wind drew upon her strength, clawing at Gawen, forcing him to stay down. Eager to please and remembering how it had been used before, it pried its way into his mouth and down his throat. Rowenna could see the moment panic flamed to life and blazed in his eyes, as the wind stole his breath and carried on. Her power was nearly in control now—that frigid sea had risen to her shoulders, to her neck, and soon she would go under and be nothing but craft and fury.

Blood seeped from Gawen's nose, and he began to jerk as his body vainly attempted to expel the jubilant wind.

With a small, broken cry, Rowenna tore herself from that inner sea, and it required all her strength to leave the icy black water behind. At once the wind stilled and returned to frolic about her.

Rowennarowennarowenna, our love our light our dark-hearted girl. We would fly for you, would die for you, would kill for you, make heart's blood spill for you.

Stricken, Rowenna hurried past Gawen, who still lay on the chapel floor coughing and gasping. She ran into the night, not slowing her pace as she wove through the maze of the castle proper. Mired in her own thoughts, Rowenna paid little attention to where she was going, but her feet knew the way. They brought her through the menagerie, down a long alley, and past the back entrance of a noisy kitchen.

She'd slowed a little, skirting the shadows along the castle proper's thick curtain wall, when someone reached out from a doorway and snatched her inside.

It was like second nature already, to call the wind. A gale came screaming through the door, but even as it did, whoever had touched Rowenna released her.

"Stop that, scold," Gawen hissed urgently, voice still raw. At once she let the wind die, everything in her anguished over how this had become her instinct so quickly. To call the wind. To use it as a weapon in her own defense.

Edging around behind her, Gawen shut the door and lit a taper. They were in a small, stone-walled room with no windows. Two other doors led out into unknown parts of the castle.

Stepping back, Gawen shook his head at Rowenna.

"You're a menace now," he said, running a hand through his dark hair. "I mean, you were before, but it was with your words. Now it's with your craft, too."

Rowenna felt as if she would drown, not in the fathomless sea of her own power, but in regret.

"Are you all right?" she breathed. "I can't—Gawen, I didn't mean to hurt you."

He shrugged. "Didn't I tell you to? There's no lasting harm done, and hopefully that was a good enough show for whoever Pendragon had watching."

Tears pricked at the back of Rowenna's eyes, and her blistered hands began to tremble. "You don't understand, I could have killed you. I was a moment from doing so. I'm just what my *màthair* always thought I would be."

Frowning, Gawen stepped forward and put his arms around her, and Rowenna hid her face against the rough wool of his pullover.

"Here now," he said. "Just because you *can* do something, doesn't mean you will. You've got a craft in you that can bring about damage, but I was brought up to be a knife in the dark. It's for both of us to choose what we do with that power—how we use it, and who we use it against. It doesn't wield us, scold. We wield it."

"What were you even doing in the chapel?" Rowenna sniffed. "Why did Torr Pendragon know you'd be there, and why did he want me to kill you?"

"I'm looking for my father," Gawen said. "Like I told you I was at first. Now that you're here to deal with Torr, the promise I made my family will be kept sooner or later, and my father can't fault me for searching. I knew Torr Pendragon's aware that I'm in the city, but I thought it'd be harder to track me down, given I'm a swan by day. And I've taken care not to let anyone untrustworthy know my business, so I can't see how he found me. I was supposed to meet Elspeth tonight—she knows of a guard in the castle dungeons who might have news of where my father's being held."

A chill swept over Rowenna.

"Elspeth," she said. "I heard Elspeth's been put in the dungeons herself. Torr must have found out about the meeting from her."

Gawen looked as if he might be sick. "She's loyal to a fault, scold. For her to tell him anything . . ."

His voice trailed off, and they left the truth unspoken. That Torr must have tormented Elspeth beyond endurance for her to give away a friend's secrets.

"What if—" Gawen began, but he was cut off. The door flew open with a loud retort to reveal Steward Greaves standing on the threshold, a flintlock pistol cocked and at the ready in one hand.

Chapter Twenty-One

"Not again," Rowenna groaned.

"Not mute after all," Greaves said triumphantly. "I saw you in the chapel, witch. I saw you fail to kill this rebel, and heard you speak to him."

But before the words were fully out, Rowenna's wind had slammed the steward's arm holding the pistol against the door-frame, so hard she could hear bone snap. Gawen moved forward too, quick as thought, and before Rowenna realized what had happened, he'd drawn his crimson-stained knife out from between Greaves's ribs.

The steward crumpled to the ground. Slowly Rowenna and Gawen turned to each other, eyes wide.

"You killed him," Rowenna whispered, still hardly able to believe it had happened before her very eyes.

"It's not the first time I've killed a man," Gawen said grimly. "And it won't be the last. We'll have to do away with him, though. We could weight him down with rocks and throw him in the river."

Rowenna shook her head, thinking hard. "No, I've got a better idea. I know someone who can help, and there'll be no worry over his body washing up somewhere, or a search for a murderer starting up. But we'll need to move him."

Gawen slipped through the door and, after a few anxious minutes, returned with a handcart. They bundled the body into it and covered it with Rowenna's cloak, and she led the way through the dark toward the menagerie. Rowenna wasn't sure which would be worse—if Torr caught her with Gawen MacArthur, known rebel, or with the dead body of his steward. She wasn't interested in finding out, and her heart beat rapidly in her throat. It was a comfort at least, to have Gawen's company and be joined together in their crime—that is, until the scent of peat and woodsmoke rose up.

The sound of the handcart trundling along stilled, and when Rowenna turned, Gawen was in his swan form already. The hours the boys spent as their full selves each night had rapidly dwindled to only a few, and Rowenna chafed at this distraction from her curse-breaking work.

Taking up the handles of the cart, she pushed it along herself, though it was slower going. At last she reached the tall hedge of the menagerie and carried on into its heart.

The *fuath* stood curiously at the bars of its cage, wicked head cocked to one side, vast eyes gleaming in the dim.

What do you have there, little fish? the creature asked Rowenna. *What do you have that smells like a man's heartblood? Have you braved the dark within you? And why does the black swan show the sheen of something cursed?*

Glancing from right to left to ensure they were truly alone, Rowenna threw back her cloak, exposing the lifeless body of the steward. The *fuath*'s lips parted as it bared its fishhook teeth in a barbarous smile.

Oh, we have wished that one dead for years now. Well done, min-now. Well done, indeed. And what will you do with his bones?

Rowenna put her head to one side. *I didn't kill him. The one in the swan's body did. But I had thought to give you the steward's remains, as a gift.*

An odd, rippling sound spread throughout Rowenna's mind, and she recognized the *fuath's* laughter.. The creature drew itself up to its full height. Though it was starvation thin, it still stood a foot and more above Rowenna, but she stared up undaunted.

And why, the *fuath* hissed, *would I help you hide this killing?*

Because perhaps someday, I'll help you in return, Rowenna offered.

The creature in the cage scoffed at her, an audible noise like a wave breaking on rock.

Perhaps today, Rowenna thought, growing desperate. *If you hide the manner in which the steward was killed, I'll let you go free. On the condition that you leave Inverness without taking a life.*

Open the door, the *fuath* said invitingly, *and bring your dead thing in. Once you do, I'll consider it.*

Rowenna knew it to be a ruse. The monster hadn't even bothered to hide its intentions well—perhaps it wanted her to know. They were taking a measure of each other now, in a way they'd never been able to before. Though the swan at Rowenna's side made small, anxious sounds and ruffled his feathers unhappily, Rowenna called the wind and slipped it into the cage's lock.

A sharp click rang out. The *fuath* stayed preternaturally still as Rowenna swung the door open and, with a concerted effort, maneuvered her handcart inside. But once she'd got it in, a metallic whine and a bang signaled the shutting of the door.

She was closed in now, with the *fuath* grinning wickedly, its webbed, many-jointed hand still on the doorway. Rowenna began to tremble as she recalled the manner of her mother's death.

What is it you fear so about me, minnow? the *fuath* asked. *You've reeked with fear since the day we first laid eyes on each other. Yet we're alike in some ways. Both creatures of power and hidden depth, who could put an end to anyone in this castle if we chose. If cold iron did not bar our way.*

It doesn't bar mine, Rowenna shot back defiantly, knowing that if she'd spoken aloud, she'd not have been able to keep her voice from shaking. *That's where our likeness ends. I'm still free to do as I please, while you're a prisoner here.*

Again the *fuath* laughed, like water chattering over rock. *Your freedom is an illusion. How many times must I tell you? You will never be rid of Torr Pendragon—not until he lies in a pool of his own blood. Until you burst his lungs with your craft or someone else makes an end of him for you.*

Even as it spoke, the *fuath* edged around the handcart that lay between them, its movements so small and fluid, they were barely visible. Had everything in Rowenna not been attuned to its actions, she'd never have noticed. But her focus was fixed on the monster, and the wind swirled restlessly about her, murmuring warnings as it had done in Neadeala before all Rowenna's curses began.

Beware, beware, dark-hearted girl.

Like lightning on water, the *fuath* struck. But Rowenna was equally quick. She thrust her wind at the creature, and a jolting shock ran through her as *fuath* and craft collided. It was more than a matter of using the wind now, or seeing what it saw—Rowenna felt what it felt, as if they were one, as if it was an extension of her own person.

A choking odor of salt and cold stone rose up, emanating from the *fuath*. And Rowenna's faithful wind was forced to draw back, pushed toward her by the monster's power. Even on land, the beast was strong and cunning and possessed of craft, and Rowenna let out a voiceless gasp as the *fuath* drew closer. Yet once the wind reached her, it held, surrounding Rowenna with a whirling, impenetrable shield, making her the eye of her own small storm.

"I am water," the *fuath* said to Rowenna, and she had never heard it speak audibly before. Even the creature in Mairead's skin never used its true voice, but her mother's sweet, stolen tones. If the *fuath*'s thoughts were like water running over rock, its spoken words were laced with the distant roar of waves—with treacherous power, of the sort that could break ships and drown strong men. "And wind will not prevail upon water for long, little fish. It will only make it wilder, and lend it strength in the end. Who are you to stand against me, with your craft of feeble air?"

It reached for Rowenna, elongated fingers prying apart her wind and setting it to unraveling like so much knitwork. With a soft, wordless cry, the swirling breeze began to fail.

Rowenna felt herself and her wind losing power even as the

fuath gained it, and the devastating recollection of Mairead's last night rose up in her.

You're like the sea, Mairead said, still herself, still whole, still beloved, *because it seems yielding at first, but even rock wears away before salt water in the end.*

Saltwater girl.

Little fish.

Cailleach.

Witch.

Our love, our light, our dark-hearted girl, the wind grieved as it slowed and gentled around Rowenna.

And last came the echo of Gawen's voice.

It's for both of us to choose what we do with that power—how we use it, and who we use it against. It doesn't wield us, scold. We wield it.

Turning inward to the restless sea of her craft, Rowenna waded in unhesitatingly, though the memory of the deaths and damage she'd already wrought lay like darkness within her. She went in among the breakers, until they buffeted at her waist and her neck and she went under entirely, suspended in a weightless, lightless world where there was only power. Above her, wind troubled the waters, and rather than draw on its strength Rowenna fed it her own, siphoned from this endless shadow realm.

Saltwater girl.

Little fish.

Cailleach.

Witch.

I am all of this and more.

The *fuath* traced the line of Rowenna's jaw with one finger, just as the creature in Mairead's skin had once done. But this monster wore its true form, fingers tipped with hooked and murky claws, and Rowenna felt a stinging burn and the trickle of blood as the creature's touch broke skin.

I am all of this and more. I choose where my craft starts, and where it stops, she repeated to herself from within the depths of her own dark sea. Reaching out, she cupped the *fuath*'s wicked face with one nettle-ruined hand, pantomiming its motion.

For a moment she saw hesitation in the creature's deepwater eyes.

Rowenna smiled.

And threw all her power into the faithful wind.

With the roar of a summer storm it tossed the *fuath* back. The monster hit the opposite cage wall with a sickening sound of impact, but it was tough and fierce and hardy, and writhed against the grip of the wind, hissing and spitting, a feral light in its gleaming eyes. Bit by slow bit, the scent of salt and stone rose up again. The *fuath* freed itself and straightened. But its power and Rowenna's were matched—they stood facing each other, with the length of the cage and the body of the steward between them, and neither could bridge the gap.

At last Rowenna gestured to the body of Steward Greaves.

This is for you, she thought to the *fuath*. *Do with it what you will.*

With a twist of wind in the lock, she stepped out of the cage and left it open. Around her, the air stilled as she drew back her power. Within herself, she broke the water's surface and stepped out from the fathomless depths of her craft, undrowned and tremulous with success.

The black swan flew to Rowenna at once, furious and anxious over what he'd seen. She caught him in her arms, holding him close. Nodding to the open door, she addressed the *fuath* once more.

There's your freedom, as promised, she told the creature. *And with it you may also do what you like.*

Before stepping out of the menagerie, Rowenna looked back. The last thing she saw in the gray dawn light was the *fuath*, still standing within the iron bars of its cage, staring down at the steward's body with a thoughtful expression on its cunning face.

Chapter Twenty-Two

Rowenna spun nettle fiber until dawn broke and she was too weary to sit upright, and then she fell into an exhausted sleep, one arm thrown over Gawen in his black swan form.

She woke not an hour later to Torr Pendragon standing over her. He was glancing curiously about himself, at the hut's spartan interior, and when Rowenna sat up slowly, Torr smiled.

"Ah, little witch, I didn't like to wake you, not when you've already spent a good part of the night working on my behalf. I'm having a bit of new trouble, though, and I could use your help."

For the first time since Rowenna had known him, Torr was dressed like a would-be king. His breeches and jacket were night-blue velvet, heavily embroidered with gold, and white lace foamed from his sleeves and his collar. Seeing him this way, Rowenna hardly had to push against the influence of his ward—his smile, which had once seemed honest to her, was now a wholly calculating thing. And she wondered at how he'd ever appeared simple and trustworthy, when he held himself with absolute confidence—the posture of a man who'd never been naysaid, and who was accustomed to power.

"Come with me," Torr said, holding out a hand. "Let me show you what I need."

Rowenna went. He led her up the hill, through the green

loveliness of late spring, and into the castle proper. There were exhausted-looking servants lounging about, who all snapped to attention as they passed, but Torr paid them no mind. He brought Rowenna to the tall hedge around the menagerie and paused.

"There was . . . an incident, in here last night," Torr said. "I was holding a banquet in honor of my nobles and my troops—perhaps you heard the music. And while everyone was otherwise occupied, the *fuath* escaped."

Rowenna feigned shock.

"It killed Greaves," Torr said peevishly. "Most inconvenient. He'll be impossible to replace. But here. I'll show you."

And together, they stepped through the door in the hedge.

Rowenna stopped short on the threshold. The *fuath* crouched in the middle of the cage-dotted courtyard. Half a dozen red-coated bodies littered the open space around it, torn limb from limb. Gore slicked the creature's arms to the elbows, and dark blood ringed its vicious mouth.

At the sight of Rowenna, the *fuath* bared its fishhook teeth in a wicked grin.

What was it you said? the creature asked her silently. *Take no lives and go freely? Instead, I choose to take them, and to stay. I see something in you,* cailleach. *Something not of the wind and the air, but of the sea. A hunger and an edge. A longing to be free. You will pit yourself against this tyrant before long, and I would be here to watch when you do. So I will stay, on the understanding that you owe me my freedom, and I will expect to gain it in the end.*

Rowenna turned to Torr with a question in her eyes, as if she had not heard the *fuath* and did not know what was expected of her.

"You're a witch," Torr said impatiently. "Obviously the beast has made short work of my guards. I could shoot it, or waste more men to return it to its cage, but that's foolishness when I have you. Use your craft, and put the monster back."

Rowenna stepped forward. She intentionally kept her gaze from straying to the horrifying spectacle of the mutilated bodies. Instead, she focused on the strange, familiar face of the *fuath*.

And once her back was to Torr, she gave it a disapproving look.

They would have killed me, little fish, the *fuath* thought at her immediately. *You will take life too, someday, so do not pretend to be more righteous.*

I don't pretend to be more righteous, Rowenna answered. *But I think you should have left. You're a fool to wait on me—you have no idea how often I've failed before.*

You won't fail, the *fuath* told her as she stopped with bare inches between them. *There's salt water in you. I scented it and tasted it in your craft only hours ago. You're more like my kind than you wish, minnow.*

Why wait to see me kill Torr Pendragon? Rowenna asked. *He's done you wrong, and he stands just there. Why not kill him yourself? You have craft of your own, with which to unmake his ward.*

A look of disgust crossed the *fuath*'s wild face. *Do you think we're alone? Do you think he has ever entered this place unguarded? There are a dozen archers waiting to strike me down if I touch him. I have not survived a cage this long to throw away my life when I might keep it yet.*

Rowenna glanced up. As the *fuath* had said, liveried men with longbows could be seen in the windows or on the battlements of every tower that overlooked the menagerie.

He thinks me a mindless beast, the *fuath* said. *Unaware of such things, and unthinking. But you. You know better. You know the cleverness of my kind.*

Aye, I do. Rowenna bowed her head to the *fuath* in respect, as she had never yet done to Torr. *You are clever and wicked and a force to be reckoned with. But you've made your choice, so to live, you must go back to your cage.*

"Can you hurry this along?" Torr said from back by the hedge, stifling a yawn. "I was up all night politicking, and I'd like to get to bed. Besides which, I've got to dispatch someone to deal with the body you left as a present for me in the chapel."

Tamping her anxiousness over Torr's last comment down, Rowenna bowed lower to the *fuath* and held out a hand, as if they stood in a grand ballroom and she was asking for the pleasure of a dance. The creature put its head to one side. For a moment, it looked more alien and other than ever. Then it mirrored Rowenna's movement and took her hand, and she led it to the cage. The *fuath* did not hesitate on the threshold—did not show the slightest reluctance at giving up its new freedom. But Rowenna could feel a tremor go through the long, murderous fingers gripping hers.

Your hands, little fish, the *fuath* said as Rowenna locked it in once more. *I have meant to ask—what is it you do to your hands?*

I'm breaking a curse, Rowenna answered evenly, though somehow, having bars between them again caused her pain. *One of your kind set it upon myself and my brothers. It's why I cannot speak, and why the black swan you saw seemed like more than just feathers and bone. We've all been altered by the craft laid upon us, and I must unravel it. But a price must be paid to unbind a curse wrought with blood, and this is the manner of my payment.*

For a long moment, the *fuath* simply looked at Rowenna. There was nothing in its wide, pale eyes. No judgment. No remorse. No pity. But no hunger, either. No malice.

I'm sorry you must do a thing that hurts, the creature said at last. *Give me your hands, little fish.*

Without a second thought, Rowenna reached through the bars.

This will not mar your craft, the *fuath* promised. *It will fade in an hour or two, but it is what I can give.*

Rowenna watched as it took her hands in its own and bowed its head. A bright tear fell from each of the *fuath*'s eyes, landing on Rowenna's upturned palms. She sucked in a sharp breath at the burn of salt water against her skin, but then a numbing coolness spread from her fingertips to her elbows. Tears sprang to Rowenna's own eyes. She had not known a painless moment since beginning her curse-breaking work, and though her feet still ached and stung, this was the most relief she'd had in weeks.

Nodding, the *fuath* let her go. It slunk away and folded itself into a shadowed corner of the cage, and Rowenna could feel its dreams and yearnings from where she stood.

The sea.

The waves.

The lightless depths.

To be free and fierce once more.

Turning back to Torr, Rowenna found him watching her narrowly.

"There's a devil in that creature, and an answering devil in you, girl," Torr said, his voice uncertain. "The only question is, will yours be one I can use?"

In response, Rowenna dropped into a low curtsy, standing on the gravel among the grisly remains of the men the *fuath* had killed.

But she kept her head low, to hide the rebel light shining in her eyes.

Chapter Twenty-Three

The soft, airy bundles of flax fiber that once lined the walls of the hut had been replaced with skein upon skein of yarn, and Rowenna began to knit. Most of the sting had been leeched from the witchnettle by now, and after a few days her hands scabbed over and started to itch.

Torr was too preoccupied to see her—something to do with his nobles and the people of the Highlands and the seeds of rebellion he could never quite crush. But Rowenna knew she was on borrowed time. Sooner or later, the tyrant's attention would turn back to her, and he'd push her to use her power for violence again. It had been one thing to brave her own darkness in matching craft with the *fuath*. It would be another entirely to do so with the intent to cause harm. Rowenna feared drowning. She feared breaking her craft. She feared losing herself entirely.

When she finished two shirts and nearly completed a third, the moment of Torr's renewed attention came. And it was worse than Rowenna could possibly have imagined.

She sat in the sun with her swans gathered about her, her hands ceaselessly moving. Only a few yards away the River Ness slipped by, laughing and chattering as it ran over rocks. The wind frisked about too and murmured contentedly.

Rowenna, Rowenna, our saltwater love, our light.

Rowenna knew a moment of near happiness—the pain the curse-breaking had given her was better now, and the work itself almost done. Before long, her brothers and Gawen would be restored, and together they could plan to deal with the monsters who still haunted their paths.

But as if fate had ordained that Rowenna's happiness must never go unblighted, the tramp of booted footsteps sounded on the castle hill. She glanced over one shoulder. Torr Pendragon was headed her way with a closed-off, displeased look on his face. Half a dozen guards surrounded him, and two of them forced along a skeletally thin man in shackles.

"Did you think because I've been occupied elsewhere I would not learn you failed me? That you did not do as I asked you to in the chapel?" Torr said in an accusatory tone as Rowenna scrambled up, dropping her knitting in her haste and shoving it under the chair and out of sight with one foot. "There was no body, yet I was very clear about my desire for whoever entered that place to meet his end. Perhaps I've been wrong about you all along. Perhaps you don't have the makings of a saint—you're just a filthy witch like the rest of them."

Frustration fairly vibrated through Torr. Rowenna had never seen him so, and icy panic washed over her. Wrapping her arms around her waist, Rowenna pleaded with her eyes.

Torr stepped closer, until he was so near, Rowenna could feel the fury wafting off him in waves.

"I don't like to think that you'd deliberately disobey me," Torr said. Rowenna shook her head vigorously in answer. "Then it's something else? Were you ill? Did your craft fail you? Did you lose your nerve?"

Rowenna nodded at the last, her thoughts racing. Torr Pendragon might be volatile, and a tyrant, but he still desired her power and saw her as innocent and unschooled in it. Perhaps she could play upon his pity.

"I thought so," Torr said triumphantly. "Do you know, for all your gifts, I've sensed from the beginning that you have no taste for blood. What saint would, after all? But did not our Lord bleed and die on our behalf? Are we not saved by blood?"

Rowenna could not keep her eyes from cutting to the hunched man in shackles.

"Look at me, swan maiden," Torr ordered, and she fixed her gaze on his face. "Without people who were willing to shed blood, we would never have received the Lord's gracious atonement. Would you deny the world a glimpse at God's greatness by hiding your light? By quenching the miracle of your nature?"

He was speaking as much to the guards as to Rowenna. They stood impassively by but were surely listening, as were Rowenna's swans, and her skin crawled at the thought of having such an audience to her craft. To the darker, wilder parts of herself.

As if to underscore Rowenna's discomfort, Torr stepped forward and lifted her chin with one finger. His touch repulsed Rowenna in a way that even the *fuath*'s did not, and she fought down an urge to shrink away.

"Do you see this man?" Torr turned Rowenna's head toward

the shackled prisoner. "He is the very last rebel in my dungeons who fought at Drumossie. All the others I've had executed for their crimes. But this one—for some reason, I've kept him alive, though until now I wasn't sure why."

Rowenna set her jaw and fixed her eyes on the man. His skin was the color of sour milk, and sores showed beneath the torn places in his ragged clothes. She could hardly see his face beneath an overgrown tangle of beard and black hair, but she felt his gaze catch and hold hers. Rowenna would feel it forever, the shock of that look he gave her, which was at once despair and relief and resignation. There was none of her own fear mirrored in the prisoner's face, and that was the one shred of mercy Rowenna grasped at.

"Swan maiden," Torr murmured beside her, and she began to tremble. "Be the righteous right hand of God. Kill this rebel for me."

Hot tears spilled from Rowenna's eyes, and she shook her head. She was neither murderer nor saint. Justice and judgment and death did not lie with her, and she'd never wanted them to.

"It's all right, lass," the prisoner rasped through cracked lips. "Do as you're bid."

"Shut your mouth, MacArthur," one of the guards growled, forcing the chained man to his knees. Everything around Rowenna narrowed to a single point—to the face of the prisoner before her as she heard his name. The prisoner's gaze was still locked on hers, and the strength in it was all that kept Rowenna's knees from buckling.

Behind Rowenna a vicious hiss sounded, followed by a com-motion. She turned and found the black swan trying to fight his way to the kneeling prisoner, while the white swans held him back, edging him toward the river. A sob rose in Rowenna's throat, and she swallowed it ruthlessly.

"It will be a mercy, what you're about to undertake," Torr said, his words slow poison in Rowenna's ear. "This pathetic renegade has nothing and no one left. His eldest son died in the battle he survived. His wife and daughters I burned while he watched. And the last of his children fled this city like a coward."

"All you see is a body," the prisoner reassured Rowenna. He let out a low grunt as one of the guards struck him in the back with the butt of a musket. But the man carried on doggedly, determined to speak his piece. "My soul died weeks ago."

Rowenna clenched her hands into fists, until her nails bit into the newly healed skin on her palms. Knowing who knelt before her, she'd rather die herself than take his life.

"Hurry it along," Torr said to one of the guards, his voice drip-ping boredom. And Rowenna cried out as the guard unsheathed a short knife and drove it into the prisoner's emaciated belly.

Blood spilled out over the guard's hand, staining the prisoner's rags and running down to the thirsty ground.

"He's dying now," Torr said sharply. "But you should know this, swan maiden—I've been in many a battle, and it's a terrible thing how men linger after a wound to their gut. It can take days, and they pass in agony. It's in your hands, to decide how long this rebel has, and how much pain he must endure."

To Rowenna's horror, Torr stepped around her and lowered himself onto the chair next to the door of her meager hut by the river. It was obvious he intended to wait, until nature took its course or Rowenna decided to hurry things along.

Or until the black swan trumpeting madly on the river escaped her brothers and met his own death on the blades of Torr Pendragon's guards.

The wind, which had been slowly slinking about Rowenna's ankles, sensed her fear. It sprang up and worried at her, causing the door to the hut to bang open and closed.

Rowenna, the wind whispered, *a little thing, a peaceful death, a gentle stealing of the breath.*

The guards had backed away from their prisoner, who still knelt, hunched over his wound. They started forward as Rowenna moved toward the dying man, but Torr stopped them.

"No," he said lazily from his place by the hut. "Leave her be. Let my little mute swan do as she will. Perhaps presently, she will show you all the power of God."

Rowenna dropped to her knees before the prisoner. The wind swirled about them in gusts and eddies as her intention began to shift toward it. Even here at the end, Gawen MacArthur's father lifted his head to look at Rowenna and spoke words that belied the hopelessness in his dark eyes.

"I'm sorry, lass," he said, his voice a fraying thread. "You don't deserve this."

The prisoner kept utterly still as Rowenna leaned forward. She wished she could offer him something. Some last spark of hope. The knowledge that his son was alive and well. But she was bound to muteness as Gawen was bound to swan form, and so she had nothing to give besides the last bitter mercy of a swift death.

Rowenna reached out and pulled the prisoner's head down, so that his forehead rested against her own and he could look nowhere but into her eyes. She wanted to tell him not to be afraid, to reassure him that this would be the quickest and most painless thing done to him since he'd walked onto Drumossie Moor that fateful day. Without a voice, though, she could only show him.

So Rowenna summoned the wind.

And deep within, she stepped into dark water, where the bottom dropped away beneath her. All was suspension and lightlessness and despair.

There was no violence in Rowenna's killing. Just her urging fingers, and the wind, and an inexorable push that lasted the span of a few heartbeats. The life in the prisoner's eyes faded out, and he slumped against Rowenna as blood seeped from his nose and from his parted lips.

Rowenna lowered the body of Gawen's father to the ground. She was drowning on the inside. There was no light, no up nor down, and she could not breathe. She would never emerge from this dark and fathomless sea again.

"Well, that's it then," Torr said. Disappointment undercut the words, and Rowenna heard him get to his feet. The guards stood at attention and waited as Torr Pendragon paused at Rowenna's side.

"Next time make it showier," he told her curtly. "What use is a miracle if no one sees it happen?"

Rowenna watched through a haze of tears as Torr and his guards retreated back up the hill, leaving her with the sad, crumpled body of Gawen's father. When the door in the curtain wall shut behind them, the clamor on the river grew to a fever pitch. Turning, Rowenna saw the black swan beat its strong wings and take to the sky, an arrow pointing west.

From down in the dark, Rowenna was struck with a desperate knowing. She could not let him go. Not if the curse was to be broken. Not if he was ever to be his full self again, or if her brothers were to walk free. Elspeth had said all the swans must be loosed from their curse together.

Calling up her wind, Rowenna drew the swan back to her. He beat his wings and fought every inch of the way, but at last her wind settled him down on the river once more.

Defeated, he hid himself among the reeds.

Rowenna stayed where she was, on her knees by the prisoner's lifeless body, until the sun went down. Only once did she stir herself, to get up and fetch her curse-breaking work, for every minute was precious and must not go to waste. It was instinct to her now, to continue this task. Shadowed hours slipped past, during which she could still see the glimmering shapes of her snow-white brothers, keeping watch over Gawen along the dusky river. She could feel the invisible band about her throat that kept her wordless, and it drove her on, hands moving thoughtlessly as this unbinding craft, this work of pain and love and restoration, took shape beneath her fingers.

Inside, she still hung in the deeps, lost in the sea of her own consuming power.

At last, when the moon rode high above, there came the smell of home and hearth. Away in the gloom, the white swans shrugged off their cursed forms and turned to boys. Among the reeds, Gawen did too. Rowenna heard brief splashing and a muttered curse.

Then her brothers appeared before her, Duncan rubbing at a newly forming bruise on his jaw.

"I tried to keep him here," Duncan offered. "But he'd have made it a fight if I'd pressed him. I'm sure he won't go far."

Rowenna swallowed. *She* wasn't sure. And though she had her voice now, it still felt as if her throat might close.

"Finn, don't look," she managed at last, a pleading note behind the words. Little Finn nodded solemnly and tore his horrified gaze from the body still lying on the turf.

Duncan dropped down beside Rowenna and put an arm about her shoulders, pulling her close.

"Liam will look after things," he offered. "He'll see the man's given a decent burial, and treated kindly in death."

For a long while, the four of them sat in silence. It was Liam who spoke at last.

"Duncan," he said heavily. "There's a spade behind the hut, from before we came. Can you do the digging?"

Duncan got to his feet without a word, and presently the rhythmic sounds of a spade cutting into the rich river soil began.

"Finn." Liam beckoned to their youngest brother. "You've seen

Father Osric and me carry out funeral rites before. Do you think you can help with that?"

Pale and wide-eyed, Finn nodded.

"Enna—" Liam began, but Rowenna shook her head.

"I can't stay for the burying," she managed to get out. "I can't, Liam. He shouldn't have me here, when he goes into the earth. I'll cast a shadow over it—taint things, somehow. I'm going up the hill to pull the last of the nettles I'll need for the curse breaking. I thought I had enough, but I've come up short. And I can't . . . I won't be able to live with myself if this happens again. It's time to finish my work. We've got to get out of here."

Before any of her brothers could stop her, she rose to her feet and hurried away, up the hillside between the fragrant pines and verdant undergrowth.

Rowenna was halfway to the castle when Liam caught up with her.

"Enna," he said in his gentle way. "Wait a moment, won't you?"

Reluctantly she stopped. Her fingers itched for work, her hands crying out for occupation, even if it meant the burn of nettles. Anything, anything, to keep her mind from endlessly replaying what she'd just done.

"Look at me." There was something implacable and irresistible about Liam's determined gentleness. After a moment, Rowenna did as she was told. She could feel it, though—that her eyes were lightless and bitter, devoid of hope that any of this would yet end well.

But Liam refused to quail before the darkness in her gaze.

"Rowenna Mairead, I've known you since the day you were born," her eldest brother said. "Do you know what my first memory is? It's not Duncan. Not our father, or even *Màthair*."

Rowenna waited as he spoke, but his words sounded strange and faraway, meant for someone else and not for her.

"I remember you," Liam went on. "Our mother put you in my arms, the morning after you were born. If she said anything to me, I can't recall—I was so small myself. But I remember your face, and your black hair, and the way you looked up at me. I remember knowing that in my arms I held a complete and perfect thing—something entirely outside and apart from myself."

Moonlight filtered down on them, drifting between the pines. Rowenna stood immobile, and a fragmented, desperate part of her wished that she could hear Liam's words and take them to heart. But the rest of her was still drowning in salt water and craft, unwilling and unable to make the landfall that might save her.

"I know we've been at odds," Liam said. "I know you and I look at the world and see it in different ways. But what you've been doing on my behalf, and for Duncan and Finn and Gawen? To me that's an act of God. Complete and perfect, like you were the first time I saw you. I don't care how you've gone about it, or what craft you've used—there's God in your hands, and in your work. I'm only sorry I haven't told you sooner. Because I know you, Enna, and even if I'm hard on you, I know you'd never do a thing out of wicked intent. What you did today had no malice in it. You were an instrument of mercy, however it may feel."

"Sometimes intent doesn't matter," Rowenna said, wrapping her arms around herself, to be smaller, and to ward off the nighttime chill. "All that matters is what you've done."

Brushing past him, she carried on up the hill, toward the castle and the chapel graveyard choked with nettles. This time, Liam let her go.

Chapter Twenty-Four

In the moonlit chapel graveyard, Rowenna looked down at her hands and sighed. Scabbing blisters and still-bloodied cracks ran across her palms and between her fingers, stretching past her wrists halfway to the elbow. They were better than they had been, though, and now here she stood, about to do damage again.

Reluctantly Rowenna went to the largest clump of nettles. She tore stalks up by the roots until her arms buzzed with pain and sweat ran down her shoulder blades to the small of her back. It felt, as ever, like penance. Like the only hope she might have for absolution, and so even as her half-healed hands split open and bled, Rowenna continued her work.

Rowenna, Rowenna. The wind worried at her, twining through the headstones. *Take care, take care, dark-hearted girl. Something wicked this way comes.*

Rowenna shook her head to clear it. Something wicked had already come, but it had been from within, not without. All those years, her mother had been right. She was unfit to wield her own craft. She was as dark and dangerous and treacherous as the monster that had stolen Mairead's life.

Kneeling, Rowenna tied a bundle of nettles together with the whip-thin upper section of one stalk. She moved stubbornly on to the next patch as the wind tugged at her. There'd be no going back to the hut tonight without everything she needed to finally break her brothers' curse. It was time to see this work over and done with.

"What are they for?" Torr Pendragon asked mildly, and at the sound of his voice, Rowenna snapped upright. He'd appeared from God only knew where and sat on one of the tumbledown headstones, holding a half-eaten apple. It was their first meeting all over again, and if Rowenna had known what she did now, she'd have taken her family and run to the ends of the earth before falling into his clutches.

"You know they call them witchnettle," he went on. "I'm surprised you'd risk being seen gathering them. You seem very reluctant to do anything else out of the ordinary, at least when I ask it of you."

Torr got to his feet, tossing the apple aside. He went to Rowenna and took one of her hands in his own, turning it over to look at her ravaged palm. Rowenna stared at him with wide dark eyes as the wind soughed and sighed about her.

I could end you now, she thought. *I could force the wind down your throat and turn everything inside you to blood and tatters, and I would be a hero. Not a soul in the Highlands would do other than thank me.*

But the sick memory of how it had felt to end Hugh MacArthur's life lay at her center and kept her from reaching out to the eager breeze. Within, she was still miles from land, still floundering in that endless internal sea, and she had not truly drawn breath since she'd used her craft to kill.

"I wonder about you, swan maiden," Torr said, his voice laced with concern. "If you're really the saint I'd hoped for after all, or if, like all the others, you're just a common hedgerow witch."

Rowenna flinched as he traced slow circles across her palm with one finger. "I have a task for you, little swan. One final chance to prove the Lord is with you, and that you're fit to have a place at my side."

Torr raised his head and glanced over to the arched graveyard entrance. "Would you bring her ladyship in?"

Rowenna watched as a dozen guards entered the graveyard. In the midst of them walked Elspeth Crannach.

At first, it seemed to Rowenna that the older girl had her head down and her hands clasped out of modesty. But as she stepped out of the shadowed archway, Rowenna caught the glint of metal shackles around her wrists and neck, and the thick iron chain that bound them together.

"Do you remember what I told you about witches?" Torr said to Rowenna as he motioned to the guards to push Elspeth toward them. "I said there are worse things in this world. What is it I named as the first?"

Rowenna could not answer, but Elspeth gave her a voice. Torr's mistress tossed her head with a clank of iron. She shook the long loose hair back from her face and answered with a single biting word.

"Rebels."

Rowenna stole a look at Elspeth. Every other time she'd seen the girl, her self-control had been flawless. But now the chains that bound her were made of metal, rather than duty and self-possession, and though her beautiful face was marred by spreading bruises, Elspeth Crannach's discipline had turned to fire.

"Yes," Torr said, a scowl darkening his face. "Rebels. And for all the kindness I've shown you, my lady, you proved to be a rebel and a traitor after all—the very things I cannot abide."

By the time he turned to Rowenna, his usual smile was back in place, though she knew it now for what it was—a wicked and deceitful thing. "So. Here it is then. A chance for you to prove your true nature, swan maiden. I will not force your hand again—I want to see you choose. To show your mettle. Here is my mistress, disgraced and guilty of the worst sort of treachery. Of plotting my death, and planning to use you as the knife in her scheme. Whatever happens, she's already dead on her feet. But you—you have a great opportunity, and a grand chance."

Rowenna swallowed. The wind played about them, rustling the witchnettle, murmuring Rowenna's name as it waited for clear instructions from the girl it had baptized with seawater the day of her birth.

"You see, I've grown tired of waiting for you to find your courage and your calling," Torr Pendragon said. "I won't hold off any longer. Unless you do as I bid, and kill this rebel who stands before us, she will burn. She'll walk to the stake tomorrow, and if you disobey me, when she goes, you'll go with her."

Rowenna looked from Elspeth to Torr, and the wind stirred her black hair. She knew there would never be an end to this. That if she did as she'd done with Gawen's father, letting Torr push her into violence she'd never craved, that there'd always be someone else. And to claim she'd been made to act as a weapon was no absolution. Not when it was in her to refuse.

So in the deep places of her spirit, where her darksome craft dwelled, Rowenna made herself heavy and dropped like a stone. She sank through the lightless sea until her feet touched bottom, and there, with all the crushing weight of her own power bearing down upon her, Rowenna called the wind.

Blood willingly given is what's needed for warding work, Elspeth had taught her. *Either the making or breaking of it.*

And had Rowenna not bled willingly for weeks now?

The wind came readily, whirling about her at once. She curled her blistered and bloodstained fingers, gathering the wind, beckoning it to her. Elspeth's face went pale as she sensed the scope of Rowenna's power—the depth and darkness of what she'd become—and Torr smiled to himself in a satisfied way.

That smile faded, however, when Rowenna turned her full attention on him. She could feel the subtle nature of the ward that protected Torr—the weft and warp of it, the delicate way Elspeth had bound it together.

Summoning her wind, Rowenna threw it at Torr. It roared across the graveyard, and he stood unmoving, with a pitying smile on his face, because Rowenna's power could not touch him through the protection of his ward.

But it was not Torr himself Rowenna had sent the wind and her power against. Elspeth had once been a marvel in her power—she'd built a wall and a ward of infinite grace and complexity. Rowenna's craft, by contrast, was neither delicate nor complicated. It was a straightforward, furious thing, a knife and a hammer and a cudgel. A bludgeon that could not be withstood. The air shimmered, pulsing and warping as Rowenna's wind beat itself at Elspeth's creation. Over and over her power battered that clever and beautiful thing, slipping in at the chinks, relentlessly taking advantage of any and every weakness.

Though it seemed a lifetime, only moments passed before an audible sound of rending and tearing filled the air. Joyous and ruthless, Rowenna's craft shattered Elspeth's work as if it were an edifice of glass. And in the absence of a ward, the wind threw Torr six feet, pinned him among the overgrown weeds, and slithered down his throat.

It took only that brief moment of panic for Rowenna to teach Torr more than he'd ever taught her. For the first time in his treacherous life, he knew a brief foretaste of death, schooled by Rowenna's craft.

Then she drew back her power.

Reluctantly the wind returned to her, twisting around her ankles like a friendly cat. Torr gasped and choked, color flooding his face. The white of his left eye had gone blood red, and when he fixed his gaze on Rowenna, there was a hatred she'd never seen there before. It chilled her, and yet at the same time, set triumph to singing in her bones.

He would never treat her like a plaything or a pawn again.

"Take them both away," Torr rasped furiously. "Lock them up and ready a pair of stakes. Oh, and give the witch a bed of nettles to wait on, since she loves their touch so."

Guards converged upon Rowenna and Elspeth, and neither of them fought—Elspeth because she already stood in chains, and Rowenna because she refused her own darkness.

Refused to be, at the last, what her mother had feared, and what so many believed or wished her to be.

⁂

Not a breath of wind could reach the dungeons beneath Inverness Castle, which had been there since long before Torr Pendragon came north and expanded the old fort that topped the hill. It smelled of earth and mildew and rot in that place belowground, where not a scrap of sky or sunlight was visible. There was only the gutter of torchlight and occasional groan of a prisoner, though Rowenna could see no one from within her cell. She could, however, see the guard station, next to the narrow stairway that led up and out of the labyrinthine prison corridors.

The floor of Rowenna's cell was carpeted with the nettles she'd gathered in the chapel yard. Shivering, she cast about herself. At the far side of the cell stood a bucket for waste and a small clay pitcher of fetid water. Taking the pitcher, she sat down and began to work. If it came to it, she'd die at this undertaking—at the task of trying to set her brothers and Gawen free. But she'd need a miracle to see it done. Though she had her nettles, the three finished shirts and the fourth, which was still incomplete, were all hidden away in the hut by the river. And she had no spinning wheel. It would take an act of God for Rowenna to finish her work now. Or at least, of a servant of his.

Perhaps she could speak to the latter, though, if she bided her time.

Rowenna could not soak the nettle stalks, nor afford to waste a drop of precious liquid, so she stripped the leaves, then poured water into the palm of one hand. She ran her damp palm along the length of the stalk, until it was wet enough to split apart, revealing the fibers within.

Soaking nettles like that was slow and agonizing work. Hours crawled past, and by the time the last stalk lay split on the cell's stone floor, Rowenna was too afraid to look at her palms for long. She'd done more damage than ever before, and dampened the final few stalks as much with her own blood as with water.

Spreading the nettles out across the floor, she gathered up her skirts and peeled her stockings off before beginning the task of breaking the fiber free. It was nearly a relief to feel the pain transfer in part from her hands to her feet, and she listened absently to the sound of the guards' low voices as she trod back and forth, back and forth.

Rowenna was on her knees pulling flax free of the broken nettles when the door to her cell opened again. A guard set down a plate with a small heel of dried bread and a raw turnip on it, and shook his head at her.

"Filthy witch," he muttered, and Rowenna was sure she looked the part. The sweat had dried on her after her work in the graveyard, her hands were a mess of blood and torn skin, and her feet were all over blisters. But she carried on gleaning nettle fiber until it lay in clouds about her, ready to be spun.

Panic set in for a moment then. With no spinning wheel and no drop spindle, there'd be no way to process the fiber into yarn. Rowenna drew in a deep breath and shut her eyes. She let the burning pain in her hands and feet rise up like purifying fire and clear the cobwebs of exhaustion from her mind.

In the darkness of her own making, she heard the guards more clearly. The night had worn on into day and back to night again as Rowenna worked, and they were about to change over. The newest warden muttered away about the weather.

"... night's black as pitch," he said. "Fog's come in off the river, too. Watch yourself out there—it's cold and dark as midwinter."

As Rowenna overheard them, she felt the band around her throat loosen. It was well past midnight then, and she was free to speak. Scrambling to her feet, she hurried to the iron door and rattled at the bars with raw fists.

"In here!" Rowenna shouted. "I'm in here, and I haven't confessed, and I want a priest."

"Going to be a long night for you," the guard heading off duty said. The night warden stumped over to Rowenna's cell door and squinted at her through the bars.

"You're the witch?" he asked dubiously.

Rowenna nodded. "Aye. But I've changed my mind about it. About the devil. Whatever I'm meant to have done wrong. I want to confess, but I'll only do it to one priest."

"They told me you were mute," the night warden said, and Rowenna shrugged. "We've got a priest already, who hears prisoners' confessions. You can say your bit to him."

"No," Rowenna snapped. "I won't confess to just anyone. Down at the wharves there's someone who writes and reads messages for hire. He's trained for a priest, and I know him. He's called Liam Winthrop—have him fetched here so I can say my bit. And tell him . . . tell him I need to finish what I've started. He'll know what that means."

"You don't give the orders here," the night warden grumbled, beginning to turn away. "Make your confession to our prison priest, or you won't be making it at all."

Rowenna snaked one ruined hand through the bars of the cell door and snatched at the warden's shirt.

"I will curse you," she swore to him, all her sharpness honed to a razor edge. "I will set a fire in your bones that never burns out. Your every waking moment will be an agony, and sleep will offer no reprieve, because each night when you lay your head down, your dreams will be filled with the deaths of those you love most. You will never know an instant of rest or comfort again, because you denied me this one thing I'm asking for, so that I can unburden myself before I die."

As Rowenna raged, the distant wind, shut out of the prison by a thick door at the top of the narrow stairs, screamed at the hinges and slammed itself against the impenetrable studded oak.

The guard blanched, and Rowenna heard a resigned voice come from the cell beside her.

"She can do it, you know," Elspeth said. "She nearly killed Torr Pendragon last night. I shouldn't like to cross her, myself."

"I'll send a page," the night warden muttered, and when

Rowenna let him go, he hurried out of arm's reach.

"I want to confess to her priest too," Elspeth called after the warden. "I know the one they send down to the prison. He's a pig with wandering hands and loose lips. Witch, can I be shriven by your priest?"

"Of course you can," Rowenna answered.

The warden hurried to the top of the stairs, calling for a page, and Rowenna turned back to the puzzle of her spinning.

She scrabbled about among the broken pieces of nettle stalk before finding one that was longer and smoother than the rest, with a notch scored at the top where it had only snapped halfway. Rowenna took a few strands of her precious fibers and tied a loose bit of stone to the bottom of the nettle stalk for a weight. It would be unwieldy and cumbersome and difficult to work with, but it would serve her for a drop spindle, at least.

In the absence of a chair or a cot, Rowenna got to her feet, leaned her weight back against the wall, and began to spin. The resulting yarn was lumpy and uneven, stained rust red in places by her hands, but it was all she could do under the circumstances.

Rowenna spun, and spun, until the cell around her blurred and her fingers moved through habit rather than conscious will. With half her mind she saw the dungeon below Inverness Castle, and with the other, the wild places of Neadeala, where Mairead stalked across the moors. She looked more monstrous now, and less human. Her face was all angles and sharp edges, her mouth a stark scarlet line. Rowenna watched with a dim, muffled horror as Mairead followed after Cam. Her father sobbed as he walked, occasionally calling for his lost children. But they were all gone away, off in Inverness breaking their own curse, and Cam was left alone with his. Mairead's uncanny eyes gleamed in the moonlight as he stumbled. The monster in Rowenna's mother's skin surged forward.

"Enna."

In her cell, Rowenna jerked back to full consciousness, dread resting in the pit of her stomach. Her makeshift spindle was still spinning, the nettle fiber nearly gone, and skeins of yarn lay untidily at her feet.

"Liam," Rowenna breathed.

Her oldest brother stood at the foot of the prison steps, and the night warden eyed him skeptically. "You don't look much like a priest."

Liam rose to the occasion at once, giving the warden a long-suffering look. "Do you think priests are born in cassocks? It's two in the morning."

"And the pair of you know each other how?" the warden pressed.

Rowenna bit at her lip. Liam could bring himself to bend the truth, but she'd never yet heard him tell a bald-faced lie.

"She's my sister," Liam said.

The warden stiffened. "I don't know if that's right, then. No one else gets to see family."

"Curses," Elspeth Crannach murmured from inside her cell, sparing Rowenna the need to threaten again.

The warden's objections melted away.

"Very well," he said. "You'll have an hour between the two of them. But no more."

Warily the warden approached Rowenna's cell door.

"Hands to yourself," he growled, and Rowenna gave him a narrow look.

"My hands are busy," she shot back. "Don't worry on that count."

Disgust marked the warden's face as he saw the damage Rowenna had done to herself over the course of her brief imprisonment. He fiddled with the heavy iron door and its ponderous key, until Rowenna heard the grating of the latch. Then Liam was ushered in, and the door locked behind him.

"Confessions are heard in private," Liam said flatly when the guard moved to return to his post, within easy earshot.

Heaving a disgruntled sigh, the warden took a torch from the wall. "Very well. I'll be in the storeroom. But I'll have the door open, so if she makes trouble, you call me. Understand?"

"Perfectly."

Then the warden was gone, retreating down the stone corridor. Liam's composure fell from him, and when he turned back to Rowenna, confusion and fear and pity were all plain on his face.

"Dear God, Enna, what happened? How'd you end up here?"

Rowenna did not look up, still busy with the spindle. "I crossed Torr Pendragon. It was always going to come to this. They'll burn me soon, as a witch or a rebel. But I want to see you and our brothers free first. I want to finish my work."

She'd hoped her voice would stay steady as she spoke, but it came out ragged in spite of her best efforts.

"Did you bring what I asked for?" Rowenna said. There was no use focusing on her troubles, no matter how grim they might be, when she hadn't yet broken the curse.

In answer, Liam slipped a satchel from his shoulder and took out the three shirts she'd completed, as well as the fourth, which Rowenna had only half finished. She looked from the poorly spun yarn at her feet to the final shirt and blinked back tears. For all the care she'd taken with the others, this one would be badly done, if she managed to finish at all. What that would mean for whoever wore it, and whether it would keep her from breaking the curse, Rowenna could not guess. But she knew it could only cause harm.

If it had been Duncan who'd come to her, she'd have been able to hide the truth from him—that perhaps she'd be unable to complete her task before going to the stake. Liam, however, saw straight to the heart of her.

"You'll never finish it in time," he said. The words came out low and toneless, and Rowenna glanced up at him, agony burning in her eyes.

"I tried, Liam. God knows I tried."

The spindle dropped from Rowenna's swollen hands, and she began to sob, laid utterly low by the thought that when it counted most, she might fail to save her brothers, as she'd been unable to save Mairead. In an instant Liam had his arms around Rowenna, her face pressed to his shoulder.

"Here now, *mo laochain*," he said, his own voice unsteady. "We'll find a way to get you out of this, I swear."

"Don't make promises you can't keep," Rowenna chided through her tears. "You know you'll only feel guilty over it. But

I wish I could fix things for you and the rest of the boys before the end. Can you come, in the morning? All of you? Not because I want you to see what happens, but because whether I've done the curse-breaking or not, I want to *try* to set things right."

"Nothing could keep us away," Liam said. "But I swear to you, Enna, we won't let you burn. I know you and I haven't always agreed, but we're family. I can speak for every one of us when I say we'll lie dead before they put a torch to you."

Liam, normally the most circumspect of them all, had never looked or sounded more like a stubborn, ferociously loyal Winthrop than he did in that moment, but Rowenna stepped back and shook her head.

"Please don't say such things," she begged. "Just be there, so I have a chance to end this."

He nodded, and Rowenna wiped at her eyes with one sleeve.

"Are you going to give me my last rites?" Rowenna asked. "I don't care if you're not truly a priest yet. None of that matters to me, and I won't be shriven by anyone else."

Liam pressed a hand to his mouth, and for a moment, Rowenna thought he might be sick. But he collected himself, squared his shoulders, and shook his head.

"I won't," Liam said, sharp enough to match Rowenna at her fiercest. "Perhaps I should, but I refuse, because you're not going to die. We're not going to lose someone again."

Rowenna could not help but think of Gawen, who'd lost everyone, and wondered if her brothers would be able to find him before morning. Something in her ached terribly at the thought of her stray. Had she known this was where she was headed—a prison cell and a witch's stake—she'd have kept him at arm's length and spared him yet another loss.

"Are you nearly finished?" Elspeth called from behind the stone wall of the adjoining cell. "Only I don't want to go to my grave without confessing."

"Go on then," Rowenna said, fighting back the fresh tears that brimmed in her eyes. "I'll see you in the morning."

But Liam stayed where he was, staring down at the pile of knit shirts and roughly made yarn on the stone floor. "Rowenna, promise me something."

"What?"

Liam bent and picked up the shirt Rowenna had only half finished, and hadn't a prayer of completing before dawn.

"This is mine," he said. "Make sure you remember. I don't want you to give it to any of the others."

In her fog of weariness, focused on the task at hand, Rowenna hadn't yet considered that she'd have to choose from among her brothers and Gawen. One of them would have to be given the worst of her work.

He handed her the bit of knitting, his shoulders tense. "Don't forget, Enna. That's for me, and no one else."

Liam called for the warden, and by the time the door grated open and he stepped out, Rowenna had resumed her spinning, only one small bundle of fiber left before she could begin to knit.

Chapter Twenty-Five

Rowenna bent silently over her work as the prison guard changed once more. Not long after Liam's departure, the iron band had closed around her throat, and she knew herself to be voiceless again.

But she did not need her voice for the task at hand. Only her nimble fingers and unflagging will. Before leaving, Liam had told the night warden sternly that Rowenna's witchwork must be burned with her, or it would set a curse on all who touched it. He'd never told such a straightforward lie before and stumbled over his words once or twice, but the warden took it for fear.

The night warden repeated the story when the guard changed and told it with more conviction than Liam had. Rowenna stayed where she was, her cramped hands working clumsily, binding together a misshapen and ugly garment. She tried to compensate by putting the full force of her goodwill and affection into the simple stitches that were all she could manage.

At last, a commotion sounded at the top of the narrow stair that led out of the dungeon. A contingent of armed guards trooped down, leaving the door to the outside world open behind them. In a desperate rush, wind howled down the stairway and into Rowenna's cell, where it tangled about her.

Rowenna, Rowenna, Rowenna, it wept. *Our love, our light, our dark-hearted girl.*

My dear, my own, my darling, Rowenna sorrowed back at the wind, even as it slipped images to her, of an open square at the heart of Inverness where two witch's stakes stood waiting. Whatever lay ahead, though, it was a comfort to have the wind with her, twining about her ankles and wrists.

"Gather up your witchwork, then," the day warden barked at Rowenna as the guards stepped forward to escort her up the stairs. Rowenna hastily stuffed her shirts and her yarn back into the satchel Liam had left and pulled the bundle over one shoulder. They were forcing Elspeth from her cell too, and the girls glanced at each other, a long, bleak look passing between them.

Then it was up the stairs and into the broad light of day. A wagon lined with benches and chains waited in the alleyway the prison entrance led out to. Elspeth and Rowenna sat and kept their eyes fixed on each other as guards lifted their skirts roughly and shackled each of them by the ankles. The moment the guard's hands left her, Rowenna dug into the satchel and took out her work once more.

"No one has ever deserved to break a curse more than you do, Rowenna Winthrop," Elspeth said quietly.

Rowenna nodded her thanks but could say nothing in reply.

With a jolt, the cart began to move, and they were off, headed toward the heart of Inverness and the waiting stakes. Elspeth sat pale and resolute, praying through the rosary with a crucifix and beads that Rowenna recognized with a small shock as Liam's.

Rowenna herself knit feverishly. All that was left to be done on her last shirt was the final sleeve, and though it looked a terrible mess, she hadn't expected to get even that far.

As they rattled through the city, people leaned out of windows or stopped on the roadsides to watch their passing. Rowenna didn't know what she'd expected, but it certainly wasn't this. The Highlanders waited silently as the wagon went by, their faces by turns grieved or stoic. Occasionally, someone raised a hand, as if to honor their going. There was a sad resignation about them all, and Rowenna wondered how many times they'd seen wagons pass by in just this fashion, perhaps bearing their own family or friends.

At last the square came into view ahead. Rowenna's sleeve was only half-done, but she hurried to cast off, not willing to risk the shirt beginning to unravel. She stuffed the garment back into her satchel and slung the whole thing over one shoulder, so that her hands were free.

"Are you afraid?" Elspeth asked faintly as the wagon jolted into the square and they caught a first glimpse of the murmuring crowd, and the stakes with dry wood piled high about their bases.

Rowenna nodded. She was sick with fear, though half of it was over her brothers and Gawen, and the thought that they might be left still cursed after her death.

The wagon drew to a halt, and Elspeth gave Rowenna a last desperate look as the guards who'd followed behind them approached.

"I wish you could speak to me once more before we burn," she said. "It seems a shame to go to your death without a chance at having a last word. And I'm sorry that Gawen and I brought you into this. I'm sorry for so many things."

But all Rowenna could do was smile sadly. Elspeth sighed, and there were tears glimmering in her wide, frightened eyes.

"I've held this off for so long," she said. "For years, and yet it came at last."

When the guards loosed the shackles at their ankles, Rowenna impulsively stepped forward and wrapped her arms around the other girl. Elspeth let out a stifled sob, and they clung to each other, until one of the guards prodded at them.

"Here now," he muttered. "It's time."

Rowenna pulled away. With one blistered thumb, she wiped the tears from Elspeth's face. She wished harder than ever that she could speak and remind both of them to be brave, and to hold their heads high.

But Elspeth spoke the words instead. She lifted Rowenna's chin and squared her own shoulders.

"We've done nothing wrong. Nothing to be ashamed of," Elspeth said. "We go to our deaths knowing that, at least. He can't take that from us."

Elspeth's eyes cut to a place behind Rowenna, and she turned to find Torr Pendragon sitting on a carved wooden chair near the edge of the crowd. Guards surrounded him to keep the gathered Highlanders away. He watched the girls in the wagon dispassion- ately, as though he knew neither of them at all, and they were about to do no more than walk across the square.

Anger licked at Rowenna, burning through the fog of her fear.

Perhaps it was a comfort to Elspeth to know she'd die blameless, but it was no comfort to Rowenna herself. She let fury at her own ill treatment build and build, even as the guards pushed her forward and she was forced to walk across the cobbles to the stake where she'd meet her end. But anger carried her, and she went dry-eyed and sure-footed across the empty space the crowd had left.

The gathered watchers were subdued as guards chained Rowenna and Elspeth to their stakes, fastening them by the ankles and the waist. The people of Inverness, it seemed, had no taste for burnings, having seen far too many of their own die in flames.

With the girls' arms left free, Elspeth held tight to her rosary, endlessly whispering her prayers. Rowenna clutched the satchel full of her work and scanned the waiting crowd, desperate for any sign of white feathers, or an elegantly curved neck.

But there was no trace of her family, of her swans. Though Liam had promised, and it was their last best hope to be freed of the curse, it seemed her brothers had failed to find Gawen at the end, and so she would once more fail too.

Rowenna's throat burned. She heard a sharp gasp from Elspeth as from somewhere within the crowd, the executioner appeared. He wore a black hood and carried a thick torch. Torr gestured to a brazier of hot coals that rested beside his chair, and the executioner approached.

Briefly a wild impulse rose up in Rowenna. To use her craft and burst his lungs. What did it matter now, if she broke herself to pieces or drowned in that lightless inner sea, in an attempt to work violence? But it would prove her a witch and a murderer, and besides that, guards with crossbows stood watch in a dozen windows. Even she would not be able to put an end to them all. Instead she would wait till the very last, for a chance to save her swans.

As the executioner plunged his torch into the coals, the wind rose up without Rowenna's bidding. Desperate and keening, it beat against the executioner and the torch in his hand. Three times the hooded man struggled to light the torch, and three times the wind snuffed it out. Tension rippled through the waiting crowd, and from somewhere hidden among the watchers, a man's voice rose.

"For shame! God himself doesn't want those girls to die."

Torr Pendragon was on his feet in an instant, rage etched across his face.

"Fetch some pitch, and be quick about it," he snarled at the nearest guard.

Though Rowenna's hands shook so she could hardly hold the needles, she took her unfinished shirt out and carried on, haphazardly adding stitches to the last sleeve as best she could. It was habit now, and a lifeline. Even if her brothers didn't appear, she'd at least end her life trying for them.

Between stitches, Rowenna couldn't help but steal frantic glances at the crowd and the sky. But there were no swans, no gleam of white. As the wait dragged on and grew interminable, Elspeth's voice rose, sweet and tremulous from the stake beside Rowenna. She recited the Our Father, over and over again, and Rowenna supposed it was the girl's anchor, just as the curse breaking had become her own.

Angry murmurs rose from the crowd at the sound of Torr's disgraced mistress praying. But before they could become more than baseless discontentment, the guard who'd been dispatched returned, bearing two buckets of pitch.

One he set down before the executioner, and the other he brought across the square, to where Elspeth and Rowenna waited. Without looking them in the eyes, he dumped the bucket's contents over the dry wood piled at Rowenna's feet.

So she would burn first, and Elspeth would be made to watch.

More scattered cries of "shame" rose from the crowd, but though the wind lashed at the executioner's pitch-soaked torch, it could not extinguish the gout of flame that flared up. At last the hooded man took his place before Rowenna.

Elspeth fixed her eyes on the sky, as if she could see beyond it to heaven above. But Rowenna focused solely on binding off the ugly, knotted stitches she'd made, which had almost—but not quite—finished the sleeve of her final shirt.

"You see before you two young women accused of witchcraft and rebellion," Torr Pendragon said, his voice ringing loud across the square. "And as we all know, it does not become us to suffer a witch to live. Accordingly, I consign these unholy creatures to fire, to be burned until they are dead."

Rowenna could not breathe as the executioner stepped forward and lowered his torch to the dry wood stacked about her. Even at the last, the wind fought him, battering the man and quenching any new flames that tried to take hold of the dry wood. Its voice was a lament, a funeral dirge.

Rowenna, Rowenna, Rowenna. Our love, our light, our saltwater girl.

The torch caught a ribbon of pitch, and unquenchable fire sprang up. Immediately the wind died down, collapsing in on itself so as not to feed the flames. Acrid smoke rose around Rowenna, and though she could not yet feel the fire, she knew it was only a matter of moments before the first tongues of it licked at her skin.

Leaning her head back against the stake, she wept bitterly. Through the haze of grief and panic and smoke, she heard the sea, endlessly breaking against the cliffs of Neadeala. She smelled the briny wind that blew over the heath. And when she opened her bleary eyes, she thought she saw the froth of whitecaps as they shattered to pieces on the rocky coast.

But it was not the foam on gray waves that gathered about her, nor was that trumpeting din the sound of squabbling wyverns on the cliffs.

Rowenna's swans had come.

Chapter Twenty-Six

In their wild, winged shapes, Rowenna's brothers and Gawen landed all about her. With thick-skinned feet they scrabbled at the piled wood and scattered it across the cobbled square. Rowenna fought back panic as flames licked at them, but they were a flurry of feathers, never in one place long enough for the fire to do harm. At last they'd extinguished every one of the embers with their strong wings and broad feet, and they stood before her in a graceful crescent. The crowd had gone utterly silent, though tension and expectation hung so heavy on the air it felt as if a storm was brewing.

With trembling hands, Rowenna drew the first of the nettle shirts from her satchel and beckoned to Finn in his fledgling form. He stepped forward, stretching out his slender neck, and Rowenna slipped the shirt over his narrow head.

Next came Duncan, but Rowenna paused for a moment when Gawen and Liam stood facing her. She glanced down at the remaining shirts—one perfectly worked, the other misshapen and unfinished. And Rowenna knew what she ought to do.

She knew that of all the boys, the one who could best bear up under misfortune was Gawen MacArthur, her dark-hearted stray, who the wind had cast up on the shores of Neadeala like a gift.

Her brothers had been kept safe and sheltered, first by Mairead, then by Rowenna herself. They'd felt grief, yes, but they did not know pain or suffering the way Gawen and Rowenna did. They had not yet wandered into darkness and learned to claw their own way back to the light.

It ought to be Gawen who was given the unfinished shirt, Rowenna knew. Yet standing in the square at the heart of Inverness, bleary-eyed from smoke and bound to a witch's stake, with her hands still bloody and cracked from the work she'd undertaken, Rowenna found she could not give another inch. To once again hurt the boy the sea had given her was to hurt herself, and she could not bear to take one more agony upon her own shoulders, or to place it upon his.

So Rowenna gestured to both Gawen and Liam to come forward and made her choice. She slipped the finished shirt over Gawen MacArthur's head. Liam bowed to her, his bill brushing the ground, and then Rowenna gave her eldest brother the worst and most uncertain of her work, woven of fear and a night in prison and skin stripped from her own pale hands.

A billow of fog surrounded the swans, bringing with it a gust of briny air—the clean, saltwater scent of the ocean, and the peat-and-grass aroma of Neadeala's moors. From somewhere within the fog, Rowenna heard an anguished sound, and then the mist cleared and her breath caught and tears stung her eyes.

This time, she had not failed, or been found wanting.

Her brothers wore their human shapes once more, clad in nettle shirts. Gawen held up Liam, who stood half fainting. At his feet lay the severed wing of a swan, and with one hand Rowenna's oldest brother clutched at his left arm—or rather, at what was left of it. It had been shorn off at the elbow, and blood rushed from the wound, drenching the shirt Rowenna had made.

In that moment, Rowenna wanted nothing more than to collapse onto the cobbles—to sob and shake over the good and ill that she had worked. But chains still bound her, and the crowd stood entirely silent around them. When Rowenna glanced frantically away from Liam to Torr Pendragon, she found a mire of emotions warring in the tyrant's eyes.

Desire. Envy. Anger. Awe.

Rowenna knew she could not falter or give him the least advantage. So for the first time in Inverness, she wielded the last of her powers. No longer robbed of her voice, Rowenna Winthrop opened her mouth and spoke.

"I'm no witch," Rowenna said, the words ringing clear and true across the square. "Since coming to Inverness, all I've ever done is work to undo a curse. Weeks ago, a monster dragged itself from the sea to harry the shores of the place I call home. It stole my mother's skin, and turned my father against me. It rendered me voiceless, and forced me from my land, and tried to curse my brothers and myself to become wild beasts. But I tempered its work—not as well as I might have done, if I'd known better, but as best I could at the time. Since then, I've fought every day to free my family. I have bled and suffered to finish this task. And now that I'm free, I swear before all of you and before God himself—I stand here blameless of any crime."

With Torr's gaze fixed on her, Rowenna did not dare look at Liam, or entreat someone in the crowd to help. Instead, she kept her head high, her shoulders set, and refused to falter beneath the tyrant's burning stare.

At last, Torr rose to his feet and, hands in his pockets, walked slowly across the square. The silence shattered as angry muttering rose from the gathered crowd. The tension in the air had turned to barely restrained hostility, and Rowenna knew that though she stood chained and unarmed, she was defenseless no longer.

As Torr approached, the Winthrop boys and Gawen backed away. While Rowenna spoke, Gawen had pulled off his belt and made a tourniquet of it for Liam's arm. Finn stood staunchly by, small and pale, holding his own nettle shirt tightly to Liam's terrible wound.

When Torr reached Rowenna, shouts rose up from the waiting crowd, and several dozen of the Highlanders surged forward. Torr's guards hurried to stop them, but neither Rowenna nor Torr himself paid the chaos any mind.

They kept their eyes fixed on each other, and for the first time in Torr's presence, Rowenna felt not a twinge of fear. Instead, a rush of triumph washed over her as he dropped to one knee.

"A miracle," Torr called out. "God be praised."

The hostility of the crowd melted away as they broke into a riotous cheer. But Rowenna stood with tears pricking at her eyes. Her desires had not changed—she did not want to be a miracle or a saint, nor yet a devil or a witch. She knew herself to encompass all those things, while remaining unbound by them, and she wished only for the freedom to be herself alone—not darkness or light, but something in between. A girl with power, who could wield it as she saw fit, rather than as others would have her do.

So it was that Rowenna and her brothers, along with Elspeth and Gawen, were all bundled onto the wagon that had brought the girls to the square. There were no shackles this time, though mounted guards surrounded them. Rowenna sat with Liam's head on her lap and her heart in pieces. No sooner had they managed to get her eldest brother into the wagon than he'd lost consciousness, and the sight of his gray face tore at Rowenna.

But though hot tears scalded down her face, Rowenna was also watching. She saw how Torr rode on ahead, in company with several guards. Circumstances might have changed, but the fact that Elspeth and Gawen had conspired to kill Torr remained. Two of their number were rebels and would-be assassins. Rowenna knew that though she was farther from death now than she had been at the stake, none of them were any closer to freedom.

At the castle proper, they were hurried into the main hall, where Torr stood waiting, flanked by guards and with a stranger at his side.

"This is my physician," Torr said, gesturing to the stranger. "He'll see to your brother."

Several guards had Liam on a canvas stretcher, and Rowenna cringed at the sight of him. There was so much blood. *Too* much blood. She could do nothing but nod her head in agreement.

"Wait," Rowenna begged as the physician and the guards

began to file away. "Where are you taking him? I want to know where he'll be."

"Safe is where he'll be," Torr answered tersely.

"I don't want him left alone." Rowenna glanced from Liam to the rest of her brothers and back again, caught between them. "There should be someone with him."

Before anyone of the Winthrop boys could speak, Elspeth stepped forward.

"I'll go," she said, pressing a kiss to Rowenna's cheek. "I'll look after him, swan maiden. I swear to you, I won't leave his side."

Rowenna nodded, unable to speak past the tightening in her throat, and Elspeth followed the stretcher and the physician out of the great hall.

"If you'll follow me," Torr said, the words coming out clipped and angry as he led the rest of them to the castle's main stair.

They traveled up, past mazes of corridors and more rooms than Rowenna thought it possible for a building to hold. At last Torr stopped in a quiet and abandoned hallway, far from the busyness of the castle's more populated areas.

Rowenna shivered. It was a good place to tuck away people who were meant to be forgotten, and who, once forgotten, could be got rid of.

One of the guards bent over a lock, opening the door to an enormous and windowless room fitted with several cots. A single lamp burned on a small table, casting long shadows across the stone walls. Perhaps the room was aboveground, but it was no less a prison cell than the one Rowenna had spent her last night in.

Finn stepped anxiously inside at a muttered word from the guard. Duncan followed with reluctance, but Gawen balked on the threshold, seeing that Rowenna had not yet gone in. They had not spoken since his father's death, and Rowenna could not bear to look him in the eye.

"We go nowhere without her," Gawen said flatly.

Torr let out a weighty sigh. "You're not in a position to give orders, boy."

He gestured to one of the guards, who pulled a short, thick cudgel from his belt and stepped forward.

"Stop, *please*," Rowenna begged. She moved away from Torr and took Gawen's face in her hands. He still smelled of river water, and of wool and unbleached linen. The feel of his skin and the warmth of his nearness centered her, lending her strength she sorely needed. And when her gaze met his, she found no bitterness or accusation there.

Only fathomless grief and longing.

You've become the very last straw, his eyes seemed to say, an echo from the night he told her the whole truth. *Losing you would be the thing that breaks me.*

"I'll be all right," Rowenna murmured to Gawen. "We'll all be all right—I promise you."

Both of them knew it was a promise she couldn't make in good faith; nevertheless, Rowenna spoke the words. They were a prayer and a petition—an attempt at speaking a better world into being, right there before the guards and Torr Pendragon. Gawen put his arms around Rowenna and held her close. She could hear his heart racing and feel his breath stirring her hair.

"It wasn't your fault, scold," he whispered. "I don't blame you. I never will. And I forbid you to die, or come to harm. I need you to live."

"That's enough now." Torr's voice had an edge to it, and Rowenna pulled away from Gawen at once.

"Do as you're told," she bid her stray, knowing he might refuse a command from Torr Pendragon, but he would not refuse one from her.

This time, no threat was needed to get Gawen through the door and into the windowless room. He went, albeit slowly, and with a long look back at Rowenna. Then a guard slammed the door shut and slid a heavy iron bolt home.

At once Torr seemed easier. He leaned against the wall and tilted his head to the side as he watched Rowenna.

"Well then, witch. Now you've found your tongue, will you tell me your name?"

"I will not," Rowenna answered. She stood straight and unrelenting, fury and fear singing through her veins after coming within an inch of burning. "*Witch* will do."

"That was quite the display," Torr said easily. "I think you've reminded the Highlanders that they've got a backbone, and a will of their own, and those are things I prefer for them to forget."

Rowenna gave him a narrow look. "What use is a miracle, if no one sees it happen?"

A muscle twitched in Torr's jaw. Once again, Rowenna caught the expression she'd seen in the square.

Desire and envy. Anger and awe.

"Aren't you afraid?" Rowenna pressed. "You've seen what I can do, and the misery I can bear up under. Why not simply open the castle doors, and let me be on my way?"

As Torr smiled, something cold and unpleasant slithered down Rowenna's spine.

"Little swan," he said. "You haven't been paying attention if you've not yet noticed what I do with things I fear."

He raised a hand, and at the end of the corridor a guard slammed the heavy oak door shut. It cut off the tendril of wind that had been playing about Rowenna's ankles and plunged them into darkness.

Rowenna flinched as a torch flared to life. Torr beckoned, and another guard came forward, bearing a burlap sack. The harsh sound of metal on metal echoed down the corridor as the guard drew two objects out of the sack.

A pair of gauntlets, made all of a piece and fused together to keep the wearer's hands immobile.

And a scold's bridle, crafted of rough metal and designed, with its iron spikes that fitted into the mouth, to still Rowenna's tongue once more.

Chapter Twenty-Seven

Torr Pendragon's guards chained Rowenna to the menagerie wall and left her there. The customary crossbowmen were visible in a number of windows, and so she made no effort to free herself. The hours crawled slowly by as the sun traced its way to the western horizon, and in spite of the bridle and gauntlets, Rowenna dozed. Exhaustion and defeat pushed her into sleep, her very bones craving unconsciousness.

In dreams, she found her way home.

This time, Mairead stood on the rocky shingle of Neadeala's harbor, under a starless night sky. Cold waves lapped at the beach and at the bodies Mairead had laid out along the shoreline.

There were six of them in total. With her heart in her throat, Rowenna scanned the bloodless faces, searching for Cam and praying she would not find him. Relief and guilt flooded through Rowenna when she found her father missing, and presumably still alive.

Rowenna watched as Mairead muttered something to the sea, her deepwater eyes gleaming in the low light. At the sound of Mairead's voice, the waves surged higher against the shore, lifting the waiting bodies and bearing them away.

Wind twined itself in Mairead's golden hair, sighing mournfully.

Rowenna, it still sang, across the hills and cliffs of Neadeala. *Come back, come home, return to us. Our love, our light, our dark-hearted girl.*

Mairead looked up, and for a moment it seemed as if her luminous eyes fixed on Rowenna, seeing across the void between them. This time, she did not reach out to put her finger to Rowenna's lips. Instead, she tossed her fair head, turned on one heel, and stalked back inland, toward the beleaguered cottages scattered along the coast.

Rowenna woke still in chains and with a mouthful of blood. The Highland wind shifted about the menagerie anxiously, muttering wordless things. Overhead, a thin silver moon had risen, and wisps of cloud scudded across its bright face. At the far end of the shadowy gravel yard, the *fuath* paced, its sinuous form moving from one side of the cage to the other. Familiarity had inured Rowenna to the fact that it was of a kind with the creature in her mother's skin, and when she stirred, the *fuath* stopped dead.

Little fish, it said silently to her. *You're alive?*

Aye, Rowenna answered. *For now, at least.*

She felt something from the creature—a vast ocean of relief.

Why did you not kill him? the *fuath* asked urgently. *I overheard guards speaking. They said you had him within your power—that you could have ended him. That you had a chance.*

Rowenna tilted her head back to rest against the wall, wincing as the scold's bridle bit into the soft flesh of her mouth.

I killed someone else, Rowenna said. *With my craft. The tyrant pushed me to, and I have the strength for it, but it felt like drowning. I'm afraid of the dark, beloved. Afraid of the deep. If it once gets into me, I will never be the same. It will be the death of who I am, and the birth of something dangerous. But I want to live as I am,* fuath. *God in heaven, I want to live.*

You're a fool, the fuath thought with unaccountable softness in its voice. *The dark and the salt and the deep will give you such power as will make a legend out of you.*

I don't want it. Leaning forward, Rowenna spat. She let out a low groan, then leaned back again, gingerly resting her head against the menagerie wall. With no work to do, no urgent task burning at her, she felt every one of the manifold pains that plagued her body. So she sat in the dark and ached and wept, while the wind vainly tried to soothe her and the *fuath* set to pacing once more.

Midway through the following morning, Torr came to meet Rowenna as was his habit. Despite the lengths he'd gone to in attempting to render her harmless, he still arrived escorted by a contingent of guards, and his archers lurked at every window. The guards hung back as Torr crouched in front of Rowenna and peered at her.

"How was your night?" he asked coolly, as if she'd spent the time in one of the castle's spare bedchambers. "I trust you mulled over your position here."

Rowenna gave no answer. She fell back on the silence that she'd always relied on with him and worn like a protective cloak. He did not deserve her craft, and he did not deserve her voice.

"Here's the heart of the matter," Torr said. He dropped his head down farther, forcing Rowenna to meet his gaze. "You know I want to make use of your power. I've been more than straightforward about that. And yet you resist. I could make your life so easy, witch. All I ask from you is a few favors in return—a death now and again—and you will be unassailable. Your brothers will be safe. I could even find it in my heart to cut loose that Highland cur you've made a pet of, though he deserves no second chances from me."

The wind rattled the gravel near them anxiously, and Torr's eyes darted away from Rowenna's for a moment. She shifted, and when he looked back, her dark gaze burned at his.

Even chained to the wall in iron gauntlets and a scold's bridle, Rowenna saw the truth of things. Torr Pendragon was afraid of her. And he could not suffer the things he feared to walk free.

So he'd cage her, either with metal bars or threats or promises. However he did it, he'd see her bound and beholden, unable to get clear of him no matter how badly she wished to, or how hard she struggled.

"My physician's seen to your brother. Liam Winthrop, he said his name is." Torr's voice was reasonable, coaxing even. "What's left of his arm has been stitched up, and he's resting easy. Better than easy, actually—he'll have as much laudanum as he needs so long as he's healing. And the youngest boy, Finn? We could make a courtier of him, or a diplomat. Whatever you prefer. I can find positions for Duncan, too, though he'd need a bit more polishing than the others, judging by the talk we had."

The wind twined about Rowenna, mourning softly as the *fuath* at the menagerie's heart hissed in frustration.

The sea, the deeps, the darkness, death and drowning was all the sense Rowenna could make of its thoughts.

"I'll send the MacArthur boy away, but won't make trouble for him," Torr went on. "He'll have to go far—across the Channel to France, or better yet to the Americas. But he'll live, in spite of what he's done. If you truly have the heart of a saint and you wish it for her, Elspeth could go with him. What do you say, witchling?"

But Rowenna was looking past Torr, to where the wind rustled the clipped yew hedge that grew around the base of the *fuath*'s cage.

"Girl," Torr barked. "I want your answer. Will you help me or won't you? Yes or no. Speak the word, so I know whether your family should live or die."

Let me go, the *fuath* said. *Let me do what you could not, minnow.*

Across the menagerie, the fretful breeze toyed at the latch on the cage, tugging it back bit by bit.

No, don't, Rowenna begged the wind, her eyes fixed on the *fuath*. She was agonizingly aware of the waiting guards, and of the archers looking down upon the courtyard. But the wind, which loved her, had a will and a mind of its own.

The *fuath* stilled, ceasing its irate pacing. All of its vicious, predatory attention fixed on the latch.

Rowenna watched the *fuath* watch the latch, while Torr Pendragon watched her. And when her devoted wind pulled the latch free, she turned her attention back to the tyrant, though the heart within her chest was breaking.

"Never," Rowenna slurred around the spike of the scold's bridle.

"I will never do as you bid." For good measure, she spat a mouthful of blood at Torr, and his face twisted with fury.

"Guards!" Torr began.

But there was a deafening clang as the *fuath* burst from its cage. Quicker than water and deadlier than lightning, it flowed across the graveled yard in a blur of scales and limpid limbs. The whining of crossbow bolts filled the air, but so swift was the monster that they sank into bare gravel, failing to find their mark.

"Witch, make it sto—" Torr began tremulously, but the *fuath* keened, a bone-chilling sound that reverberated from the walls and drowned out the tyrant's words. The creature's deepwater eyes flashed to Rowenna.

Then it was on top of Torr Pendragon, bearing him to the ground . . .

Mairead Winthrop on the shingle, at the bottom of the rain-slick burn

and wrenching his head back . . .

another fuath's *hands, tangled in Mairead's golden hair*

as with a gleam of fishhook teeth and malice . . .

the lantern glow of monstrous eyes, the sound of breaking bone

the monster snapped his neck.

A dam of grief and regret and yearning broke open within Rowenna, and in response to it, the wind roared forward, not to kill, but to make the *fuath* the eye of its storm—to afford the only protection Rowenna could give. She watched, helplessly, as her wind did its work and sent another volley of crossbow bolts awry.

But then the guards on foot descended upon the *fuath*. Even her wind and the creature's wild fury were not enough against so many men. Though the wind raged and the *fuath* moved like quicksilver, Rowenna felt the very moment a sword pierced its side. The pain was so sharp and fresh it was as if she herself had been run through, and a wordless cry tore itself from her throat. Again and again, the sensation came, until the wind calmed and returned to mourn around Rowenna, because it had failed in its work and could no longer bear to be parted from her.

The swarm of guards thinned and scattered. From somewhere beyond the menagerie, other noises were rising up—shouts and pistol shots and breaking things.

Rowenna was left alone, still in chains, her eyes fixed on the lifeless body of Torr Pendragon, and on the *fuath*, which lay in a spreading pool of its own blood. Now and then, the creature's chest rose and fell with a shudder.

little fish, it thought at Rowenna, and even its unspoken words had grown very faint. *do you remember the sea?*

In answer, Rowenna sent it a flurry of images. The boundless expanse of the Atlantic, its cold lightless depths, breakers on the shore, the glory of sunset gilding a watery horizon.

The *fuath* sighed.

listen well, little fish. Its voice was a broken thing, a wave that had shattered into a thousand disparate drops. *you have lived and unbound curses, and now I will tell you how to survive the deeps within. I will tell you how to end your monster.*

Rowenna listened, with all her mind and with all her heart.

When the *fuath* fell silent again, it fixed its pale-moon eyes on Rowenna and nodded its fearsome head.

Gently, so gently, she sent her wind slipping across the gravel. At least she could hold the creature this way, as it passed.

But by the time Rowenna's wind brushed against the fallen monster, it was already gone.

Hours slipped by. Even from the menagerie, Rowenna could hear intermittent shouts from within the castle, followed by running feet and the occasional sharp retort of a matchlock pistol. But she could not call out, and the chains that bound her held fast despite the wind's best efforts, so she stayed as she was—a lost thing waiting to be found.

Once a contingent of red-coated guards ran through the menagerie and halted in shock at the sight of Torr Pendragon and the *fuath*. Rowenna sat up straighter, wondering if they'd have pity on her. If they'd set her free.

"So it's true," the officer among them said gruffly. "They told me he was dead, either at the hands of his witch or his monster. Well, let him lie there. He was no good master in life, and deserves no loyalty in death."

"What about the girl?" one of the soldiers asked.

"Leave her, too," the officer said. "She's a menace herself. And we've no time left—Foster's called for a retreat, and we're headed south for home. It'll be good to see the back of this godforsaken northland—it's no fit place for civilized folk. Pity those of us who don't get word of the retreat, for they'll undoubtedly all be dead by morning."

Though Rowenna pleaded with her eyes, they carried on and left her as she was.

The sun had slipped to the western horizon when at last another clamor and a scuffling sounded down one of the alleyways that led into the menagerie. Rowenna could not hold back the small, helpless noise that escaped her as Gawen stepped into the gravel yard, forcing a uniformed guard before him with a knife to the man's throat.

"The keys," Gawen barked at the guard, who fumbled at his belt for a heavy key ring. "Drop them."

The ring fell to the ground with a heavy clank. Gawen shoved the guard back into the alleyway, out of Rowenna's field of vision. She heard the brief sounds of a struggle, followed by several moments of wet gasping. Then Gawen returned, wiping blood from his hands.

He bent and picked up the keys but froze at the sight of Torr's and the *fuath*'s remains.

"What *happened* here?"

Rowenna shook her head. For the first time since entering the courtyard, Gawen really looked at her and saw the scold's bridle and the iron gauntlets. His jaw set, and something dark etched itself across his face.

Gawen crouched before Rowenna and fumbled with the keys. She could feel the outrage radiating off him, and it made his hands unsteady. Catching Gawen's eyes, Rowenna hummed the first few bars of "Queen Among the Heather," and after a moment he calmed.

The third key fit the scold's bridle, and with infinite care, Gawen removed it, easing the spike from Rowenna's mouth.

"Tapadh leat," she breathed. "Thank you."

The second to last key fit the iron gauntlets, and Gawen let out a long breath at the sight of Rowenna's hands, which had swollen overnight. She set them in her lap and looked at Gawen, and he looked at her. They stayed that way for what seemed a very long time. Darkness and pain and loss passed between them, and Rowenna knew that for the rest of their lives, there would be this moment, binding the two of them together.

As desperate as she'd been to have her voice back, Rowenna could not find words to tell him about the *fuath*, or the end of Torr Pendragon, and he did not speak of his father. Instead, as the moon rose above them, Rowenna leaned forward and kissed her stray, mouth featherlight against his, the taste of blood and despair still on her lips.

The wind moved softly about them, and for the first time in as long as she could remember, Rowenna's fear melted entirely away, leaving only calm and certainty in its wake.

"Will you do something for me?" Rowenna asked Gawen. "Now that your tyrant's dead and our curse is broken, will you come with me to kill my monster?"

"Aye," Gawen said simply. "There's nowhere I wouldn't go with you."

Chapter Twenty-Eight

In a stolen cart, the Winthrops and Elspeth and Gawen rattled out of the chaos of Inverness. The city was back in the hands of the Highlanders now, and the looks of those they passed were so fierce, Rowenna doubted Inverness would ever fall again.

Sitting in the back of the cart at Liam's side, Rowenna watched him slip in and out of consciousness. The journey would have been agony for him, were it not for the generous dose of laudanum Elspeth had given him from a bottle she'd pocketed upon leaving the castle. Elspeth and Finn sat up near the wagon box, talking in low voices with their heads together—she was telling him stories of her own brothers and the mischief they'd gotten into when they were alive and young. Gawen and Duncan, who'd apparently resolved to be allies, sat on the box together, taking turns with the reins whenever one grew tired of driving the skittish horses.

As they left the city behind and made it into the sun-washed glory of the Highlands countryside at dusk, Liam's eyes fixed on Rowenna's face.

"Well, saltwater girl," he said with a faint smile, using Mairead's old nickname for her. "You've done the impossible, and saved us all."

Swallowing past a pain in her throat that was part of no curse, Rowenna shook her head. "Don't, Liam. I didn't save you, at least not the way I should have. And there's still *Athair* to think of."

"I'm happy enough as I am," Liam said, reaching out to take one of Rowenna's hands with his own. His grip was weak, but she held fast to him, just as she'd always done with each of her brothers. "I'd have traded a piece of myself to be rid of that curse in a heartbeat, if it had been what was required. I'm only glad I could be a help and share in your work, at the end."

Rowenna smiled down at him, though she had to blink back tears. "*Màthair* always said you were the best of us, if I'd just find a way to understand you."

"Don't know about that," Liam said, his voice already beginning to slur and his eyes to drift shut again. "I'm not . . . not sure I'm even cut out for a priest, truth be told."

And it was not Rowenna who held his gaze in the moment before he passed out of consciousness once more, but Elspeth. She still wore Liam's rosary about her neck, and her face as she spoke to Finn was brighter and more unguarded than Rowenna had seen it yet.

Before long, they'd turned off the main road and into a pine wood. A bridle path through the forest led to a clearing, within which stood a stone house, smoke curling from the chimney.

Rowenna recognized the woman standing on the doorstep at once—Elspeth's mother, who the wind had shown her in memory. Scrambling out of the wagon, Elspeth threw herself into the older woman's arms.

"Your brothers will be safe here with the Crannachs if you want to carry on, scold," Gawen said, his voice low as he turned on the wagon box to look at Rowenna. She was filled with a heart-deep gratitude for the understanding that existed between them—that she need not say there'd be no stopping and no rest for her till she saw the last of her kin safe. But it pricked her still, to think of leaving Liam and Finn behind.

"I'll stay and look after everyone," Duncan offered, seeing Rowenna's uncertainty. "Can't see as I'd be any good against a monster when we've got a witch in the family. But you must promise that you'll send word the moment you've finished what needs to be done, Enna."

The way Duncan spoke—with pride and satisfaction and approval—leached all the sting out of the word "witch," and Rowenna thought she might never mind hearing it said again.

"Come here to me," she said him. "You too, Finny. I want to look at all three of you before I go."

Duncan and Finn joined her beside Liam at the back of the wagon. Just as she'd done the night after the curse had been laid upon them, Rowenna pressed a kiss to each of their foreheads.

"I'd move the world for any one of you. Don't ever forget it," she said, and the sharp edge to her voice only served to keep it from shaking. Her brothers nodded, for of course they knew and would not forget—hadn't they seen Rowenna do as much for them with her craft already?

"Ready, scold?" Gawen asked.

"Yes," Rowenna said firmly. "I'm ready."

The stolen yoal they'd left in weeks ago brought Gawen and Rowenna back to Neadeala. Within sight of the village's familiar coastline, Rowenna stood at the prow and squinted. Stone cairns dotted the cliffs and the shingle along the harbor. She could feel craft rolling off them—a raw, powerful magic that set her skin to crawling and her stomach to roiling. It was a ward of sorts, but nothing like the subtle protection Elspeth had wrought for Torr, or the wards Mairead as her true self had made. Those felt clean and soft and strong, while this was all headache and nausea and jagged edges.

Beyond the line of wards lay a dense, unnatural wall of fog, so thick and heavy that not a glimpse of the village or the moors could be seen. Mairead had hemmed the people of Neadeala in like sheep, cutting them off from the outside world entirely.

At the sight of it, Rowenna let out a long breath.

"All right, scold?" Gawen asked, and Rowenna nodded.

I need your help, she thought to the wind, which spoke to her, and to the sea, which had baptized her at birth. But here in this cursed place, where the tainted power of Mairead's wards radiated out and out, neither the wind nor the sea answered back.

There was only Rowenna, alone with whatever innate craft she possessed, here at the edge of the world. She thought of her mother. Of how, before her death, Mairead had secured the power of her wards with the blood of swans.

I stand here in need of an offering from something wild and pure to make fast my ward, and protect this land.

"Drop the anchor," Rowenna told Gawen, trying to sound more certain than she felt. "We're going ashore."

Gawen did as he was told, and Rowenna lowered herself into the waist-deep sea. Immediately the waves began to rise, working against the tide and with unnatural speed. They lapped hungrily up Rowenna's chest, reaching for her neck and then her chin. She struggled toward shore, but her feet left the seabed as the water grew too deep for her to stand.

It felt like a perfect mirror of the sea within, which she sank into when attempting to push her craft further into darkness. Some ineffable force bore down on Rowenna, pushing her under. She heard Gawen call out in alarm and took a great gasp of air before submerging entirely.

Then a furious blast of wind surged into the harbor, beating the rising water back. Rowenna regained her footing as the waves dropped, finally leaving the boat they'd come in grounded and Rowenna standing on dry shingle.

The wind twined about her, singing its welcome song.

Our love, our light, our dark-hearted girl. Our salt, our fire, our light in deep water.

Rowenna let the untamable breeze into her. For a moment they were one, and she saw the small world Mairead had wrought beyond her ward. The cottages, cold and dark and unwelcoming. The villagers standing on the shingle, fear in their eyes and hunger written across their faces. Mairead herself, standing before them, at once wolf and shepherd to this anxious flock. The land itself, aching like a broken limb.

Beloved, Rowenna sang back to the wind. *Let us right these wrongs.*

When Gawen joined her, she turned to him.

"Give me one of your knives," she said, and without hesitation he handed over one of the daggers from his wrist sheaths.

Clutching it tightly, Rowenna walked along the shore. Her soaked skirts clung damp and heavy about her legs, but she paid them no mind. In spite of the sickening feeling the wards projected, her wind had returned, frolicking about her like a faithful hound, and she would never be entirely at a loss when they were together.

Approaching the first cairn, Rowenna eyed it critically. She reached out with the part of her that could speak to the wind and to *fuathan,* that could sense craft and work in power. She could feel the texture and contours of this vast, far-reaching magic, the tightly bound, rough-fibered knots of it.

Whether she could break it or not, Rowenna wasn't sure. But she meant to try.

An offering from something wild and pure, Mairead said from within Rowenna's memories. *To make fast my ward and protect this land.*

An offering from something wild and pure, Rowenna echoed, as she drew Gawen's knife across each of her ravaged palms. Thin lines of crimson blood beaded to the surface of her skin. Tucking the knife into her belt, she set her hands flat atop the first cairn.

At once, a twisting sense of decay flooded through her. Of deep water and drowning and things laid to rot at the bottom of the sea. But Rowenna took a breath and called the wind. It flooded into her once more, and she let their powers join together, a counterpoint, a joyous union, a partnership, and a dance.

Together, Rowenna and the wind drained the power from that cairn, until ink-black salt water poured from the rock itself and the very stones shattered beneath her hands. A mountainous billow of cold, wet fog poured forth from behind the bounds of the ward as it failed and foundered. At long last, Rowenna could see with her own eyes, rather than the wind's, what had become of her home. The rooftops of Neadeala appeared, then the cottage windows, and finally, the people of the village standing like wraiths upon the shingle.

Mairead stood at their head, as the wind had shown her, with Cam a few steps behind. At the sight of Rowenna, Cam's eyes went wide and his face pale, but he stayed where he was, as if rooted to the spot. Alone among the village's residents, Mairead seemed healthy and well, all gold and cream and blush pink, though a look of fury twisted her beautiful face. Those at her back were sallow-skinned and hollow-eyed, with a haunted air about them.

"So she returns," Mairead said, her voice sweet and clear. "Having set the devil loose among us, she would look on her handiwork, and put an end to you all."

"Gawen, go to my father," Rowenna said quietly. "If anyone comes near him, put a knife in them."

At once he was off, and Rowenna stood alone save for the wind, facing the monster in her mother's skin.

"Hello, *Màthair*," Rowenna said, the words devoid of emotion. She recalled what Torr had told her in the menagerie—that the touch of a *cailleach* could strip a *fuath* of its glamour and reveal its true form. "Won't you come and give your own daughter a kiss?"

With a smirk, Mairead stepped forward.

"Kiss me if you will, child."

Still holding fast to the blade Gawen had given her, Rowenna took one of Mairead's hands in her own and pressed a kiss to her cheek.

Nothing. No slip of the glamour the *fuath* wore. No frowns or gasps rippling through the gathered villagers as they caught a glimpse of the monster beneath Mairead's skin.

"You've grown stronger," Mairead murmured. "But did you not think I would spend the time growing stronger too, and in securing the good faith of the people you left behind?"

Pivoting on her heel, Mairead turned to the gathered villagers. She smiled at them, fair and golden and reasonable, and to a one they fixed their eyes on her. Only Gawen watched Rowenna steadfastly, and Cam's eyes flickered back and forth in agonized uncertainty, between his daughter and the semblance of his wife. Rowenna could *see* him trying to fight off Mairead's insidious glamour, and it tore at her.

"It's been a hard spring in Neadeala," Mairead said. There was understanding and pity in her words, and a stomach-turning tendril of dark craft. "A spring of unaccountable deaths and works of evil. And where, my lambs, did it begin?"

"When *she* left," George Groom shouted, pointing at Rowenna. He was as ready now to level accusations at her as he had been to taunt her true mother. No *fuath*'s craft was needed for that.

Mairead's smile grew sadder. "Not when she left. Go back further. Father Osric, I think you've discerned it."

The priest stepped forward. He clasped his hands piously, but his eyes when he glanced at Rowenna were blank, and he spoke as if by rote. "The night this witch claimed her mother died our troubles began. Her brother Liam confided in me—said his sister swore she'd seen a devil. That was the first evil to come to our shores, witnessed only by her. And she claimed it had killed her mother, but here Mairead stands. So what congress did the girl have with that demon? What is it she wanted to hide?"

"I saw her," Mairead answered, voice low and sorrowful. "I saw her that night, dancing on the cliff tops with the devil himself, both of them in an ecstasy. And when she realized she'd been seen, Rowenna herself pushed me to what she hoped would be my death."

But Rowenna, standing by and seething, was weak and voiceless no longer. Mairead's attempts to render her powerless, both in life and after death, had failed. And she would not suffer accusations any longer.

"Enough," Rowenna snapped, taking a step toward Mairead, who had walked away from her to address the villagers gathered on the shingle. "You've slandered me for the last time. And those gathered here may not be able to see you for who you are, but they will before the end. They'll know you for the demon you claim I've had congress with—for a liar and a monster and murderer, who crawled onto these shores to make a meal of my people. We'll have no more of you, beast. It's time to drag yourself back into the darkness that spawned you."

Mairead tossed her gleaming hair, disdain twisting her mouth.

"For a daughter to speak to her mother so," she said, a hurt note creeping into her voice. "I'll give you one last chance to leave us, Rowenna Winthrop. Your very presence here is a plague and a curse. You're not wanted, and if you stay, I'll be forced to use my old power on God's behalf. To end you, before you can do more damage."

Even though Rowenna knew it was the *fuath* speaking and not Mairead, something in her twisted as the words "you're not wanted" came from her mother's own mouth. But she squared her shoulders and shook off the pain of it. She'd come through worse. Been called worse. Broken curses and stood bound to a witch's stake.

"I go nowhere," Rowenna said, the words low and dangerous. "I've come back for one reason and one reason only—to free my father and the rest of these people by casting you into the sea you came from."

Mairead drew closer. Her eyes gleamed with a deadly, deep-water light. For the first time, she spoke words for Rowenna alone.

"Little fish," the *fuath* taunted. "Drive me into the waves and I will only return, again and again. I will bear a grudge against you and this land for all my long years. Your grandchildren's grandchildren will know the fear of me, and every one of them will die by my hand. Leave me alive and I will be a mad dog at your heels, the shadows on your path, the ice in winter. You will never be free of the fear of my return, just as your mother never was. And yet she could not put an end to me. All she had in her were feeble wards and charms. She was never enough to serve as my end. No witch ever has been, for you are all less in power than you once were."

In answer, Rowenna called her wind. It roared down the cliff tops, tearing past the gathered villagers with such force that they were driven to their knees. As it came, Rowenna infused it with her own sharp power, honed through pain of the body and anguish of the soul. The strength of that wind was such that when it struck Mairead, she stumbled back a full five paces and had to throw her arms up to shield her face.

The creature in Mairead's skin let out an inhuman snarl and, with a sudden downward motion of her arms, unleashed her own craft. The smell of cold stone and salt water Rowenna had learned from Torr's *fuath* poured out onto the air, and in the harbor the sea churned like boiling water, pulling itself away from the shore and gathering into a devastating wave. It came rushing back in, a wall of dark water bent on swallowing the entire beach—on engulfing every one of the people of Neadeala and sucking them down into the depths, where the *fuath* might pick at their bones until she grew tired of them.

Panic surged through Rowenna. Tearing her attention and her wind away from Mairead, she sent everything in her out to the harbor, out to the sea, to shove and push and harry the oncoming water, stealing its power drop by drop, stilling its dreadful rush, softening it to no more than a wave.

That wave crashed against the shingle in a foaming surge, breaking into frothing white water around Rowenna and the *fuath*'s knees. But it stopped just short of the people of Neadeala, who cowered at the edge of the beach, and they were left standing upon dry land. Rowenna caught sight of Alice Sutherland waiting with her family. There was recognition and a desperate plea for help in Alice's eyes—she, at least, had shaken off Mairead's glamour and realized the mortal peril facing Neadeala.

Help us, she mouthed silently, and Rowenna nodded.

"Well done, little fish," the *fuath* purred. "You have made yourself into an enemy to reckon with."

The creature circled Rowenna with slow, measured steps, and Rowenna turned as it did, keeping her face toward it at all times.

"How long can you fight, I wonder?" the *fuath* asked. "And what will it take to break you? You cannot stand against me forever. I am old, witchling—older and more powerful than you can comprehend. I have outlasted far worse than this little sparring match."

Summoning its craft, the *fuath* sent a ferocious blast of it at Rowenna, who was forced to set the whirling wind around her as a shield. Sea-foam and pebbles and sand formed a cloud within the maelstrom of joined powers, and for a moment, Rowenna could see nothing else. There was only this—craft matched with craft, the *fuath*'s ancient and indomitable, but Rowenna's young and fresh and furious.

Within the whirlwind, Rowenna felt something—a sudden jolt. A sinking of the heart. At once she fought off the *fuath*'s power and let her wind die so that she might see.

There stood Mairead, among the villagers. A knife wound scored one of her graceful arms, cut clean through the woolen-work of her kirtle, and black blood soaked the fabric, seeping out from the wound. Gawen MacArthur lay on the shingle at her feet, terribly still, with blood trickling from his ears and nose.

And before Mairead was Cam, driven to his knees, his graying tawny hair caught in one of Mairead's fists while she held Gawen's knife to his throat. His eyes cleared for a brief moment as he fixed them on Rowenna. But it was only an instant before they hazed over again, any trace of recognition fading away.

"*Athair,*" Rowenna whispered. She could not even look at Gawen after that initial glance—it hurt too much. She could not think on that just yet.

At the word, Cam's face twisted, as if with pain. But still no spark of recollection resurfaced.

"*Athair,*" Rowenna said, louder this time. "It's me. It's Enna. I've come back for you."

"Yes, good," the *fuath* chuckled malevolently. "Coax him into casting off my magic and remembering his failings before he dies. That will be the cruelest cut of all."

"*Athair,*" Rowenna repeated. "I'm here, and I love you, and I'm going to save you."

Slowly the comprehension she longed for lit Cam's eyes, but with it came raw horror.

"Rowenna?" he rasped. "God in heaven, Rowenna, this is no place for you now. We're a cursed place and a cursed people. Get out while you can."

The *fuath* bent, so that Mairead's sweet face was next to Cam's.

"I will kill you," she murmured to him. "And when I've done it,

I'll kill the witchling, too, and lap up her blood. Then I will unbind the memory of every soul here, so that all they remember is darkness and fear, which I will tell them was brought about by your wretched child. They will believe me, and cleave to me, and I will be the wolf among them for generations."

The intemperate wrath that rose in Rowenna at the sight of Mairead holding her father so set fire blazing in every part of her. Without stopping to think or to doubt, she retreated into that inner part of herself where her craft dwelled. She waded unhesitatingly into its fathomless night-dark sea, until there was nothing but water and emptiness and loneliness on every side. Then she took a breath and dropped like a stone.

As it had been with Gawen's father, she sank and sank, until the weight of her own power threatened to crush her and it felt as though she would never know the touch of the wind or light again. But this time, Rowenna had not been pushed into an act of desperation. She was not about to undertake the last, most bitter work out of a sense of grief-stricken mercy. This time, she was brimful of righteous anger and the knowledge that if she did not do what was required, there was no other recourse for her family or for the people of Neadeala.

Rowenna Winthrop, for all her darkness and sharp edges and faults, was all they had.

And within her lay the secret Torr's *fuath* had imparted in the moments before its death.

You will not overcome the long dark of your craft by wishing for some other help or light, the creature had said, lying on the gravel

313

of the menagerie as its wide pale eyes began to cloud over. *You will only manage this last work by becoming that light yourself.*

Then it had shown her a vision and a memory of its kind in the ocean's secret heart, where sunlight never shone. The *fuath*'s people gleamed with an unearthly luminescence of their own, monstrous but beautiful, unquenched by the depths. Their radiance drew all the creatures of the darkness in—the things that dwelled below flocked to them, enchanted by the light, and met death between the *fuathan*'s merciless jaws.

Rowenna knew that she did not have it in her to become monstrous. Though it was what her mother had feared, and what Torr had desired, her heart bent to the ordinary. To a life lived freely and gladly, with those she loved at her side.

But she could become light. Hadn't she been doing so in small ways all her life? By keeping the worst of her temper in check. By cherishing her brothers. By serving as a help and a companion to her mother. By knitting the family together in the wake of Mairead's death. By holding out hope to Gawen MacArthur. By braving pain day after day after day while breaking her brothers' curse. And by giving Gawen's father the mercy of a gentle end.

I am more and less than others have wanted or feared, Rowenna thought, still suspended at the breathless center of her own craft. It tasted of salt on her lips and sounded of silence—not even the faithful wind could reach her, this far into herself.

I am neither witch nor saint, yet both at once. Dark-hearted the wind named me, and dark-hearted I am, yet I will cast a light to drive away the last shadow, and set a fire to burn away the very sea.

In the depths, Rowenna spread her arms wide. She smiled into the darkness and, as she'd done so often with the beloved wind, invited that darkness in.

With a turbulent rush, the sea of her power flooded through Rowenna. It burst the dam of her dark heart and suffused her every part—bone, breath, and spirit. And though it was dark, Rowenna shone with it. She blazed like a ship's lantern, like a beacon fire, like a lighthouse on a cape.

Opening her eyes, she smiled at the *fuath*, too, as it stood on the shingle with a knife at her father's throat.

"If I were you, I would let him go," Rowenna said sharply, and because the sharpness was a part of her, it was also a part of the light. The words blazed out as an injunction, and reluctantly the *fuath* dropped the knife and stepped away, unable to withstand the force of Rowenna's order.

Rowenna went to the creature. She stood before it, with Cam still on his knees beside them. With Gawen still motionless on the shingle.

"You," she said, "will never wear my mother's shape again."

Reaching out, Rowenna set one hand on either side of Mairead's lovely face. A shock ran through the *fuath*. Terror and hatred filled its cornflower-blue eyes as they widened, and widened, and became staring deep-sea orbs. Its cherry mouth split and lengthened, lips thinning out to nothing, no longer able to hide rows of fishhook teeth. Limbs elongated, fingers stretched and grew extra joints, and mottled scales broke through as the last of Mairead's shape sloughed from it like shed skin.

The *fuath* stood before the villagers unmasked. Their cries and sobs and frantic prayers broke over Rowenna like water over rock. She grasped the creature by the back of one unnatural arm and the nape of the neck and dragged it, hissing and furious, into the sea.

When they were waist deep, Rowenna stopped. Though the *fuath* writhed in her hands, her power and her grip were sure. She was shot through with light and darkness, altogether beyond the comprehension of those who'd doubted her or sought to pit themselves against her growing craft.

Rowenna knew, in that moment, that she could accomplish what her mother had feared and what many desired. She could end the *fuath*'s life—kill it with water or air or her raw, flaming touch. How did not particularly matter. Her craft would remain unbroken by the act. She would remain unbroken by it.

But it was not her choice. It never would be. Her sharpness and her love, her darkness and her mercy, were bound up with one another. They were pieces of the ward and the curse that was her own nature, and she could not be other than who she was.

Had Mairead seen her daughter clearly, she would never have been afraid.

"Little fish," Rowenna hissed at the *fuath*, bitter and merciful all at once. "So you named me and so you will be. Don't doubt that I could kill you—I have that strength in me and more. But I choose to put the lie to your words instead. To show that in the end, I am not bound to your will or your certainty. I follow my own path, and I will lay you under the same fate now that you laid out for my brothers."

The *fuath* struggled, eyes fixed on Rowenna, its expression frozen in a rictus of fear.

"I curse you," Rowenna Winthrop snapped, power cutting through the words as the wind and the sea churned about her, joining their craft to her own. "I curse you to become smaller and less. To be bound to a thousand forms, every one of them little and mindless and powerless. Your lives will be short—no more than the span of a year—and during that time, you will be hunted to the ends of the sea as you have hunted my kin. Over and over, you will die in terror, but it will not be by my hand. That one mercy I grant you at the end."

Drawing the *fuath* up so that its vicious face was near her own, Rowenna shook her head.

"You never should have touched my mother," she said, her voice low and fierce.

And with that, her power swelled, forming a curse fit for a monster. The creature in her hands fell apart, disintegrating into a shoal of glistening silver minnows. They fell to the surf like raindrops, inconsequential in their size and fear and desperation.

For a moment they hung in the water about Rowenna, a constellation of insignificant stars. She stirred, and with a few gleams of sun on scales, they panicked and were gone.

Rowenna turned. Everything within her felt weighted with lead, but she forced one foot in front of the other and waded back to shore. The heady power in her was fading, but work still waited to be done. Hurrying across the shingle to where Gawen lay, she dropped to her knees at his side.

"Stray," Rowenna whispered, cradling his head in her hands. He lay so still, struck down by the *fuath*'s power, but she had broken that in the end, and surely she could right this very last wrong. "Come back to me. I forbid you to die—you're my light and my darkness and everything in between. I won't let you go."

Bending, she brushed her lips gently to his and put all of her remaining strength into that kiss. She'd broken a curse once for this boy already, and the craft she did now, with her mouth and her will and the remnants of her power, had a subtlety to rival even Elspeth's clever ward. It was a work to heal, a work to summon, a work to rattle the gates of death itself.

But some forces were beyond even Rowenna's ken and skill. The moments passed, and Gawen stayed as he was, white faced and motionless on the shingle. Tears filled Rowenna's eyes as she felt it all over again—the familiar rush of defeat. Of hopelessness and incomparable loss.

The first sob wrenched itself from her. Then she was weeping with a wild abandon, for all the things she'd suffered and for this boy, who'd lost everything and carried the fate of the Highlands, yet still managed to make her feel warm and safe and seen.

Cam's hand settled on Rowenna's shoulder.

"Enna, my love," her father said heavily. "You must come away. Let Father Osric see to him, and come home with me."

"No!" she snarled, and hugged Gawen to her. "I won't. You and the boys are safe now, but I can't lose him. I refuse."

Moving to crouch in front of her, Cam sighed. There was

kindness and understanding written across his face, and oh, how Rowenna had missed him.

"Enna, I know how deep this sort of loss can cut. But sometimes, as hard as we will it, we can't change fate."

Sniffing and blinking back tears, Rowenna shook her head stubbornly.

"No," she repeated. "No. What use is being who I am if I can't change fate? Get everyone away. Leave us alone."

With pity in his eyes, Cam got to his feet. A few words from him and the crowd on the shingle melted away.

"You know where to find me, if you need me," Cam said. "I'll be waiting for you, and for your story."

Then he himself stumped off, in the direction of the Winthrop cot. Rowenna was left to herself on the shore, with the body of the boy the sea had brought to her.

Shutting her eyes and setting her jaw, she took that well-known journey inward. She reached for her power—moved to the shore of that inner sea—

and there was nothing.

Only an ocean floor gone bone dry, a chasm where once boundless salt water had been. She'd spent her power in its entirety, and while it might come back to her in time, it would not be soon enough for her stray.

Nothing was left to her now but her voice and her will, and the hope that those might be sufficient.

"Stray," she said, pressing kisses to his face. They carried no craft now and were only the caresses of a girl brokenhearted over a boy. "Please, stray, I'm begging you. You're not allowed to be lost."

It was an echo of her words at Drumossie, when she'd not yet known what he meant to her—only that there was some darkness of the soul they shared.

Rowenna, the wind sighed. *Our love, our light, our dark-hearted girl.*

And rushing into her, it brought the vision of a little work. Of blood and salt water and the wind's power, rather than her own.

Shaking, Rowenna hurried to do as she'd been told. To flex her cut hands until blood flowed once more and to run the blade of Gawen's knife over his palm before clasping his hand between her own. She bowed her head and let bitter tears drop onto their fingers, mingling with the blood there as the wind twisted about them, muttering and murmuring in its wordless way.

My heart, my love, my dark-hearted boy, Rowenna keened with it, until they were one and the same. And the wind, with which she had done violence and stolen lives, slipped itself gently down Gawen MacArthur's throat.

Again and again it worked at him, with infinite care, setting his chest to rising and falling in a pantomime of life. Rowenna lost her own breath as she watched the color return to his face. As she felt the whisper of his pulse begin beneath her hands—barely a thread at first, but strengthening bit by bit.

Gawen MacArthur opened his eyes and looked at her.

At first, there was only that.

"Now then, scold," he said at last, still lying on the shingle with the solicitous wind worrying over him. "Have you saved your family?"

"Aye."

"And killed your monsters?"

"Aye."

He sat up, wincing a little, and Rowenna recalled his first days in the Winthrop cot, surly and broken to pieces on a bed before the hearth.

"And have you found your true love?"

Rowenna hid her face in her hands.

"All right, all right," Gawen said, gentle humor in his voice. "I shouldn't tease."

"No, you shouldn't," Rowenna scolded, letting her hands drop so that he might see the fresh tears in her eyes. But they were no longer of sorrow or loss. "I thought you were dead, you great fool. You *were* dead. It would have broken my heart—it did break my heart, and I need a moment to put the bits back together."

Gawen fell silent. Rowenna inched over to him, and he put his arm around her shoulders. They sat together, staring out at the wide, restless sea. The afternoon sun had come out, warm with summer, and it made a glorious thing of the water, gilding every inch of it with diamond fire.

"Better?" Gawen asked presently.

Rowenna nodded.

"You called and I came," Gawen told her. There was no humor in his voice this time, only earnestness. "I always will, Rowenna Winthrop. Living or dying. If you want me, I'm yours."

"I do," Rowenna breathed.

And when Gawen kissed her, it was victory. It was the bittersweet taste of living through darkness and trouble and coming out whole—of one story ending while a new one shone on the horizon, just about to begin.

Before them, the sea murmured its constant song.

Around them, the wind whispered.

Above them, the gulls sounded their wild and lonesome call.

And for the first time in as long as she could remember, Rowenna Winthrop felt whole, and glad, and free.

Acknowledgments

Writing novels is a solitary pursuit except for when it's not, and this one came into being with a lot of help. Lauren Spieller, my incredible agent, has been a tireless advocate for Rowenna's story, believing in it even when I didn't myself. It's been an absolute pleasure to hone and revise and polish alongside the talented Nicole Fiorica, even if I think I've eternally disappointed her by never having Rowenna and Gawen doze off and then wake up together. My critique group also indelibly shapes every story I write—Anna, Jen, Hannah, Joanna, and Steph, I would not survive publishing without you. And my one and only alpha reader, who gets to see the words before anyone else does, deserves a million thanks for cheering on this book and literally everything else I do—Mom, you're the best.

Perpetual gratitude goes out to all the rest of the wonderful people in my life who support my odd writing habit, and who have done so since before a single word of mine went to print. Tyler, thank you for being my person and for the thousand loads of laundry you've done in the Aftertimes. Moo and honk. Amy and Breanne, thanks for the lifetime of fun and interpersonal drama and spectacular interpretive dances. Dad, thank you for always having the back of everyone in the family—none of us ever doubt that you're on our side. Ashley, thanks for the entire novels of all-caps yelling we text back and forth.

And thank you, too, to everyone in the Twitter writing community. There are far too many of you for me to list individually, but I love getting to talk books and chickens and writing and soup and life in general with all of you on a daily basis.

Lastly, writing in the middle of a pandemic is hard. Writing in the middle of a pandemic while trying to look after two small human beings and teach them things like how to read and multiply is harder. But in every way possible, my girls make the perpetual balancing act of writing and parenting a joy. The lion's share of the credit for this novel goes to them—my lockdown warriors, who greet every day with good humor and a sense of adventure no matter the circumstances. It is my absolute privilege to be their mom, and without their enthusiasm, zest for life, and support, you wouldn't be holding this book in your hands.